Choices for Jamie
By: Angela Rigley
ISBN: 978-0-908325-27-6

Bluewood Publishing Ltd
Christchurch, 8441, New Zealand
www.bluewoodpublishing.com

To Dawn
Kind regards
Angela Rigley

Other books in this series:

Looking for Jamie

A Dilemma for Jamie

School for Jamie

Also by Angela Rigley:

Lea Croft

**For news of, or to purchase, these and other books from
Bluewood Publishing Ltd please visit:**

www.bluewoodpublishing.com

Choices For Jamie

by

Angela Rigley

Dedication

I dedicate this book to Eastwood Writers' Group for their support and encouragement for my writing, and also to my newest granddaughter, Violet.

Chapter 1

Puffing out his chest, trying to raise his head high, Jamie Dalton walked along the corridor with Oswell Peel. "It's not fair, Saint Clements. You've grown so much. You must be at least six inches taller than me now."

Oswell smiled. "Yes, Dalton, my aunt says she can't keep pace with me. I noticed even Anthony Robins has overtaken you. He used to be the shortest in the class, didn't he?"

"Yes, he did." Jamie chewed his lip. "I'm so glad this is our final year, aren't you? That we only have two more terms after this one?"

He didn't receive a reply for a while, and thought his friend hadn't heard. Before he could repeat it, the door opened behind them and Silas Brown appeared, surrounded by his cronies.

"Oh, no," Jamie murmured. "Not him."

"Just ignore him," hissed Peel.

That would be easier said than done. The bully still made him shudder in his boots, even though he hadn't caused any real trouble since the event when he had forced him out of the window some three years previously.

"Good day, Quackers. I see you've shrunk even more." Brown turned to his mates. "Do you think his mother—?"

"Don't you start on him," Oswell intervened, standing in front of his friend. "Jamie told me how he fell out of that window, and why. It's not too late to report you to Mr Trout, you know. Just because you've escaped retribution all this time, doesn't mean you couldn't still be expelled."

1

"Huh, it would be his word against mine," snorted the bully, backing off. "Nobody would believe the little runt. And, anyway, your *Jamie* hasn't the balls to report me."

"Maybe not—but I have, so just watch yourself."

Brown walked off, his nose in the air, his mates whispering to each other as they hurried after him.

"That will make them think twice." Oswell pulled Jamie by his sleeve through the door ahead.

"I would've stood up to him, Peel. I would. You didn't need to fight my corner, but thank you, anyway."

"We have to stick together, we underdogs. We mustn't let the bast…sorry, bullies overcome us. My aunt says they are weak, that's why they act as they do. We must show them we are strong."

"Yes, I know, but…"

"Come on, it's English Literature this morning, my favourite. We don't want to be late on our first day back."

Jamie thanked his lucky stars that Oswell had remained his friend. Oswell still enjoyed the company of Prince Nasir from time to time, but the prince had made a new friend, another member of the Indian royalty, so had less time for him. Jamie still had not made any other friends, and his hero, Alexander Bank, had left at the end of the previous year. Nobody had taken his place in Jamie's affections, so he only had Peel for a confidant.

* * * *

Saturday afternoons the boys lined up in twos and walked, crocodile fashion, towards the woods or other local places. Jamie usually loved these excursions.

Oswell Peel had chosen his prince friend to walk with, so Jamie turned to Anthony Robins. "Do you want to partner me, Tony? You might as well. We could be the Tiny Two."

2

The other boy laughed, and stood in the line next to him. "Tiny Two, eh?" He pushed back his shoulders as if to try to make himself taller, but then let them slump again. "I suppose that sums us up."

They began walking, their coat tails flapping in the strong breeze. Jamie's hat blew off and he ran to pick it up from the hedge bottom.

"Keep in formation, Dalton," shouted the master, Mr Ewart, who Jamie had heard arguing with one of the other masters as to whose turn it should be to supervise that day.

"Tell that to my hat," whispered Jamie to Anthony once he had regained his place.

He received a snigger in reply.

"Silence," yelled the master. "You may talk all you wish once we reach our destination."

"Where are we going today? Do you know?" Jamie murmured, holding his hand up to his mouth to muffle his voice.

Robins shook his head and whispered back, "I wasn't listening when he told us."

"Me, neither. We…"

He didn't finish what he had been about to say for the master marched up from the back and glared at him, walking alongside so he couldn't continue.

Why does he always pick on me? thought Jamie. *I can hear other boys chatting behind us. He isn't telling them to be quiet.*

They continued in silence for a mile or so, Jamie's natural exuberance kept in check by the presence of the master, walking up and down, glaring at him whenever he came close, until a large bird with white markings on the underneath of its wings flew overhead.

"Hey, a buzzard!"

Everyone looked up. Mr Ewart came hurrying to him. "Dalton!"

"But, sir, there's one of my favourite birds—a

buzzard. I wrote a story about one and came first in class with it. Don't you remember?"

The master glanced skywards. "Um, yes, of course. But…"

"Sir, couldn't we stop and watch it for a while. See, there's another one. In fact, there are three, circling up there. Look, they hardly ever flap their wings."

"We don't need a biology lesson, Quackers," came a hated voice from near the front.

"I'm not… It's just…"

"All right, everyone, you may take a breather." The master clapped his hands.

Jamie grabbed Anthony's arm. "Aren't they magnificent? I saw one once actually kill and eat a crow. It was stupendous."

His friend grimaced. "Thanks for that, Dalton. Just what I need when I'm already feeling queasy."

"Oh, sorry, Tony. I didn't realise you weren't well."

"I am not unwell—just as I said, a little nauseous. It'll pass."

Jamie peered into his face. "I hope you're not sickening for something. I had measles a few years ago. That was horrid. I still can't hear very well."

They watched the hawks fly higher and higher until they became mere specks in the sky.

"Anyway, Dalton, please don't call me Tony. My mother scolds my father for doing so, even though he argues that I was named after my grandfather, and he was always known as Tony."

"Is he dead then?"

"Who?"

"Your grandfather, Tony?"

"Yes, he died about two years ago. That was when my father began to call me by the shortened name."

Jamie took the apple he had saved from the previous evening's supper from his pocket, bit into it, and then held it out to his friend. "Want a bite?"

Anthony shook his head.

"It might clear your sickness. They say, 'An apple a day keeps the doctor away', don't they?"

"Do they? I hadn't heard that. But thank you, I'll decline the offer."

Jamie wiped the juice from his chin. "I don't have any grandparents. They are all D.E.A.D. Do you have any others?"

"Yes, my mother's mother. She lives down in Sussex, though, so we never see her, except at Christmas."

"Sussex? Why would she want to live all the way down there? That's the other end of the country, isn't it?"

"It is, and I don't know why. My auntie lives there as well. Her husband comes from that part of the country. I suppose my grandmamma went to live with her when my grandfather died."

Jamie nibbled the remains of the fleshy fruit so only the core remained. As his hand neared his mouth for the final bite, Anthony's eyes widened. "You're not going to…?"

"What?" he mumbled, popping it in. A piece of the sharp core stuck between his bottom front teeth. He reached inside his mouth and eased it out with his finger nail. "I hate it when it does that, don't you?"

"I wouldn't know. I don't eat the core. My mother says it is the height of bad manners and, anyway, the pips are poisonous."

"Are they? Poisonous, I mean? They never done me no harm."

Oo, dear, I said that wrong. I wonder if he noticed.

From the raised eyebrows and rolling eyes, it appeared the other boy had, but he didn't say anything.

Oswell Peel came across.

"You don't even have any parents, do you, Peel?" Jamie asked.

Peel squinted at him, screwing up his forehead. "I beg your pardon?"

"Don't mind him, Saint Clements," interrupted Anthony. "He's being his usual dopey self."

"Hey, I'm not dopey. I'm just interested in other people, that's all." Jamie stuck out his bottom lip. "If it hadn't been for me seeing those buzzards, we would still be walking up that hill. Just think of that." With slumped shoulders, he stalked off.

Me, dopey? Why would Robins think that? I thought he liked me.

The master clapped his hands and called everybody to pair up again. Jamie glanced over his shoulder to see if Anthony was coming towards him, but he had walked off with Oswell Peel to the front of the line.

See if I care. I'll walk on my own.

With his head high, he followed behind the others, whistling through his teeth, hands in pockets, until he caught up with the master who had been counting the boys.

"Where is your partner, Dalton?" the master asked, stepping into line with him.

"He's with somebody else, sir."

"So, why don't you run ahead and join him?"

"I like being on my own, sir. I can't fall out with anybody, then."

"As you wish, Dalton. I had better go and see what those boys up there are doing." The master hurried off, leaving Jamie once more to ponder why his friends had such a low opinion of him. Kicking a stone, he grimaced as it hit the heel of the boy in front of him.

A cross face turned. "Hey, watch what you're doing."

"Sorry."

The boy murmured something to his partner and they both giggled.

I don't need their company. Damn the lot of them, and I don't even care if that's swearing.

Rounding a large rock face, he saw a ledge about three feet up. He hung back until the rest of the group had disappeared around the corner. "They won't miss me if I have a rest on that," he murmured as he climbed up and stood gazing down at the scene below him.

What a view! Miles and miles of undulating hills and fields spread out in front of him.

This is even better than the view we have at home from the top field.

"And there's the buzzards again," he exclaimed as three large birds soared high above on the thermals. "I knew I was right to stop. This must be what they can see all the time."

Taking in a deep breath, he watched the magnificent trio circling around and around, until one of them dived down, clearly seeing some prey—probably a vole or small mammal. There weren't any crows about, so it wouldn't be one of them. Leaning forward to see if it succeeded, his foot slipped in the shingle on the narrow ledge, and he lost his balance.

* * * *

Tillie straightened the new blue curtains that had replaced the worn ones in the nursery and listened to the sound of her baby, Joseph Michael, snuffling in his cot behind her. How ecstatic her husband, David, had been, even more so than at Daniel's birth, for some reason she couldn't fathom.

She ran her fingers over the wallpaper. Pretty blue flowers had replaced the peeling yellow paper, so the room had a clean, fresh feel to it. The old dapple-grey rocking horse still stood in the corner—its real horsehair mane and tail somewhat dilapidated. Daniel frequently rode on it, but Alice considered herself too old for such childish occupations, now she had reached the lofty age of six.

Nanny came in with Daniel, a healthy three-year old.

"Mama," he squealed, holding out his arms. "We been to lake."

"I shall have to come with you next time. What did you see today?" She picked him up and gave him a kiss.

"We seed…um…what we see, Nanny?"

Tillie laughed, remembering how she had tried to wean Jamie off saying 'seed' instead of 'saw'.

The nanny shook out her shawl and hung it over the back of a chair. "We saw a heron."

"Yes, a hellon."

"Why, that's wonderful, my darling. I hope it's still there when I come tomorrow."

He nodded, going across to his toy box and taking out a battered train.

"Where's Alice?" Tillie asked, as the nanny helped him set up the track.

"She went to see her papa. He said he had a surprise for her."

"Oh, do you know what it could be?"

The nanny looked up at her with a look of indignation. "No, ma'am. How would I know, if you do not?"

Shaking her head at the woman's insolence, she rued the day she had engaged her. Why did she have so much misfortune with her children's carers? Not one had come up to her expectations. Cecelia had been found dead in the river several weeks after she had run away. In a way, Tillie felt responsible for her death but, deep down, she knew it had had nothing to do with her. She hadn't sacked the woman. She had just left, taking some of the family silver with her, rather than face the consequences of her actions. The silver must have been sold, because the police never found it.

This particular nanny, Maria, had only been in the household six months. The glowing references had not prepared her for the daily arguments. She deemed the woman to be too strict. Her children needed love and pampering, not the cold, seemingly emotionless attitude portrayed by the woman.

"Joseph is sleeping." She didn't continue, for her intentions were no business of the nanny's. Bending down to give Daniel a kiss, she ruffled his blond curls, and went out.

What could David be showing Alice? Where would they be? First, she tried his study. Empty. Then the library—likewise. Where then? The lounge was also clear, and the morning room, and she found Betsy in the dining room, putting away the china.

"Betsy, have you seen the master or Miss Alice?"

"No, ma'am, not this past hour," the maid replied in her high, squeaky voice, a huge grin on her face as usual.

Even more intrigued, she tried her last hope, the kitchen, although she didn't imagine for one minute they would be in there.

Maisie looked up from the pie on which she had been placing cut-out pieces of pastry in the shapes of leaves. "Ma'am?"

"Maisie, have you seen the master? He seems to have disappeared."

"Yes, ma'am. I think he took Miss Alice down to the paddock." The scullery maid's violet eyes looked big in her small face. She had matured from the shy little girl who had come to work there to help Freda before they had known the old cook had been ill. Now fourteen years of age, she was an asset to the household, and a hard worker who used her own initiative. No complaints could ever be heard about her from the other staff. In fact, Tillie reckoned her to be well-loved by everyone.

"Oh, of course," she replied, recalling her husband saying something about a new pony for Alice's birthday a few weeks previously. It had slipped her mind until the mention of the paddock, as it had not materialised at that time. She didn't think he had mentioned it recently, though. But, maybe, she had not heard. He often complained about her being too engrossed with their young boys to take in what he said.

But why hadn't he invited her to accompany them? Admittedly, she had been otherwise engaged, feeding Joseph, but surely, he could have waited until she had finished?

She opened the back door and lifted her face to the warm sunshine. An Indian summer had replaced the wet, miserable weather of the previous months, and she wanted to make the most of it.

That's probably what David thinks, she mused as, tying her bonnet ribbons, she stepped outside.

David and Alice could be seen down below, her daughter riding a beautiful palomino. Tillie thought the pony she already had, that grazed in the field at the side, still suited adequately, but her husband insisted she needed a larger one. Their daughter only had to flutter her eyelashes at him, and he became as putty in her hands whenever she asked for anything. She had become a little minx at manipulating him.

Hurrying down towards them, she gasped as Alice almost fell off when she attempted a small jump. How could David allow her to try such a feat? Increasing her pace, she reached them as her daughter pulled up.

"Look, Mama." Alice wheeled the pony around in a circle, her head held high, obviously showing off. "Isn't she wonderful?"

"Yes, dear."

David hobbled across, his blue eyes brilliant, a huge grin on his face. She had been about to admonish him for not waiting for her, but could not bring herself to do so when she saw the happiness exuding from him. To her surprise, he kissed her. Her shoulders relaxed and she kissed him back.

"It's lovely," she replied tamely.

"I'm going to call her...um." Alice stopped and tapped her chin with her forefinger, in the manner David often did when thinking. "What did I say, Papa? I've forgotten."

He laughed. "Do not ask me, you have changed your mind six times already." He linked arms with Tillie as Sam came towards them. "That is enough for today, Alice," David began but then sighed as she flicked the reins and trotted over to the other side of the paddock.

Tillie shook her head, calling, "Alice, obey your father this instant. Come back now, if you please." She turned to David. "You really must be firmer with her."

"I know."

Alice returned, her bottom lip jutting out. "Can't I have five more minutes, pleeease?"

"Five more minutes would not hurt, Tillie." David unlinked his arm and took hold of the rein, saying to Alice, "Three minutes, all right?"

Tillie could see Sam smiling. His own three-year old daughter, Eleanor, would soon be able to ride the smaller pony. She called across to him, "I would wager you are not so soft with your girls, Sam, and I know my sister would not allow you to be."

He ambled over to them. "It is becoming harder to say no to Eleanor, I must admit. Ruby insists I do, though. But she is very obedient, and rarely needs scolding."

"Just wait until she's six, like this little madam. I can't believe how wilful she can be."

David clicked his tongue. "She is not wilful, my dear, not in the least. You are too hard on her."

"Well, not as hard as the nanny." She didn't enlarge, for her attention was averted by a scream. She had taken her eye off her daughter for a second. Looking across towards the sound, she saw her lying on the ground, the pony standing quietly at her side. They all rushed over as she sat up.

"Are you hurt? Oh, my poor baby." She helped Sam pick her up as David caught up.

"How did it happen? Is she hurt?" he gasped, leaning heavily on his crutch.

The child's lip quivered as if she couldn't decide whether to cry or put on a brave face.

"I think she's fine, aren't you, darling?" Tillie cupped Alice's face with her hand, looking into her blue eyes.

Alice nodded.

"Are you sure you have not injured anything, your legs or anywhere?" persisted David with a worried expression.

Sam set her down and she waggled her arms. "No, Papa, I don't think so." Putting her thumb in her mouth, she looked at the pony and frowned.

"The pony wasn't too hard to handle, was it?" asked Tillie.

"Oh, no, Mama." Alice looked down with a guilty expression, and then leaned her forehead on its flank, stroking its soft neck.

Tillie turned her to face them. "So how did it happen?"

The thumb came out. "You weren't watching." The thumb went back in and she looked away.

"So, you thought you'd do something to attract our attention? Is that it? You stupid child. You could have done serious damage to yourself. Don't you ever do anything like that again." Tillie yanked her away, but David pulled her sleeve.

"No harm has been done. Do not be too severe on

the child."

"David, she has to learn she cannot have her own way all the time. Let's take her home before anything else untoward happens." She took Alice's hand and walked off.

David turned to Sam, who had picked up the pony's reins. "Thank you, Sam, if you could unsaddle her and wipe her down."

Tillie didn't wait to see if he followed. How could she curb her daughter's wilfulness if her husband didn't back her up? David was already more severe with Daniel, chastising the little boy for the slightest misdemeanour. And what about Jamie? For the few short weeks he spent at home each holiday David practically ignored him. During the summer she had noticed her oldest son had changed.

I suppose he's just growing up, she thought as she pulled Alice along.

"Mama, you're hurting me."

"I beg your pardon?" They stopped and she let go of her hand. "I'm sorry, sweetheart. My mind was miles away."

"Are you missing Jamie?"

How did a six-year old know? She rolled her eyes. "Yes, dear, but he'll soon be back, won't he?"

"I do, too. I miss him. I wish he didn't have to go away."

Bending down, she gave her a hug. "I know, darling, we all do. He's our…" What could she call him that wouldn't make her daughter feel jealous? "He's your wonderful big brother."

"Mm. When can I have another ride on my new pony?"

"We'll see. You need to prove to me that you can be well-behaved, otherwise you might not."

"But Papa bought her for me." Tossing her blonde

13

curls, the child yanked her hand away. "It isn't up to you. It's Papa's decision."

Taking a deep breath and biting her lip, Tillie let her run off, and turned to see if David had followed, but he had disappeared. She blew out her breath and followed Alice to the house.

A few days later, Tillie found Joseph awake in his cot, looking around. Maria seemed to be ignoring him, continuing to fold his clothes, so Tillie picked him up. "Didn't you see he was awake?"

The nanny didn't cease her chore or even look up. "He wasn't crying."

"That isn't the point, Maria. It's time for his feed."

"Well, I say, if he's hungry, ma'am, he'll cry, so leave well alone. I would have come to find you as soon as he did so."

Shaking her head at the nanny's attitude, but seeing the logic in her words, she sat on her stool and gave him a cuddle. His face lit up as his little mouth broke into a smile.

"You certainly are a happy baby, aren't you, my darling? A lot more aware than Daniel at your age, and thriving wonderfully. I don't need to worry about you." She then added, "Please, God, at any rate. I don't want to tempt the fates."

The nanny held up her hand, her forefinger and second one entwined. "No, you don't want to do that. Those fates can be very unkind at times, as I've come to discover."

"Really, Maria? In what way?" Tillie realised she didn't know much about the nanny's past life. It had not occurred to her to ask before. Maybe something had happened to make her so belligerent.

"In every way imaginable, ma'am, but I don't want

to bore you with the details. I'll go and see if Missus Wright has brought Daniel and Alice back yet. I thought they would have returned by now." She went out, closing the door behind her.

Joseph began to whimper, so Tillie put him to her breast, humming quietly to him as he fed. How lovely to sit there, just the two of them, in peaceful harmony. Through the open window she could hear birds chirping, a blackbird singing the loudest, reminding her of Jamie. He loved their song.

A soft breeze ruffled the curtains and she hoped they weren't sitting in a draught. Maybe she should draw them to when she changed the baby over to the other side. She swivelled round, so her body shielded him from any possible ill effect.

Ruby had taken her two other youngsters for a walk. Tillie had protested that they would be too much of a handful, but hadn't been able to dissuade her. Her two beautiful nieces, Eleanor and Elizabeth, resembled their mother, with their grey eyes, but she could also see a similarity to their father, Sam, the groom. Tillie had never thought him particularly handsome, but her sister adored him, and sang his praises daily.

Maybe I should do the same for my husband, she thought. *I admit I don't do so often enough. I love him with all my heart, but he can be so unbending at times, so obstinate.*

"But we don't want to be negative today, do we, little one?" She finished feeding Joseph and put him on her shoulder, rubbing his back, as she stood up and looked out of the window.

"And there he is, your papa, striding out purposely across the meadow. I wonder where he's going." Pondering at his direction, she tried to suppress the image of Christine Harrison, the beauty David had been thinking of marrying before she herself had come on the scene. Rumours abounded that she had split from her husband, and that her sister, Grace Harrison, had returned to live with her.

"How odd, isn't it, Joey, that two sisters married two brothers?"

Gently laying the baby in his crib, fast asleep once more, she turned back to the window. David had gone. She had no reason to distrust him. He jokingly mentioned the lady's name sometimes, but she knew in her heart of hearts that he would never betray her. He was a man, though. Could any of them be trusted to remain completely faithful?

Banish such thoughts from your mind, she told herself, as Daniel's voice filtered through the window. Pushing back the curtain, she could see him playing with a small brown puppy on the lawn. She smiled at his squeals.

Checking that Joseph still slept, she hurried downstairs and out through the door.

"Mama, look." Her son threw a small stick and the puppy ran after it. "Me keep him?"

"Where's Nanny?" Surely he couldn't be out there on his own?

He shrugged and tussled with the puppy once more.

"She's just gone upstairs," came a voice from the bower.

"Ah, Alice, I didn't see you there."

"Auntie Ruby asked me to say goodbye. She had to hurry off."

Tillie looked around as if to confirm her daughter's words. "Oh, did she say why? I'd been hoping to have a word with her."

Her daughter chewed her fingernail. "I can't remember."

Tillie walked across and gently pulled Alice's finger away from her mouth. "Don't do that, sweetheart. You'll make it sore."

"But it's too long. It vexes me."

Tillie smiled. "That's a grown-up word for a six-year old."

"I like it. Jamie said I should try to learn one new word a week. That way I'll increase my volcab…voculabrory." She tossed her fair curls. "Whatever the word is."

"I think you mean 'vocabulary'."

Alice hunched her shoulders, not attempting to repeat the word.

"Yes, he's always done that, always loved learning new ones, probably still does. I'm pleased he's passed on the fondness to you." She gave her daughter a hug. "Where did you go for your walk?"

"We went up to the bluebell wood. There weren't any bluebells, though."

"It's the wrong season for them, my darling. It's just called that because of the magnificent show it affords in the spring."

The puppy ran into Alice's legs. "Hey, you little rascal," she said, picking it up. "Watch where you're going."

Daniel ran up and tried to grab it from her. "Mine, my puppy."

Tillie intervened before an argument could ensue, and took the dog. "Now don't go fighting, or neither of you will have it."

Alice stalked off across the lawn. "I don't want it, anyway. I have my new pony."

Tillie called after her. "Don't go. You were telling me about the bluebell wood."

Alice hesitated and then came back. "We picked lots and lots of pink and red and yellow flowers for you, Mama. Nanny said she would put them in a vase."

The mother dog came lolloping towards them with three of the puppy's siblings, all identical, so Tillie put down the puppy, which had different markings to the others, and took Daniel's hand. "How lovely. Let's go and find them, shall we?"

The flowers lay in an untidy heap on the kitchen table. "So much for finding a vase," murmured Tillie, as the cook came out of the pantry, clutching a plate of meat.

"Ah, ma'am, I was about to find something to put them in."

Tillie bunched together the flowers and lifted them to her face, breathing in the woody, sweet aroma.

"You like them, Mama?" Daniel took one and sniffed it.

"I certainly do, children. How kind of you to think of me."

Alice tugged at her skirt. "It was my idea, Mama."

"So let's find them a home before they die. We don't want your efforts to be in vain."

The assortment of different coloured daisies duly ensconced in some water, they continued to the morning room and placed them on the sideboard.

"Can we go again tomorrow, Mama? It was so peaceful up there."

Tillie smiled. Her daughter sometimes seemed wise beyond her six years. "Yes, certainly, I'll make sure I accompany you this time. A walk will do me good."

They carried on upstairs to the nursery. "I think it's time for your nap, little boy." She took off Joseph's outer clothes and shoes and put him in his bed, where he snuggled down and fell asleep immediately.

Alice picked up a hairbrush. "Will you brush my hair, Mama, please? It's so full of tangles."

"Sit on that stool, then."

The nanny came in, carrying a pile of clean clothes. "I can do that, Mistress, if you have more pressing tasks."

"I want Mama to do it." Alice turned her head away from the nanny.

"It's all right, Maria, I enjoy doing this." Tillie took the brush from her daughter, humming as she teased out the tangles, stroking from the ends upwards.

"Papa said…ouch, that hurt."

"I'm sorry. I'll try to be gentler." She eased the knot apart and started on the other side. "Anyway, what were you saying about your papa?"

"He said I can have another ride on my new pony tomorrow."

Tillie gritted her teeth. She had tried to have words again with David the previous evening, but he had shrugged her off, saying the pony now belonged to the child, and he could see no reason for her not to ride it whenever she wanted.

"I have been a good girl, haven't I?"

"I suppose so," Tillie conceded. "But don't try to jump before you can trot."

Alice's tinkling laugh filled the room. "That's funny, Mama."

"Why?"

"It just is."

Tillie couldn't see any humour in her words, so she continued brushing, her thoughts back to her husband. Despite his leg—the stump never giving him any bother—he always seemed in the best of health, but he hadn't seemed himself lately. Not ill, but his glow seemed to have faded. Maybe he'd been working too hard—not that that would be unusual—in fact, quite normal.

"Mama?" Alice brought her out of her reverie.

"Um?"

"When's Jamie coming home?"

"Not for a long time, sweetheart. He's only just gone back."

Someone else for her to worry about—her Jamie. Although he tried to convince her everything ran smoothly at school, she didn't quite believe him. Still, he only had to put up with it until the following summer. David wanted him to go on to university, though. Would he be any happier there?

"That's all the lugs out." She ran her fingers through the silky hair. "Would you like me to plait it, or leave it loose?"

"Can I have ribbons in the plaits?"

Maria came across. "I'm very good at plaiting hair, young Alice. I'm sure your mama has better things to do."

"No, it's all right, thank you, Nanny. I am very capable of dressing my daughter's hair." *That is one service I can provide for her. I'm not allowed to do much else,* Tillie wanted to say, but muttered, "What colour ribbons would you like?"

"Um." the thumb popped into her mouth.

"Blue to match your eyes?" volunteered the nanny.

The child shook her head.

"Green to match your dress?" Tillie went towards the drawer that held the ribbons.

Another shake, as the little girl pondered, looking inside the drawer. She took out a pink one and studied it, her head to one side, then put it back. "Red. This one. I want red."

"Now, are you sure?"

"Yes, Mama, red, please." The little girl sat back on her stool. "Red's my favourite colour today. Can I put my red dress on as well?"

"I don't think it's worth changing now, darling. And I thought we were saving it for our next outing?" Tillie began to weave the ribbon into the ringlets.

"When will that be?"

"We're going to visit Missus Thompson next week. You may wear it then."

"Oo, yes, I like going there. She always gives us those special biscuits with ginger pieces in them."

Tillie smiled. "Is that how you rate people? By what

niceties they can offer?"

Alice turned her head and raised her eyebrows as if to say, 'In what other way would you do so?'

If only everything in life was so easy to measure!

"There you are, sweetheart. All finished."

Alice jumped up and ran over to the mirror. "Oo, it's lovely. I'm never going to take these ribbons out. May I go and show Papa?"

"I'm not sure where he is. I saw him going across the meadow earlier, so he probably won't be back yet."

"Well, may I go and see Auntie Ruby and show her?"

Taking a deep breath, Tillie pursed her lips, and then nodded to the nanny. "The boys should sleep for another hour or so. I think I'll have a walk down the lane to see my sister." She turned to her daughter. "It looks warm out there, so we shouldn't need our coats."

"Couldn't I have put on my red dress, Mama?" Alice asked as they made their way along the lane. "Auntie Ruby hasn't seen it yet. She doesn't have one like that, with such a big bustle."

"I don't think it would be a good idea. You know how messy Elizabeth is. She'd probably wipe her sticky fingers down it."

"Oo, no, I wouldn't want that." She stopped. "But Missus Thompson has a baby, hasn't she?"

"It'll be easier to keep out of his way. Don't fret. We'll make sure your new dress comes to no harm."

They arrived at Ruby and Sam's cottage. A baby's cries could be heard through the window.

"Oh, dear, I wonder what's happening."

They went around to the back. Nappies, baby clothes, and white sheets billowed on the line, but there was no sign of Ruby. Sam would, of course, be working in the stables.

"Ruby?" Tillie called through the open door. "Are

you there?" They entered the tidy kitchen. The cries didn't abate. In fact, they seemed to be doubling. They went through to the stairs. She called again.

Chapter 2

Coming to a halt, Jamie tried to stand, but a wave of dizziness overcame him, so he rested his head on a bush. Not for long, though. Prickly spikes covered the branches. Turning his head this way and that, he finally found a semi-comfortable position.

A sensation of falling awoke him some time later. Realising he had begun to move, he grabbed onto the nearest branch, squealing as the thorns dug into his hand. He took stock of his situation. Upwards, a sheer rock face reached to the sky, no longer the bright blue of earlier, but a deep indigo, showing night time fast approaching.

He tried once more to stand, but what would be the point? He had no chance of climbing up the rock, and down below he could hear rushing water. He tried to peep around the bush to assess how much farther he could fall if he weren't careful, but a black void stared back at him.

"Oh, 'eck," he declared. "I'm stuck." He strained his ears, but the only sound besides the water below came from a sparrow above his head.

Maybe a huge eagle will come and lift me up in its talons and carry me to safety. It's a pity those buzzards aren't big enough. But even they had deserted him. *Gone home to their cosy roosts to spend a comfortable night with their families. No thought of me, lying here, dying.*

"Dying?" he cried, realising the seriousness of his situation. "No! I'm too young to die."

What about little Annabella? She was only two, a voice in his head told him.

"But that was different. She fell down a well."

And what have you done?

"Oh, my goodness." He tried to call for help but

could only manage a croak.

Nobody would have heard that, you idiot, the voice mocked.

His hand bled from the thorns—and the pain in his ankle! He had never experienced anything like it. He broke down in huge sobs, unable to keep up a brave face any longer.

After a while, he began to shiver. Darkness had fallen. He could see nothing, not even his own hand in front of his face. Wrapping his coat around him, he tried to find a comfortable position and dozed on and off throughout the night.

Birdsong awoke him. He could still see no sign of the buzzards, but he felt sure they would reappear later.

But I don't want to be here later. I hope someone will come and rescue me any minute now.

"Help! Please, someone, help me," he yelled, and listened for a reply. Only the birds. They set up an even louder chorus once they had settled down after being alarmed by his shouting.

"Help!" he repeated. "Help."

He examined his hands. Dried blood. His legs. The right one seemed fine, but the left one… Just moving it sent electric shocks through him, and his dry mouth seemed to be full of sand.

Oh, why do so many awful things happen to me? It isn't as if I'm a bad lad. It just ain't fair.

The sound of the running water below beckoned. Maybe he would be able to tell in the daylight how far down it was. He leaned out. Not very far, and he could see some small shrubs close together, so they would give him something to hold onto.

He manoeuvred himself—trying not to cry out with the pain—and slid down. The rock levelled out and he reached the river. Scooping up the water with his hands, he gulped down the cool, refreshing liquid, and lay on the riverbank.

Pictures of his sister stuck down the well flitted through his brain. "Annabella, can you save me?" he murmured. "You're up in heaven, aren't you? Please send someone to find me. Don't let me suffer the same fate as you."

A flapping of wings made him open his eyes as a heron flew past, so close he could almost touch it. "Has my sister sent you?" he called. "Because I don't think you'll be much good."

He took in his surroundings. The river meandered from behind the rock he had fallen down, and opened out towards a lush green valley, before disappearing again into the distance.

Maybe I could work my way along and find a boat or something.

His leg would have nothing to do with his plan to stand up, though. Gritting his teeth, he sat down again. "You'd better not be as bad as Father's leg," he told it. "I don't want you chopped off, like his was." Saying the words scared him. "Oh, 'eck, I wish I hadn't thought of that. Oh, please, God, don't let me have it cut off."

He pulled up his trouser leg to examine it. No cuts, no blood, but his ankle looked twice its normal size. His left hand had started to bleed again so he reached over and sloshed it in the water. Then he splashed his face.

He wondered if he would be able to drag himself along the side of the river. Maybe he could find a house or, even better, a fisherman. His attempts merely increased the pain.

I can't stay here forever, though. I've got to do something.

A copse of small trees grew farther along, almost into the water, with overhanging branches. Perhaps he would be able to find a forked branch and make a crutch.

"Like you did, Mama, when you found me that time, after you left that prison place."

He realised she had never told him what it had been like inside the prison. Whenever he asked her, she always fobbed him off, never wanting to tell him.

"But I'm old enough now. I shall insist you tell me. That is, if I'm ever rescued." His predicament closed in on him and he shivered, pulling his damp clothes around him. "I will get out of here, I will," he cried. "I must."

Hours later, he had reached the copse and found a makeshift crutch, making it more comfortable under his arm by folding his coat into a bundle and using it as a cushion. But the coat wouldn't stay put. His head fuzzy, he was forced to stop many times and rest.

On one of these rests, he thought he heard bells. He sat up, scanning the area behind him. Then a cow mooed and, within minutes, a whole herd surrounded him. He edged backwards—not frightened of them, just startled— as they wandered towards the water to drink.

They must belong to someone.

"Hello!" he shouted. "Is anybody there?"

A man he assumed to be a farmer came towards him. Jamie flopped to the ground, his muscles and bones seeming to turn to jelly. "Oh, thank you, sir. You've saved my life," he blurted out. "I thought I was going to die here, all on my own."

"What happened?"

Jamie explained.

"You've been here all night?" the farmer asked when Jamie finished.

"Yes, sir."

"Oh, deary me. Then we had better find some way of getting you back." He rounded up the brown cows and began to walk back the way he had come. "Do you think you could follow me?"

"I'll try, sir, but I won't be very fast."

Fortunately, the cows weren't in a mood for speed, either, so he kept up with them until they reached his rescuer's farm, where the man turned the cows into a pasture. "I'll just go and find my wife. I'd better warn you, she'll want to mother you."

Jamie wouldn't have minded a motherly arm around him as he sat on a tree stump and waited for his return.

I wonder if the headmaster will have informed my parents. I hope not, they'll only worry, especially Mama, he thought as he looked around him, trying to ignore the pain in his ankle. *And Father?* He imagined him shaking his head, his lips pursed, his eyes sad or angry. *Which will it be? Hopefully, not angry. I can't bear it when he gets cross with me. I go all shaky.*

A large, chubby woman with brown hair and a big nose ran across to him. "Oh, my goodness, child, however did you come to be in such a situation?"

Jamie began to recount the happenings of the previous day, wondering why her husband hadn't already told her, when she continued, "Yes, yes, never mind. What's important now is helping you back to the school. Do you think you can stand?"

"Yes, ma-am."

She put her arm under his elbow and helped him up. "There, there, what a good boy."

He wanted to protest that he wasn't three years old, he would soon be an adult, but her arm around his shoulder felt so comforting, he wanted to stay there. Resting his head on her shoulder, he revelled in the sympathy, as she patted his cheek.

"I expect I'll be in trouble," he moaned. "And all the boys will laugh at me even more."

"Surely not?" she exclaimed, screwing up her nose so her nostrils looked enormous. "Why would they do that?"

He shrugged, tearing his gaze from her nose, and heaved a huge sigh. "I don't know. They just do. But I leave next summer. It can't come soon enough."

"There, there," she repeated. "You're just feeling sorry for yourself. Ah, here's my husband with the trap.

He'll soon have you back with your friends."

Friends? He had thought Anthony to be one, but he had turned his back on him. Hopefully, Oswell would still be.

"But…but I don't feel well enough to travel, yet. Can't I…I mean, please may I stay here a little while, just 'til I feel a bit better?"

She looked at him with her head to one side, as if weighing him up, and then nodded. "Of course you can, lad. Come on, you must be parched."

"Oh, thank you, ma-am, thank you." He let her help him into the farmhouse, after she'd told her husband to leave the trap until later, and finish his chores.

"I'll bet you're starving, as well." The sight of two large slices of bread and butter lit up his eyes. "Do you like strawberry jam?"

"I love it. It's my favourite." He remembered telling his cousin, George, that when he'd first met him. But George had died, so he didn't want to think of him. Trying not to wipe jam around his face, he tucked into the feast.

"You'll soon feel better with some food inside you," she told him, wiping her hands down her white pinafore. "The farmer will take you back then."

Jamie hesitated, about to take another mouthful of the delicious food. Maybe he should pretend he couldn't eat any more. The temptation, though… Licking his lips, he looked at the red topping. Before he could give in, he dropped it onto the plate. "I'm so tired," he muttered. "I can hardly keep my eyes open." Resting his head on his arm, he closed his eyes to prove the point.

"Oh, my poor boy. I'll bet you hardly had any sleep, did you?" She put her arm around his waist. "Come on, let's have you upstairs to bed. Do you think you could make it up there?"

He gave a small nod, just enough for her to see. The

other alternative would probably be to lie on the sofa, and she would be able to keep her eye on him there, whereas, upstairs, he could pretend to sleep all day.

After a longing look back at the unfinished bread, he found enough strength to climb the stairs and into a small bed smelling of rose petals. "Thank you," he murmured. "You're very kind."

"I'll leave you to have a good sleep." She tucked the covers around him and left.

Looking up at the ceiling, he wondered if he should feel guilty, but fell asleep before he'd come to any decision.

Later that afternoon, his ankle covered in a white bandage, he climbed into the farmer's trap. As they began to pull away, his wife called, "Wait a moment. I'll fetch the lad an apple."

She soon ran back with an apple and a bottle of water.

"Thank you, ma-am," he called as the pony began to trot forward. "Thank you very much." The clip-clopping of the pony's hooves drowned out the sound of her reply. He drank the water, and then looked at the apple. What had Anthony said about the pips being poisonous? Surely not? He'd eaten them loads of times and had never died once. *Should I eat them?* he pondered. *Maybe not. I don't want to tempt providential.*

He threw the core into the bracken, blowing out his breath at the thought of what would happen when he arrived back at school. Maybe they hadn't missed him. What day was it? Sunday. He could say he had stayed behind to pray in the chapel after morning service. But that wouldn't explain his ripped trousers and cut hand. He would just have to make his way straight to the infirmary and see if Matron would cover for him by saying he had been there all night.

* * * *

Tillie found Ruby lying on the bed in a pool of blood.

"Oh, my goodness," she yelled, trying to shield Alice behind her. "What's happened to you? How long have you been like this?"

A low moan escaped Ruby as she turned a pale face towards her. "I think I may have lost the baby."

Tillie covered her with a blanket as Alice surprised her by running out the door, calling, "I'll fetch Uncle Sam." She had expected her daughter to have hysterics or, at the very least, to scream and cry.

"I didn't know you were pregnant." Tillie took Elizabeth from her cot, wrung out a flannel from the basin, and wiped her sister's brow, the baby still screaming.

"No, nor did I. Well, I wasn't sure."

"Where's Eleanor?"

"Downstairs playing, isn't she?"

"I didn't see her. Oh, my days, don't say she's gone missing." Tillie adjusted Elizabeth on her hip and ran downstairs, calling Eleanor by name, her mind filled with visions of her own daughter, Annabella, being found down the well after nearly two days of searching.

A murmur came from under the table in the kitchen. She lifted the cloth, and there sat her niece, tears running down her cheeks.

"Thank goodness you're safe," Tillie gushed, scooping her up with her free hand and hugging her close, still shaking. "You must have been scared."

The little girl nodded. "I could hear Mama crying. I don't like her crying."

Tillie gave her another hug. "No, my darling, I'm sure you don't. It must be very unusual." Her sister usually had a happy disposition, even though she had little self-confidence.

Sam hurried in the door, followed by a breathless Alice. "I found him, Mama. I found him."

"She said something about blood," gasped Sam. "Where's my Ruby?"

Tillie indicated with her head. "Upstairs."

Not bothering to take off his muddy boots, he ran up, two at a time. Alice began to follow him, but Tillie stopped her. "No, darling, you stay here and help me with these two. Take Eleanor, would you? Maybe go down the lane and pick some blackberries?"

"That would be spiffing, wouldn't it, Ellie?" Alice opened a cupboard door and took out a basin.

Tillie smiled at the use of Jamie's favourite expression, but warned, "Don't let your auntie hear you call her Ellie. You know how cross she becomes when you shorten her name."

Alice grinned at her cousin and took her hand.

"Make sure she doesn't prick herself on the sharp thorns."

"I'll look after her," Alice called.

Tillie sat the baby in her high chair and looked in the pantry for something to feed her. She had stopped crying, but whimpered now and again. "It'll have to be bread and cheese, by the looks of it," she told her. "Oh, and here's some of your mama's gorgeous strawberry jam. I bet you like that." She spread a thin layer onto a slice of bread and cut it into fingers, placing them on the child's tray, before listening at the bottom of the stairs. "Do you want me to go for the doctor?" she called up.

Sam came down, his face ashen. "No, I don't think there's much point now. I've changed her and the bedding, and she's settled down for a sleep." He sat down at the table, pushing his hair off his brow. "I didn't even know she was expecting again. This is the second miscarriage she's had in six months. We must be doing something wrong."

Tillie picked up some of the bread the baby had thrown down, and patted his shoulder. "You can't blame yourself, Sam. These things happen. I'm sure you'll have lots more beautiful babies. You're both still young."

He heaved a huge sigh. "I know you're right. I must stop feeling sorry for myself." He looked around the kitchen. "Where's Eleanor?"

Tillie told him, adding, "But I'm beginning to wonder if I should have let them go alone. What if they can't find their way back? Maybe I should go and look for them?"

He stood up. "No, you stay here, if you would. I'll go." Replacing his cap, he went out the door. "Which direction did they take?"

She tried to recall if she had noticed and scratched her head, replying, "I'm not sure. Oh, my goodness. What a stupid fool I am. I should have taken more care." She ran out, looking in both directions, calling, "Alice, Alice."

Her daughter stepped out from a bush, about twenty yards away, holding Eleanor's hand. "Yes, Mama?"

Letting out her breath in a whoosh, Tillie shook her head. When would the feelings of apprehension leave her? Surely, she should be able to let her daughter out of her sight by now? It had been four years since Annabella had died. "Are you finding many blackberries?" she murmured, her shoulders slumping.

"Quite a few."

Sam went up to the girls as Tillie went back inside to check on Elizabeth. The baby banged her hands on the tray of the wooden high chair, a beam covering her sticky face.

"Have you had enough, little one? It looks like you've thrown most of it on the floor, so I take it you don't want any more. I suppose I'd better take you home with me. Your papa will need to go back to work." She wiped the child's hands and face and lifted her out. "We'll just check on your mama before we go."

She found Ruby fast asleep, making little noises in her throat. She stroked her cheek, whispering, "I'll come back later and wash your things, little sis. You rest." Memories of her own miscarriage still haunted her at times, so she knew what her sister would be going through—only Ruby's would be twice as poignant, it being her second.

The bowl of blackberries stood proudly on the table on her return to the kitchen, and the two little girls, their mouths betraying the fact that they had eaten as many as they had picked, sat drinking lemonade.

Sam twiddled his cap in his hands. "I have a new mare I need to attend to. I don't suppose I could presume on your good character?"

"Of course, Sam. I'll take the girls home with me. Ruby's sleeping, so I'll come back later and check on her."

"Thank you so much. I shall call in now and again, when I can." He hurried out, after giving his daughters a peck on their cheeks.

"Don't I deserve a kiss?" asked Alice, her bottom lip sticking out.

"Of course." He gave her one as well, and bent towards Tillie, as if to do the same to her, but she pushed him gently away.

"Off you go."

With one last look towards the stairs, he hurried out.

Tillie put Elizabeth in her pram. Being a late walker, she could walk around the furniture, or if someone held her hands, but would definitely not manage the mile to The Grange. Her own children had been on their feet at a much earlier age, but this little one had followed in her sister's footsteps, and been too idle to bother trying until well after her first birthday. But then, Eleanor had begun to talk sooner than Daniel, so she knew no babies should be compared with their cousins, or with other children of a similar age, for they would all catch up eventually.

After closing the back door behind her, she bid Alice to hold Eleanor's hand and they set off down the lane. "Nanny will have her hands full." She smiled. "It will do her good to be stretched for a change."

They met David on the way. "I wondered where you were. I came home to find Joseph bawling his head off. Why do you have Ruby's girls?"

"Oh, David, I'm sorry. I lost track of time. We found Ruby in the throes of another miscarriage, so I've brought them with me to give her some rest."

That seemed to appease him. She sat Eleanor on the front of the pram and they hurried the remainder of the way, Alice clinging onto his coat tails when he couldn't balance properly holding her hand as she wanted him to.

Joseph's cries could be heard as soon as they came around the corner. "We'll go and find Nanny," she told David. "Did you want me for anything in particular?"

He shook his head. "No, you go. I will speak to you later."

Wondering if that meant she had committed a misdemeanour—she couldn't think she had done so—she put it to the back of her mind as she grabbed Elizabeth out of the pram and followed Alice and Eleanor upstairs.

The nanny paced up and down with Joseph, while Daniel sat playing with a jigsaw. He jumped up as soon as the girls came in, a huge grin lighting up his face.

Tillie swapped Elizabeth for her own baby, explaining what had happened before the nanny could expound on the censure Tillie had perceived on their arrival. Maria's nostrils flared in disapproval, but she took the little girl, glancing around as if she didn't know where to put her.

In a bid to relax as she fed Joseph, Tillie smiled at

Eleanor, who was trying in vain to press a piece of jigsaw into the wrong hole.

"Here," commanded Daniel. "It goes here, doesn't it, Alice?"

Alice took the piece and showed her where it should go, but she didn't want it there, she clearly wanted it in the other space. Daniel grabbed it from her and ran across to the other side of the nursery. Eleanor stood up and stamped her foot. Tillie closed her eyes and sucked in her lips. This would turn out to be a noisy few hours. She had considered keeping Ruby's girls at The Grange for a few days, but wondered if it would be such a wise decision, after all. For the time being, they would have to knuckle down and behave, though.

"Daniel, please…"

Before she could continue, the nanny had intervened by picking him up and carrying him over to his cot. "If you're not a good boy, you'll go in there and stay for the rest of the day. Do you understand?"

He handed her the piece of jigsaw.

"And that goes for all of you," she continued.

Alice gave her an indignant look.

"Yes, you as well, Miss Alice."

"I wouldn't fit in a cot." Her voice trailed off at the raised eyebrows of the nanny. She lowered her gaze and carried on to complete the picture.

The front door bell rang, and Tillie held her breath, hoping it would not be a visitor. She had too much on her plate to entertain. A few minutes later, Nellie appeared at the door with a letter.

* * * *

Jamie asked the farmer to drop him off before they arrived at school, so he wouldn't be seen, but the farmer would have none of it. "Oh, no, young man, I want to

35

deliver you into safe hands. I don't want anyone accusing me of shirking my duty."

"But I won't tell them. I promise." The cart pulled up, right at the front door. "Please, sir, don't let anyone see me like this. I'll be in right trouble." He climbed down, realising he had been defeated.

The farmer patted his arm and pulled the bell. "You didn't fall down that ravine on purpose, so why should you be in any bother?"

He shrugged, looking at the large oak door as it opened. "'Cos I always am."

The headmaster came out. "Dalton, where on earth have you been? We have been worried sick. Your parents are on their way."

Jamie groaned, kicking at a stone. "Can't you stop them? I'm fine." He looked at the farmer.

"I found him, sir, at the bottom of a ravine. Apparently he had fallen down it."

Mr Trout shook the farmer's hand. "Excuse my bad manners, sir. Thank you for bringing the boy back. If you would like to go around the back, the cook will provide you with some refreshments."

"No, sir, I must be on my way." He winked at Jamie, jumped onto the cart and drove off.

"Thank you for rescuing me," Jamie called, giving a little finger wave.

Other people, all asking questions, had come outside by the time he turned to enter the front hall. He covered his ears with his hands, trying to suppress the panic he always felt at such times.

Mr Trout steered him away and beckoned to one of the housemaids. "Please take Dalton up to Matron and ask her to examine him." He turned to Jamie. "You can tell Matron what occurred. I am pleased to have you back safe and sound."

"But what about my parents?"

"I'm afraid there's no way of stopping them now. They should be here at any time."

He groaned again as he followed the housemaid upstairs. They would be in such high dudgeon. His latest new word didn't give him any pleasure to use. He would rather not have learnt it. What would they say when they found him hardly hurt at all? They would be furious, especially Father, having been summoned on a wild goose chase.

Matron examined his ankle and replaced the bandage. "You'll live, young Dalton. Have you hurt anything else?" He shook his head. She washed the cuts on his face and hands. "So, how did it happen?"

After he'd told her the bare facts of the accident, she urged him towards the door. "Well, you'd better find some clean clothes and join the other boys as soon as they return from the walk." She checked her watch. "They should be back soon."

Close to tears, he looked up at her, gritting his teeth.

"There's no point giving me the soft eyes," she retorted. "You'll have to face them."

He breathed in and pushed back his shoulders. "Yes, I suppose I may as well get it over with. I'm not a little boy any more. I have to face up to my misfortunes."

"That's the spirit. Good lad. I'm glad to see you're growing up." Shaking her head, she nudged him. "But don't go falling down any more crevasses. See if you can reach the end of term without any further mishaps. You must have seen the inside of this infirmary more times than any boy I have ever treated."

Smiling, he went out. He couldn't help his clumsiness. In fact, he wasn't clumsy, just…what had his father once said? Attracted unwanted attention. No, Alexander Banks, his hero from the previous year, had said that. His father had said he 'fell foul of every situation'. That was it. That summed it up in a nutshell.

But it didn't solve the problem of how he would manage to remain calm when everyone started picking on him, and poking fun.

After changing into clean clothes, he dragged his feet down to the common room—fortunately empty. Sitting down with a book, but unable to concentrate, he practised looking cool and collected, telling himself he would hold up his head and look them in the eyes, that he didn't care what they threw at him. His name was James Dalton, heir to the Brightmore Estate.

Almost dropping the book, he jumped up when the door opened and the housemaid reappeared. "Ah, there you are, Master Dalton. Your parents are here in the parlour."

Here we go. Time to face the music.

With a grimace, he followed her, limping into the parlour with clenched fists, and forcing a smile onto his face.

His mother put down her cup and saucer and ran to him. "Oh, Jamie, thank goodness you're safe."

"Yes, Mama. Please don't fuss." Looking over at his father, sitting rigidly in an armchair, his lips jutting out in disapproval, he drew in his breath. "Good day, Father." He only received a nod, confirming his earlier fears. "I'm so sorry to have dragged you both needlessly all the way here. Please forgive me."

His mother hugged him again. "That's all right, as long as we know you're unscathed. They tell me you fell down a canyon. How did that happen?" She stroked the scratches on his face.

"It wasn't a canyon, Mama, it was a small ravine." He thought he heard his father give a 'Humph', but continued, "I just lost my footing and then it was dark."

"Never mind that now." His father put down his unfinished drink and made to stand. "We had better be making our way home, now we know you are in one piece."

Jamie repeated, "I really am sorry. I'll make it up to you, somehow."

"Yes, well, say your farewells to your mother. We have a long drive ahead of us."

"I need to use the um...you know...first, David. Would you show me where it is, Jamie, please?"

His father raised his eyebrows, but then he agreed. "Me, too," and they all traipsed out, followed by the housemaid carrying the tray of cups and saucers.

His parents had been at the school enough times to know where the toilet was. Maybe his mother had wanted a quiet word with him, in private.

After he had waved them off, he went back to the common room. A few boys had filtered in, but none he knew particularly well, so he picked up a book and sat with it in front of his face. His heart sank when he heard Bullimore's voice. "Dalton, come with me."

Would he be in bother, or would his housemaster be in a good mood, and merely ask him to perform a few simple tasks?

He saw Silas Brown in the distance, and slowed down. Bullimore turned to say something, but Jamie didn't reply, so he pulled his sleeve. "Dalton!"

"Sorry, sir." He had been wondering if he should finally report the bully at the end of term, for the incident when he'd fallen out of the window. What harm could he do once they had left? But, as Oswell often pointed out, Brown had not actually pushed him—none of them had—they had merely closed the window, preventing him from climbing back inside. Could they be disciplined for that? They would probably only receive a reprimand, so would it be worth it? He still hadn't reached a decision when they arrived at Bullimore's rooms.

"Remind me which book you borrowed last term, Dalton," the housemaster barked as they entered.

"Um, I had a few, sir. Why do you ask?"

Bullimore held up a brown book with the corner bent over. "This one?"

Jamie took it and flicked through the pages, trying to remember if he had borrowed that particular one. "I don't think so. I know I had 'Oliver Twist' and 'The Old Curiosity Shop', but I'm sure I didn't have this one. I might borrow it this term, though, if I may?"

Bullimore looked at him from under his raised eyebrows. "Are you sure?"

Jamie's head jerked up. "You don't think I damaged it, do you? Is that why you're asking?"

"Well, I wasn't sure."

"You know I take extra special care, since the time I dropped 'Twelfth Night', but I explained how that happened, didn't I?"

"Yes, yes, well, if you are sure, toast me some crumpets."

Placing a crumpet on the toasting fork, Jamie felt aggrieved that his housemaster should suspect him of being careless with his property. Why would he do so? He always scrutinised his books as soon as he returned them.

"So, tell me what happened yesterday."

"Oh, you mean on the walk?"

"Well, what else would I mean?"

Spreading butter on the crumpet, Jamie took a deep breath and told him the full story, even the part about the apple pips.

"I don't know, Dalton. What are we going to do with you? You are in your final year, so I feel it's too late to change you. We shall have to accept you for what you are, a…what shall we call you? An oddity. I mean it in the nicest possible way, so don't go considering yourself hard done by. Everyone's different. It wouldn't do for us all to be the same, would it?"

Jamie shook his head. Did he feel 'hard done to'?

His mama always called him 'one in a million'. Did the housemaster mean it like that?

Chapter 3

Six months later, Jamie stepped out of the carriage and looked up at the house. Snow covered the garden and the drive and he had been worried he would not be able to go home for the Easter holidays. But there he stood. Running his finger inside his itchy collar, he took a deep breath, before throwing his scarf over his shoulder and marching up to the front door. It opened and Purvis appeared, followed by Daniel. He picked up his brother who squealed, "Jamie, welcome home."

"Thank you, little brother. Where's everybody else?"

"Alice has gone to see Auntie Ruby and Eleanor and Elizabeth and Uncle Sam."

"But what about Mama?"

As the door closed behind him, his mother's voice carried down the hall. "Jamie, welcome home, my darling." She hurried towards him. He had been expecting her to be carrying a baby, but she held out empty arms. He lowered Daniel and ran to her embrace. No matter how old he grew, he would never stop wanting her cuddles. He breathed in her perfume, so familiar, so comforting, as he hugged her. As he pulled back, he thought she looked older. A few grey hairs peeped out from beneath her cap, or maybe the light played tricks on his eyes. He touched one. No, definitely grey.

"Yes, my darling, I am afraid to say my hair betrays my age, if that is what you can see."

"Oh, no, Mama, you're not old, only thirtyish." Embarrassed at his impropriety, he turned away. "How's Father?"

"He is…how shall I put it? He's very well, actually— looking forward to seeing you. He should be home soon. You know what he's like, his business demands keep him so busy. But, come into the lounge and let's have a homecoming drink."

With one more look around, to make sure his father hadn't arrived while they had been talking, he followed her, taking Daniel's hand. His mother pulled the bell to order tea. Maisie came in. The maid beamed at him, grinning from ear to ear.

Why had she come in response to the bell? Surely she should not be doing so? He looked from her to his mother and back again.

"I wanted to tell you in my last letter," began his mother, "but Maisie asked me not to. She wanted it to be a surprise."

"Do you mean…?"

Maisie rubbed her hands together and blew on them. "Yes, Master Jamie, I've been promoted to parlour maid."

"Why, that's marvellous." He reached out and, not knowing what else to do, hugged her. "It's about time. You were much too good to remain a scullery maid."

"We did think she might train to be cook," added his mother, "but she said she would prefer to do this."

"Right then, what shall we order?" Not knowing if she had had much experience, he asked for tea and cake and, sitting down as she went out, pulled Daniel onto his knee. "Now then, young man, what do you have to tell me? Have you had any adventures lately?"

The little boy laughed. "No, don't be silly."

"That isn't silly. But I suppose the snow has kept you all inside. It seems as if it has been here forever, doesn't it?"

A smirk appeared on his mother's lips. *What did I say?* he wondered.

"Me and Alice made a snowman," Daniel continued as he jumped down and tried to pull Jamie off his chair. "Do you want to see it?"

"Not yet, later maybe. I haven't had my cup of tea

yet."

His mother beckoned his brother towards her. "Jamie will play later, sweetheart. Do you want to go up to the nursery?"

A shake of the head came as reply.

Jamie recalled building a snowman, years earlier, and how excited he had been. "Does he have coal for his eyes and a carrot for his nose?" he asked.

"Yes, and one of your old caps on his head."

"Huh! I hope it wasn't one of my favourites."

Daniel turned to his mother with a worried expression. "Was it, Mama?"

Shaking her head, she smiled. "No, dear, just a tatty brown one that had no more use."

"That's all right, then, isn't it, Jamie?" The boy came back and stood in front of him, his head to one side.

Jamie sat back and rested his hands behind his head. "I suppose so. I don't expect it would fit me anymore."

"No, Mama says you've grown into a young man."

"Does she? What else does she say about me?"

Daniel climbed onto his knee, put his arms around his waist, and rested his fair-haired head on his chest. "That you're the best brother in the world."

His arms came down and he wrapped them around his little brother. "Ah, thank you. And do you say the same?"

"Mm."

He looked up at his mother and saw her beaming. He grinned. How wonderful to be back home in the bosom of his family. Thank goodness he only had one more term at school.

"Anyway," his mother said, helping Maisie as she re-entered with the tea tray, "what do you fancy doing this holiday?"

For a second he had thought her to be speaking to the maid, but realised his former friend would never have the chance to go on a trip with them again, not like the time she had accompanied them to the zoo. "If this snow stays much longer, we won't be doing a lot, will we?" He nudged Daniel off his lap and accepted the cup of strong tea, stirring in two spoonfuls of sugar. "Unless we build another snowman?"

Daniel jumped up and down. "Yes, Mama, may we?"

In between sips of her own drink, she replied, "Of course, dear."

"Alice and Joey can help."

"Joey?" Jamie wondered who the new addition to the household could be, and then it dawned on him—his youngest brother, Joseph. "Why, can he walk, already?"

"No, no, he is only nine months old," answered his mother. "He can sit in his pram and watch, though."

"Shall I fetch my coat, Mama?" Daniel ran to the door.

"No, sweetheart, not just yet. Let your brother accustom himself to being home first." She stood up and went towards him. "Come on, it's time for your nap. Say goodbye to Jamie."

"Aw, must I, Mama? I'm not tired."

Jamie laughed. "I remember using that excuse, but it never worked. I shall see you in a little while. I'll still be here, for I don't intend going anywhere."

After they had gone out, he wandered around the room, picking up familiar objects, and some not so well-known, marvelling at how his brother had grown up since the Christmas holidays. He examined a photo of Alice, Daniel and Joseph. Why had they had a photo taken of the younger children without him? He plonked it down, blowing his breath out in resentment. Come to think of it, he could not ever remember having one taken with the whole family.

His mother returned. "That's him settled. We can have a nice chat now."

Picking up the photo again, he asked, "When was this taken?"

"Oh, yes, a while back. We must have one done with all of us while you are home."

"Yes, that would be wonderful." What else could he say?

The door opened and Alice ran in, dispelling his chagrin. "Jamie, you're home."

"I certainly am." He ran and picked her up, twirling her around.

"I've been to Aunty Ruby's house," she reported as he put her down. "Did you know she's expecting yet another baby?"

"No, I didn't. That's good news." *Or is it?* he thought. *Yet another one to add to the menagerie.*

His mother took off the little girl's bonnet and fingered through her hair. She shook it, letting it cascade down her back. "Do you think my hair's grown, Jamie? Look, I can touch it from behind now." She reached around and put her head back, twiddling her fingers until they came into contact with it. "See."

"So you can. What a clever girl. Have you learnt any new songs since I last came home?"

She put her finger on her lip. "Um, have I, Mama?"

"Why, yes, there's that one about sheep."

"Oh, yes, Baa, Baa, Black Sheep. Do you know it?"

Pretending not to, he tapped his teeth with his nail. "I might need reminding."

"Even Daniel can sing it. Shall we wait 'til he's with us?"

"No, you remind me, and then I can show off to him when he comes down."

"Very well." She recited the nursery rhyme. He hadn't realised he had not taught it to her before. He had always enjoyed singing them to her, ever since she had been a baby.

They spent the next half hour singing as many rhymes as they could remember, Alice coming up with the most, until his mother patted her skirt and stood up. "I expect baby Joseph will be awake by now. Why don't you show Jamie how proficient you've become on the piano, Alice? I'm sure he'd love to hear you."

With a shake of her hair, Alice took his hand. "What a spiffing idea. Come on, Jamie."

* * * *

David leaned on the gate in the lane that ran behind the house, surveying the white fields spread before him. He had intended calling on Farmer Askew to sort out another problem, but his leg ached from trampling in the snow.

As he turned to go back, he heard horses coming towards him and female voices. Christine Harrison and her sister appeared around the bend in the lane.

"David," she squealed. "I mean, Mister Dalton, what on earth are you doing out here all alone, and in this weather? Don't tell me you are hiding from your lovely wife and all those children."

He shook his head and bowed as he replied, "Good, day, Mistress Harrison." The sight of her pretty, heart-shaped face still caused his heart to flutter, no matter how hard he tried to suppress it. He turned to her sister and nodded. "And Mistress Harrison." A grin formed on his mouth from calling them by the same name. "I trust I find you well, and your husband?"

The sister nodded. "Very well, indeed, sir, and your good wife?"

These pleasantries had to be adhered to, but he needed to return to the warm house. A chill ran down his back and he pulled his coat around him. "Very well, also, thank you, but I must bid you farewell. Be careful, the snow has drifted in places, and I should hate to have to send someone to rescue you if you fell in one." *Not that I would do so for you*, he thought uncharitably. *You could stay there until you froze.*

A smile pinned to his lips, he nodded and turned, his head down and his gaze averted from the green eyes of his former flame. Rumours abounded that Christine had left her husband, but she did not seem particularly heart-broken.

He could feel her eyes boring into his back as he walked away. Maybe she still had feelings for him. Someone had told him she had been very enamoured of him, and had been devastated when he had married Tillie in such haste. Maybe she had married her husband for his money, and when she had found out he had squandered it all, she had not been able to remain with him any longer.

Well, she need not try to get her claws into me. I love Tillie and my children. I would never do anything to hurt them. Never. He pulled his hat over his ears, and hurried back home, eager to see his family.

John, his valet, appeared. "I have been looking for you, sir. You did not tell me you were thinking of going out."

Taking off his coat, he replied, "No, it was very foolish of me to even contemplate it. I think I could do with a hot bath later. Could you arrange that, please?"

"Certainly, sir."

"Do you know where my wife is?"

"I think she is in the lounge, sir, with Master Jamie."

David threw his arms in the air. "Oh, my goodnight. How could I have forgotten?" He had fully intended being home for his oldest son's return, but circumstances had removed the event from his mind. Slinging his gloves at his valet, he hobbled across the hall as fast as he could, and would have fallen when the wet crutch slipped on the wooden floor if John had not held him.

The door opened and Jamie ran out. "Father, I thought I heard your voice."

"I am so sorry not to have been here when you returned." He followed him into the room as Tillie came downstairs.

"Come to the fire, David. You look frozen. Were you able to talk to...?" For a second, he thought she meant the ladies he had met in the lane. His eyes opened wide until she continued, "...to Farmer Askew?"

"Oh, no, I um, no. Anyway, Jamie, let me sit down and you can tell me all about your goings-on at school. Have you had any more calamities or incidents that we have not been told about?"

Jamie laughed as he perched on the arm of the chair. "No, Father, I have completed a whole term without a single mishap."

"Well, thank the Lord for that. It must be the first term we have not had to hare across the countryside after you had come to grief in one form or another." David accepted the glass of brandy Tillie offered him and drank it in one gulp.

"Oh, Father, that is unfair. I can only think of, maybe, three such episodes."

Alice jumped onto his knee. "Papa, when the snow's gone, I will be able to ride my pony, won't I?"

"Yes, of course, darling."

Jamie clapped his sister's hands together. "You have a new pony? Oh, yes, of course, you showed me at Christmas. What's his name?"

"He is a she, and her name is Starlet."

"Why, does she have a little star on her forehead?"

"No, she's a palomino."

"So, don't palominos have stars on their faces?"

From the set of his daughter's face and her blazing eyes, David could see an argument brewing, so tried to diffuse the situation. "She likes the name because she read about a pony with that name in one of her books. Am I right, darling?"

"No, Papa, that's not it at all."

"Oh, well, never mind. You can explain it all later. I would like to hear about Jamie. Have you taken any exams yet?"

"Um, yes, Father."

"Don't tell me you did not try."

"Oh, I tried very hard, but they were so difficult."

Tillie sat down on the sofa and picked up a pink garment she had been knitting. "You know he isn't academic, David. There's no point in wishing he were."

He sighed. What would the boy do with his life if he could not even pass a few exams? "Well, perhaps I could show you the household ledgers later, when you have settled in. You will have to learn how to complete them, if you want to make yourself useful once you have left school, especially as you are insistent that you are not going to university. I cannot understand it. How can you not? Unless you have changed your mind since last time you came home?"

Jamie shook his head and stood up as Tillie put down her knitting and said, "Please, David, don't start. We'd been having such a merry time earlier, singing and so on. Now you've spoilt it. I'm going up to the boys. Do you want to come, Jamie?"

"I'm staying with Papa," chimed Alice, putting her arms around his neck. "I love my papa."

Over his daughter's head, David could see Jamie looking uncertain, his head down, and his arms folded behind his back. He had not meant to bring up the subject straightaway. He had meant to leave it until the boy had settled in, but it had just blurted out. No point retracting it, though. It had been said, and he would keep on saying it until he could change the boy's mind. All Dalton men went to university. It had been a tradition in the family as long as time began. His own sons, Daniel and Joseph, would be going, and any other boys they might have. He would make sure of that.

Nudging Alice off his lap, he watched Jamie and Tillie leave. "Papa has work to do, darling, so go with your mama, there's a good girl."

Tillie held out her hand to her daughter and gave him a look from beneath her brows that showed her dissatisfaction with him. She would never understand. She had not been brought up in society. She had been a maid since she had been not much older than Alice. Well, maybe slightly older, but her father had been a miner. What had he known of such things?

* * * *

Tillie went up to the nursery, seething that David could be so insensitive on Jamie's first day home. What could she say to alleviate the state of affairs? Not much. She knew her husband's views, but could not agree with them. She had given in on the question of boarding school, but only because Jamie, himself, had decided he had wanted to go, even though it had proved to be a disastrous decision in the end. She did not feel as lenient over the university matter, and would not back down so readily. If the younger boys proved themselves to be more academic, she would bow to his greater judgement, but she knew her oldest son better than David ever would, and university would not be the best place for him.

Daniel sat playing with a jigsaw on the floor, while Joseph lay in his cot, kicking his chubby legs in the air. She went across and picked him up. "He's cold, Maria. How could you have let him kick off his blankets like that?"

The nanny looked up from her sewing. "I hadn't

realised he had awoken, ma'am."

Pursing her lips, Tillie held him out to Jamie. "Would you like to give him a cuddle?"

Alice tried to grab him. "I will, I will."

"Not this time, Alice. Let your big brother have him. He hasn't seen him for nearly four months."

Daniel jumped up. "Me, me have a cuddle."

Jamie's face relaxed and he laughed. "Everyone can have one. Come on." He held out his arms to encompass all the children, and Tillie joined in. "Let's have a group cuddle—a gruddle."

"Ha, ha," laughed Alice. "That's a new word. A gruddle."

Joseph began to whimper, clearly not appreciating the gruddle.

They broke away and Jamie went to look out of the window. "May we go out and play in the snow?"

Tillie smiled. "Yes, just for a short while."

Pulling on their coats and scarves, the three ran out, happily chatting and singing.

Even though Joseph was nine months old, she still tried to feed him herself, not that she had a lot of milk, but conception should be less likely if one still breast-fed and, old wives' tale or not, she thought it worth pursuing. Four children should be enough for any family. She did not want to be one of those mothers who had a baby every year.

Hearing happy voices outside, she sat crooning to Joseph. His shock of black hair had started to turn fairer, more like Daniel's, and his green eyes mirrored hers.

The nanny came in with a pile of clean linen and, without speaking, put it away in the tallboy.

If she can't be bothered to talk, then nor can I, Tillie thought. *I would probably only berate her for some misdemeanour.*

Noticing a button seemed to be missing from the baby's trousers, she fiddled with her free hand to try to see if it had just come unfastened, but could not find it. The nanny opened the door to exit, but she called her back. "Maria, when you wash this little one's clothes, please would you make sure all the buttons are intact. This has one missing."

Maria did not refute it, just replied, "Yes, ma'am," and went out.

Tillie wondered if she could be having problems. "Come to think of it, Joey," she droned to the baby, "she hasn't been herself for a few days. Should I ask her if there's a problem? Am I that interested? Yes, I care for my staff. I shall do so as soon as she comes back."

However, the sound of shrieking put the thought from her head. Gently easing Joseph away from her, she jumped up to look through the window. Nothing untoward could be seen at first, but then Alice ran across the lawn, her arms waving in the air, followed by Jamie, carrying a screaming Daniel. "Now what's happened?" she muttered, laying the baby in his cot and fastening her dress. She ran downstairs and found the children in the kitchen.

David hobbled in behind her. "What in heaven's name is going on?" he yelled.

Alice ran to him and put her arms around his waist. "Oh, Papa, Daniel fell out of the tree."

"Which tree?"

Tillie pushed him to one side. "For goodness sake, does that matter, David?" She picked up Daniel who had been leaning against the table. "Are you hurt, my darling?"

He nodded and then pulled up his trouser leg. "My knee."

"Let me look." She sat him on the chair and bent down to inspect him, but couldn't see any blood. "Anywhere else?"

He screwed up his face as if he had to think, and

then examined his arm. That seemed fine.

Jamie stood twiddling his fingers. She looked up at him. "Jamie, would you like to tell us what happened?"

"Well, it weren't my fault, really."

"Did I say it was? Just tell me."

"Daniel wanted to climb that big tree on the edge of the lawn, but he couldn't reach, so I lifted him up. He'd just caught hold of the branch when Alice saw a fox and squealed, making him lose his concentration, and he fell."

David sat down and pulled Alice onto his knee. "So, you are blaming your sister?"

"No, Father."

Tillie intervened. "The boy doesn't seem to be hurt. I expect the snow softened his fall. We'll put it down to youthful exuberance. Nobody needs to take any blame."

"I do not know." David sighed as he stood up and made for the door. "You have been home two minutes."

"David, I've just said it's nobody's fault." Tillie glared at him. "No one has been hurt, so we can forget all about it, can't we?" she added through gritted teeth, and then turned to the cook. "Missus Lansdowne, would you please make the children a sandwich and a drink? I left the baby on his own, and am hoping the nanny will have returned to the nursery, but need to check." She helped Daniel take off his coat and went out after her husband.

She caught him up in the hall and tugged on his sleeve. "Why do you have to belittle Jamie all the time?"

He turned with a surprised look. "My dear, I do not 'belittle' him. You still mother him too much. It is about time he grew up."

"I…" What could she say? He was probably right. She did mother him. But David did the opposite. She felt him to be too cold towards him. "Don't you remember how you used to love him, when we first married?"

"I still love him, of course I do, but he cannot stay a little boy forever. He is almost sixteen. If I had not rescued you from a life of drudgery, he would have been out working for the past five or six years, so just think on that." He looked her in the eye as if defying her to repudiate his words.

"I am aware of that. You don't have to remind me. I thank God every day. You know I appreciate everything you do." She looked away. "That's the first time you've ever thrown it back in my face. What made you do so today? It should have been such a happy day for me. Now, you've spoilt it."

"I am sorry. I…" His shoulders slumped. "…I should not have said that. I vowed to myself at the time that I would never do so. Let me make it up to you." He touched her arm, a contrite look on his face.

"How?"

He puffed out his cheeks. "I do not know. What would please you?"

She could tell his arm ached under the crutch, so steered him into the nearest room, the morning room, and they sat down. The baby upstairs needed his nappy changing, if the nanny had not done it, but she wanted to clear the air with her husband first.

"What I would really like—if the snow clears, of course—is for us all to go for a ride into the countryside, as a family. Me, you and the children. Maybe take a picnic."

"That would be lovely. The weather would have to warm up significantly, though."

"Of course, of course. Do you think you would be able to find time to do it?"

"I shall find time, my dear. Anything to make my wife happy."

She tried not to show her surprise at his words. His blue eyes shone as he smiled. She leaned forward and kissed his lips, feeling an ardour she had not felt since Joseph's birth. He kissed her back with passion, clamping one hand behind her head, and stroking her cheek with the other. As he pulled away, he indicated with his head towards the ceiling.

"If only we could, my darling, but the children…"

"I know, I know, always the children."

"Well, if you would like to…here, and risk them coming in and observing us?"

"No, do not be so silly." He laughed. "Could you imagine their faces?"

Standing, she laughed also. "And the nanny's. What a hoot that would be."

"Maybe, we should, after all, just to witness her expression?" He pulled her back down and kissed her again. She lay in his arms, not wanting to leave them—her haven. They had so few opportunities for such intimacy. She vowed she would make more in the future. Make time for cuddles and hugs, whenever the occasion arose. They were such a panacea for resolving niggles and doubts.

Chapter 4

Jamie held Daniel's hand as he took the children for a walk along the lane towards the village.

Alice walked demurely beside them. "Why wouldn't Mama let me bring the baby? I am big enough to push the pram."

"Me, too," piped up Daniel, letting go and running ahead into the trees.

Jamie called him back. He didn't want to lose him. He couldn't afford another catastrophe. As his father frequently pointed out, he'd had enough of them to last him a lifetime. When Daniel didn't return straightaway, he grabbed Alice and followed him. They found him talking to a girl. Beth! His heart almost stopped. She had grown even more beautiful than he remembered. He tried to recall how long it could have been since he'd last seen her. Easily over a year. She had grown taller, only a little, but then so had he, so the difference in their heights remained about the same.

"Hello, Jamie." Her loud, clear voice surprised him. She must have grown in confidence, too. But her green eyes—they still mesmerised him.

Alice pulled at his coat. "Who is this?" He dragged his gaze to her, wondering why she sounded so haughty.

"This, my dear sister, is a friend of mine, Beth."

"Well, how do you know her?" Her mouth turned down as if in disgust, and he thought he heard her mutter, "Dirty." Maybe her dress and shawl did not match up to their pristine clothes, but they looked clean enough to him.

A small girl whom he had not noticed until now stepped out from behind Beth. Her clothes looked even more raggedy then Beth's. Jamie grimaced.

"This is my cousin." Beth stooped down to the little girl, probably to hide her face from Alice. "She's living with us now because her parents died."

Mention of the word *cousin* brought back horrible memories. Memories of Jake and his cronies. He wondered whether to ask after him.

She forestalled him. "Do you remember my cousin, Jake, her big brother, who they sent to prison for poaching?"

He nodded, too afraid to speak, in case his name conjured up the actual person.

"Well, he's been sent to the convict land, *Austrialia*, or something like that. He might never come back, so my ma says."

Jamie breathed a sigh of relief. "I think you mean 'Australia'."

Alice yanked on his arm. "Are we going, Jamie? I'm cold."

"Yes, of course, in a minute."

"Now. I want to go now."

Daniel had been staring at Beth's little cousin. He reached over and kissed her cheek.

Alice pulled him away. "Do not touch her," she squealed. "She might have something unpleasant."

Beth's face turned angry. "She does not. What do you think we are? Animals?"

"Of course she doesn't, do you, Alice?" When his sister looked away with a hard set to her mouth, he continued, "I'm so sorry, Beth. I'd better take her home. She's a very impolite young girl. I shall have to have words with Mama about her." He knew there would be no point mentioning it to his father. He'd already cottoned on to the fact that whatever she did would be fine in his eyes.

They turned to go and he remembered his little friend, Beth's brother. "How's Bobby?"

"He's working up at the farm over yonder." She pointed towards their left. "We rarely see him."

"Oh, I'm pleased for him. Tell him I was asking after him."

With one last look at her, he made his way through the trees, back to the lane, and continued towards the village. She had made his day, appearing like that, as a vision, almost. He often thought about her, wondering if she and her family still lived with the charcoal burners. In fact, what would she be doing in the woods? How come she'd not been working? At a year or two younger than himself, he would have thought her to be in service, like Maisie, or working in the mills. Strange. Maybe it had been her afternoon off. He pondered these things until Daniel moaned.

"You're walking too fast, Jamie," explained Alice, taking her younger brother's hand in hers. "He only has little legs."

"Oh, I'm sorry. Do you want me to pick you up?"

Daniel nodded.

Jamie did so, but soon put him back down. "You're rather heavy to carry far. Do you want to return home, instead of carrying on to the village?"

"No, me want lollipop."

Jamie had promised the children a lollipop from the sweet shop if they were good. "Well, you may have one, but I don't think Alice deserves anything at all, after speaking to my friend in such a nasty way."

Alice stopped, a defiant look in her eyes. "How do you know such a creature, Jamie?"

"She's a human being, like you or me, not a 'creature'. I hadn't realised you were so high and mighty, looking down on people less fortunate than yourself. If Mama had not married Father, you would not be here at all." Realising she would not understand what he meant, he gave up and, still undecided if he should buy her anything or not, continued on the way.

A poster stopped him in his tracks, announcing the arrival of a travelling circus the following week. "A circus, how exciting!" he exclaimed.

"What's one of them?" asked Alice, still sulking.

"It's like a travelling zoo. Just look at the pictures. Lions, elephants—all sorts of animals."

"Let me see." Daniel raised his arms to be picked up. "I like animals." He looked around as if expecting them to be there. "Where are they?"

"They aren't here yet, not 'til next week," Jamie replied. "When we return home, we'll ask Mama and Papa if we can all go. Oh, I hope they say we can. I went to the zoo a few years ago. It was the best day of my life."

Alice screwed up her face. "I don't know if I want to."

"Why ever not? It would be interesting, don't you think, to see, up close, all those wild animals? Now, they are creatures."

She shook her head in disdain. "I can see my pony up close whenever I want. Why would I want to see wild things? Wouldn't it be dangerous?"

"No, or they wouldn't allow it to happen, would they?"

She shrugged and walked down the street towards the sweet shop. On a high, Jamie bought them each two lollipops and one for himself. With a contrite face, Alice accepted hers. "I'm sorry, Jamie, for not liking your friend."

"That's all right, but you must remember, not everyone is as lucky as we are to have parents who have money to buy whatever we want—new clothes and the like, even sweets. When I was a little lad, I never ate sweets. Mama couldn't afford them."

"Yes, she once told me something like that. I didn't really want to know, so didn't listen much."

"Well, just think yourself blessed."

"Me, too." Daniel took his lolly out of his mouth. "Me blessed."

Jamie tickled him under his chin. "You certainly are, young man. We all are."

"And Joseph?"

"Yes."

"And my new puppy?"

"Yes, everyone in our household."

"Even...?" His little face puckered up as he tried to think of someone else to mention.

"Yes, Daniel, as I said, everyone. Come on, it looks as if it might start snowing again. We don't want to find ourselves caught in a storm."

They hurried back, Jamie carrying Daniel most of the way. The snow from the previous week had almost disappeared, but this fall came down quickly, and by the time they arrived home, the ground was covered again.

Giggling and squealing, they ran into the kitchen. "We look like snowmen," cried Alice.

The new scullery maid, Ellen, who had replaced Maisie when she had been promoted, helped them take off their coats and mittens. "You do, don't you?" she exclaimed, her brown sparkly eyes flashing. Jamie wondered why her skin had a much darker colour than his, more like the Indian princes at school.

"Do you know where Mama is?" he asked her.

"No, Master Jamie. I've been in here all day."

"Of course, silly me." *For sure, she would have. What on earth made me say that?* "I'll just go and find her. Coming children?"

He hurried out, berating himself for being so insensitive. He had been lecturing Alice earlier, and there he was, being just as bad.

They caught up with their mother in the hall.

"Did you have a nice walk?" she asked, bending

down to feel Daniel's cold cheeks.

"Yes, Mama, and we saw some pretty girls." Daniel looked up at Jamie as if to ask him to confirm it.

His mother's eyebrows shot up. "Oh, yes, where did you see them?"

"In the woods."

"In the woods?" she repeated. "What the heck where you doing in there?" She turned to Jamie. "I thought you were going to the village. Jamie, please explain."

"And they were ragged and filthy," muttered Alice.

Jamie glared at her. The lollipop had clearly only been the means to a temporary apology.

"They were perfectly clean, Mama. Alice is exaggerating. Do you remember me telling you about a boy called Bobby, some years ago?"

A look of enlightenment covered her face. "Oh, yes, I think I do."

"Well, Beth is his sister, and the other little girl, who Daniel took a fancy to, is her cousin. Her parents have died and Beth's mother has taken her in. She's a lovely lady, her ma, very short, but very friendly."

"Oh, I see. Well, don't go getting any ideas of romance into your head, young man. Your father may have his own on that score."

"What do you mean? I'm not old enough to be thinking of marrying. I have my schooling to finish and…and…"

"Yes, yes," she ushered them up the stairs. "Forget I said anything. I should not have done so."

They reached the nursery and his mother took the children inside, while he carried on to his own room farther along the landing. What could she have meant? He could not think of any girls of his age in the neighbourhood, not suitable for his father's high standards, anyway. And he could not imagine any of them measuring up to Beth.

He flung his coat on a chair and slumped onto the bed, lying on his back, his arms behind his head. Of course he couldn't contemplate betrothal, not at his age. His father had been thirty-four when he'd married. Surely he didn't expect Jamie to do so before his twentieth birthday. *Mama must have the wrong end of the stick again. She does that a lot.* He sat up. Should he confront his father about the matter? Lying down again, he decided not to. It would be best to let it lie. The subject might not come up again.

The travelling circus! He hadn't asked his mama about that. Perhaps he should wait until later. She would probably be feeding the baby. Not much later, though. He didn't want to miss the opportunity. Just fancy seeing those elephants and clowns and other acts. The school library had a book about a circus clown and he'd read it many times. It had sounded so thrilling. He really hoped he would be allowed to go. Crossing his fingers on both hands, he felt sure he wouldn't be scared, not like the time he'd had the picture show for his twelfth birthday, and thought his parents had been eaten by a lion. What a dunderhead he'd been. But he'd grown up in the last three years. He would not make the same mistake again. Even if they looked ferocious, he would put on a brave face.

Unable to contain his enthusiasm any longer, he jumped up and ran to his father's library. Maybe there would be a book in there about clowns. After all, he had played a jester in the school play, and a jester being an old-fashioned name for a clown, it would be appropriate for him to be interested in them. Which section would it be in? He spent ten minutes searching, but couldn't find one, so gave up.

Hearing his father's voice in the hall, he ran out. "Father, do you know if you have any books on clowns?"

His father's head jerked back in surprise. "I beg your

pardon. Did you say 'clowns'?"

"Yes, Father. The travelling circus is coming to Leeds next week. I saw a poster in the village."

"What has that to do with us?"

Jamie followed him into the lounge. "Well, I would absolutely love to go and see it. So would Daniel. Alice isn't so keen. Please say we can…I mean, may."

His father sat in his armchair and stroked his moustache. "I shall have to think about that. What does your mother say?"

"I haven't asked her yet. But if you say we can…I mean, may, then she will agree to it, won't she?"

Raised eyebrows and a down-turned mouth came as his reply. "I am not so sure about that, son."

"Well, in any case, would you like me to pour you a brandy?"

"What, butter me up, you mean?"

"No." Jamie laughed as he approached the cabinet. "I just know you like one at this time of day."

His father leaned back. "That snow is a nuisance. I had intended going out."

Is he changing the subject because he doesn't want me to go? Better play along. "Yes, Father, we were lucky to arrive home before it came down heavy." He handed him the drink. "Anyway, about the book?"

"Book?"

Grr, is he being intentionally obtusive, if that's the word? "Yes, about clowns? Don't you remember I played the part of Feste in Twelfth Night? You said I was magnificent. He was a clown."

"No, I do not think I have ever seen one. You are free to browse through the shelves, though, if you are insistent on finding one."

Does that mean he's saying we can go to the circus? I'd better not push my luck, though. "Thank you. Would you like another drink?"

His father grinned. "No, thank you, Jamie, I have not finished this one." He swirled the amber liquid around in the glass, as if relishing the taste, without actually drinking it. "Your mama says I drink too much, so I need to modify the amount I have. You would not want me to be in trouble, now, would you?"

"Oh no, Father, I didn't…I mean…"

"Do not look so worried. I shall not tell her you have been trying to corrupt me."

"But…"

"Relax, I am jesting. Do you like the reference? Of course, I would do no such thing." Voices sounded from outside the door. "Ah, here she is now."

Jamie blew out his breath. The conversation hadn't turned out at all as he'd hoped. He opened the door and his mother came in.

"Ah, my two favourite men." She sat next to Jamie. "Nellie tells me dinner won't be long. I'm starving."

His father held out his hand towards her. "Well, that makes a change, my dear. You normally do not eat enough to keep a sparrow alive."

"Oh, David, that's an exaggeration. I eat ample. I don't want to put on weight and look like a fat whale. You wouldn't love me then."

Jamie wanted to bring up the subject of the travelling show, but daren't interrupt. He sat looking from one parent to the other, as if watching a tennis match.

"My dear wife, I would love you if you were the size of a house, so do not worry on that score."

Jamie laughed that time. "Ha, ha, that's funny. As if someone could be the size of a house!"

The gong rang for dinner. He helped his father stand, and they went to the dining room. During the main course, Jamie would have loved to bring up the subject closest to his heart, but his parents had a long conversation about a neighbour and his lost sheep, and he thought he'd better not butt in. However, as they enjoyed the dessert—a delicious dish of meringue and cream—he took his chance. "Mama, you like animals, don't you?"

Her spoon halfway to her mouth, she paused. "Yes, of course."

"Wouldn't you like to see some in real life?"

She finished chewing before replying, "What sort of animals?"

His father put down his napkin. "I think our son is trying, in a roundabout fashion, to ask permission to go to a show. A travelling circus."

"A what?" she spluttered.

"When we went to the village today, we saw an advertisement. Is that the right word? Anyway, a notice, saying the circus would be coming to Leeds. Oh, Mama, I would so much love to go and see it." Putting down his spoon, he put his hands in his lap, waiting with bated breath for her reply.

Her eyes lit up as she wiped her mouth. "Oh, a travelling circus. I remember going to one when I was a child. It was marvellous."

"Did you really, Mama? Does that mean we can go?"

She looked at his father. "Well, David, it would be an opportunity for us to go somewhere as a family, wouldn't it? You did promise, the other day, that we could go somewhere."

"Me?" His father scratched his head and then cupped his chin in his hand. "I had not thought about me going to such an affair."

"But you'd love it, too, Father. I know you would, and Alice. I'm sure she'll change her mind if she knows you're going."

"I shall have to consult my diary. Find out the exact details, and then we shall see." His father finished his meal and Jamie decided to leave the subject at that. Pushing too far could have the opposite effect to the one he wanted. He grinned at his mother, and she grinned back, clearly as eager as him for the jaunt.

"We wouldn't be able to take Joseph, but Daniel would be old enough to come," she continued.

He grimaced, thinking she ought to stop, as he'd decided to.

His father stood up. "As I said, we shall have to see."

Jamie tried to pull a face at her to tell her not to pursue the matter, but she must have come to the same conclusion. "Yes, dear," she muttered. "Have you finished reading today's newspaper? I would have thought there'd be an advertisement in there, wouldn't you? Didn't you see one?"

"No and no. I intend to read it now. I shall let you know if there is."

After his father had gone out, Jamie and his mother made plans for the outing, just in case the answer came back favourably. He had not seen her so animated in a long while. In fact, he couldn't remember ever seeing her so. Maybe his idea would cheer her up. She looked so sad a lot of the time. Well, not really sad, just not happy. It would be good to see her laugh and smile more, and the trip would surely do just that.

Have I actually done something right for a change?

He couldn't wait to hear his father's reply. If only there was some way of finding out straightaway. Walking over to the window, he drew back the curtain. It had stopped snowing, thankfully. That could put a spoke in the works, if the weather were too bad for them to go. "I'll go to the village again, tomorrow, Mama, and take another look at the notice, just in case Father can't find anything in his newspaper."

"Yes, dear, that sounds a good idea." His mother still sat in her chair, a dreamy look on her face. "Have you finished your dinner?"

"Oh, yes, thank you. I forgot to ask if I could leave the table. Sorry."

She stood up and walked towards him. "I remember your Auntie Ruby being scared of the elephants when we went."

"Was she very little? Say, do you think she and Uncle Sam and Eleanor would want to come? I hadn't thought of them."

"I'm not sure, in her condition."

"Oh, yes."

"But Sam could bring Eleanor, for she is much more outgoing than your auntie was at her age. I'll ask them, but I suppose I'd better wait until we have the go-ahead first, hadn't I?" Putting her arm around his shoulders, they stood together in silence, his head resting against hers. He realised he had grown taller than her. Maybe he would not be such a shrimp, after all, like the boys at school called him.

After a while, she pulled away. "I suppose I'd better go up and say goodnight to your brothers."

"Do you want me to come? I could sing to them. We learned a new song in the choir last term. I love it. It's called 'Home, sweet home' and I learned all the words so I could sing it to you. It starts, 'Mid pleasures and palaces though we may roam'. He began to sing as they went upstairs.

"I think I know that one." She joined in with him and they had almost reached the end of the song by the time they reached the nursery.

Nanny looked up in amazement as they came in singing. "Good evening, ma'am. You sound happy."

"Don't I usually? I suppose not. It must be the influence of my magnificent son, here. Are the boys asleep?"

"Joseph is stirring, ma'am. He seems very unsettled, but Daniel…"

A little voice called from the bed, "Mama."

As his mother went over to him, Alice looked up from her dolls. "May I stay up a little later, tonight, Mama, please? I'm not at all tired."

"We'll see." She kissed Daniel and settled him down, and then went to look at what Alice had been playing with—the rag doll she'd had since babyhood.

The little girl lifted it up. "Nanny had to mend her arm, it came apart. Give her a kiss to make it better." Her mother obliged and Jamie took down the other one. That had been her twin's, and it sat on the tallboy most of the time, a replica, although less battered, for it had not been handled as much.

"Does this one need a kiss as well?"

"She doesn't deserve one. She's been a naughty dolly."

"Oh, in what way?" asked her mother. "How can she possibly be naughty when she sits up there all day long?"

"She made me tear my dolly's arm. It was her fault it ripped."

"Oh, my darling, how could a rag doll make you do anything?" His mother took Annabella's doll and turned it over as if to find some flaw in it. "You must have caused it yourself. You're the naughty one, blaming an inanimate object."

"No, I'm not. It *was* her. You ask Nanny."

They all turned to the nanny, who stood near the door, a guilty look on her face. "It's time for the servants' dinner. I shall be late if I don't hurry." She ran out, almost colliding with the door jamb on her way.

Jamie sat down next to his sister. "What did Nanny do, Alice?"

"She told me Annabella's doll had her spirit inside it, so I shook it to make it come out. What's a spirit?"

"It's like a..." Jamie remembered, some years before, thinking almost the same thing. He stood up, feeling unnerved. "You tell her, Mama."

"It's part of a person left behind after they die," his mother tried to explain. "Well, sort of. You can't actually see it. Nanny should not have said such a thing."

"No, she shouldn't." Jamie hugged Alice, trying to relieve some of his own unease.

"But how did that rip your doll's arm?"

"I'd been holding my dolly at the same time, and shook her too."

"But that didn't make Annabella's doll naughty, did it? She was the innocent party."

"I don't want to play with her anymore, just in case it's still in there." Alice turned her back on them.

"Very well, I'll put her back up."

"No, take her away."

Jamie looked at his mother. She seemed as much at a loss over what to do as he was. He handed her the doll. "I'll keep her safe in my bedroom," she told Alice. "I won't let any harm come to her, just in case you want her back any day."

"I won't, not ever."

"Let's have you ready for bed. You love your new nightgown, don't you? Where is it?"

Jamie decided he'd better leave. While his sister had a sorrowful mood on her, he didn't want to bring up the subject of the circus. But what could he do?

"The candle's almost burnt down. Would you replace it first, please, Jamie?" his mother asked as he made for the door.

He found a new one in the cupboard and lit it, sniffing in the sulphur pong of the match. He loved that smell.

His mother smiled her thanks as he picked up the stub and carried it out. There should be enough left on it to light his way to the library to find a book.

An hour later, the candle having snuffed out, he gave

up once more. It didn't look as if his father had any books on clowns or circuses or anything of that ilk so, thirsty, he went to the kitchen for a drink of water.

The following morning, before going to the village, the snow having almost melted, he took Alice down to the lake with Goldie, the golden Labrador he had been given as a pup. The mother, Lady, stayed behind because she couldn't walk far.

He threw a stick. "Fetch, Goldie."

Alice picked up a bigger stick and threw it when Goldie returned. "Mama says she misses walking with Lady."

"I'm sure she does." His voice sounded deeper than usual. Even though it had broken a year or two before, it still seemed to be deepening. He didn't know if he liked it. "There's nothing you can do about it," his friend, Oswell, had said, when he'd mentioned it to him. "It's like having a hairy chest, or a big nose. You just have to accept it." At least he had neither of those.

"Oh, Jamie, look." Alice had run ahead. "It's a baby bird, and it can't fly."

Looking around for its parents, he picked it out of the grass before Goldie could get to it. "It's a blue tit."

"Shall we take it home?" She reached into his cupped hands to stroke its little blue head.

"I don't know. Its mother might be looking for it."

"I can't see her."

"She wouldn't come while we're here." He placed it into a pile of soft leaves. "I tell you what, we'll creep over to that tree, and wait to see if she comes."

They waited for about a quarter of an hour, but no blue tit came near so, becoming cold, they left their hiding place and approached the spot where they had left it.

"Oh, it's gone," cried Alice.

Jamie ferreted about in the undergrowth. "It looks

like it. Oh, well, perhaps it found its mother, after all."

"Ah, I hope so."

Goldie snuffled around and began to bark.

"What?" Jamie ran and grabbed her collar. "Have you found it?"

"Yes, it's there, look, under that branch sticking out over the water." Alice reached forward to try and grab it.

Jamie pulled her back. "Don't go near the water. Our cousin, George, fell in there a long time ago. He almost drowned."

"But we need to catch it, before it goes in the water itself. What can we do?"

"Here." Jamie gave her the dog to hold. "You stand back with Goldie. I'll try and reach it."

The bird hopped closer to the water's edge. Holding onto the branch with one hand, he leaned forward and scooped it up. "I have it," he called in triumph. Trying to gain his footing, he almost lost his balance and, for a heart-stopping moment, had visions of his body being swept down into the murky depths of the lake. Fortunately, after a wobble, he stood upright and hastened back to his sister. "Phew, I nearly didn't make it."

"Oh. Jamie, I thought you were going to fall in," Alice wailed, nearly in tears. "I was so scared."

He wanted to put his arm around her, but rested his forehead on hers, the bird cupped in his hands. "I'm fine, see."

"Did you catch it?"

"Yes." He opened his hand a little to show her. "I think we'd better take it to Uncle Sam. He'll know what to do."

"Why will he?" She trotted along beside him, having let go of the dog. "It isn't a horse."

Laughing, he replied, "I know, but he knows all about nature and stuff. Did I ever tell you about the baby fox I rescued when I first came here?"

"A baby fox?" She stopped and gazed up at him in admiration. "You rescued a fox? How?"

"It had become trapped in some wire. Sam fed it for me but it escaped."

"Back to the fields? Was it better?"

Not wanting to give her the outcome, for deep down in his heart he knew the hounds had ravished it that day, he made a non-committal reply.

"Ah, that's a lovely story." She clung onto his coat as he hurried along once more, Goldie running and jumping up beside them.

Thinking he'd better somehow warn his uncle not to tell her the real outcome, he continued, "So that's why I think Uncle Sam will help," he added.

They found their uncle in the stables, brushing down the horses. He looked up and smiled. "Hello, you two. Are you enjoying the warmer weather?"

"Yes, thank you, Uncle, but we have something to show you."

Alice sneezed. "It's really dusty in here, isn't it?"

"Yes, I'm afraid so. Shall we go outside and you can show me what it is?"

Jamie opened his hand enough to show him his treasure.

"It's a blue tit," Alice declared.

"So I see, but why do you have it?"

"'Cos it's lost."

"Well," explained Jamie, "we couldn't see its parents, and we waited for ages."

"And it can't fly," Alice persisted. "Would you look after it for us until it can? Jamie said you cared for his fox 'til that was better."

His uncle gave a look from under his eyebrows and Jamie tried to indicate, by shaking his head, not to finish the story. Sam must have understood, for he didn't pursue the subject. "I shall try, me duck, but I can't promise anything."

"Aw, thank you. Do you have anything to put it in?"

"Let me see." Sam went into the stable and called, "Yes, here's a box. I'll put some straw in it, and I think I saw an old mitten over there."

Jamie followed him in, and picked up the woollen glove. "That'll keep it warm. What can we feed it with?"

Alice had remained near the door but, holding her nose so she wouldn't sneeze again, she ventured inside. "What do baby birds eat?"

Jamie took her hand. "They eat caterpillars and worms and things."

"Ugh, where will we find them? Do we have to dig the garden?"

"Now the snow has gone, the ground will be softer, so you could do so." Uncle Sam settled the bird in the box. "But I'll try it with some warm milk soaked in bread first."

"Let's go and ask Missus Lansdowne." She grabbed Jamie's hand and pulled him outside. "Come on, Jamie."

"Very well." He turned to his uncle. "We'll be back as soon as we can. Will it survive that long?"

"I should think so."

They ran to the house, and arrived at the kitchen door, panting.

"What on earth is happening? Is something on fire?" asked the cook.

They both tried to explain at the same time.

"Calm down and tell me, one at a time. You first, Master Jamie."

He gave her the details and she put some milk into a pan and put it on the stove.

"Not too hot. We don't want to burn its mouth...rather, beak." Alice stood peering into the saucepan. "It's bubbling, look. Will that do?" She lifted it off and carried it in both hands to the table where the cook crumbled some bread onto a saucer and poured the milk onto it.

Jamie grabbed it, calling, "Thank you," as they ran back out.

Arriving at the stables, they called their uncle and opened the box. Jamie's heart pumped as he looked inside. Had it died? No. Its yellow-edged beak opened. He took a pinch of the soggy bread and put it in. It swallowed it straightaway, so he gave it some more.

Alice pushed closer. "Can I give it some?" She grabbed a large piece and, before he could stop her, shoved it down its throat.

"Not that much," he yelled. "You'll choke it."

The little bird heaved and spat it out, then pecked at the lump, picking off a small bit and eating that.

"See, it knows what to do." Alice stood back, hands on hips, as Uncle Sam came in. "We've already fed it," she declared.

"Ah, good. What are you going to do about the rest of its feeds?"

"Oh, I didn't think of that, did you, Jamie?"

"No." He grimaced, thinking his trip to the village would have to be postponed if he needed to feed it at regular intervals. He looked up at his uncle.

"Don't expect me to do it, young man. I'm much too busy."

"How often should we do it? Mama only feeds Joseph about every four hours."

"Oh, much more often than that. Have you never watched a parent bird flying into its nest every few minutes?"

He offered the blue tit another crumb. It ate it. "How will we know when it's full?"

Uncle Sam shook his head. "I don't know. When it stops taking any more, I suppose."

"We'll be at it all day and all night."

"Yes, I'm afraid so. You should have thought of that before you took it in."

"Can't we just take it back to where we found it, now it's had some food?" Alice suggested, clearly not relishing the idea of staying up all night any more than Jamie.

Their uncle made as if to go out. "It's up to you."

Jamie asked, "Could you not feed it some of the time, please, and we'll take turns doing the rest?"

"No. I really am too busy. I have two mares in foal and your father's stallion, Starlight, is ailing. I need to tend to him." A faint neighing came from a stall down at the bottom of the stable. "There he is, now. I must go to him."

Jamie picked up the bird. "Well, Alice, what do you think?"

She turned to go. "I'm hungry. I'm going home."

"You can't go on your own. Mama would kill me if I let you do that. You wouldn't want that on your conscience, would you?"

"I don't know what coscious is." She sneezed again. "I can't stay here, the dust gets up my nose."

"But I thought you often came to curry your pony. What happens then?" He walked outside with her, still carrying the blue tit in the box. "Doesn't it affect you then?"

"Well, I'm supposed to."

"Oh, I see, you haven't started it yet."

"It's been too cold. I'm cold now. Please may I go home?"

Torn between helping the bird and pandering to his sister, Jamie had to make a decision. "If we put the bird back on the ground where we found it, a fox or a stoat, or even a buzzard could find it. It wouldn't last long, then. I'll have to take it home with us."

"Yes, that's a spiffing idea," Alice retorted, making

him laugh as they ran across the grass back to the house.

The bird safely ensconced in his bedroom, he spent the rest of the day feeding it. That evening it tried its wings out and he encouraged it by placing it on a shelf. It flapped several times, but hopped into the box and settled down again.

During the night he could hear it tweeting, and every now and again would feed it some more of the bread mash, along with a chopped-up worm he had dug out of the garden in the afternoon. The following morning, worn out from being awoken so often, he dragged his weary body out of bed. The blue tit had gone from its box. Where could it be? A fluttering of wings heralded its approach to adulthood, as it flew around the room.

"Hooray, you can fly." Expecting it to want its freedom, he ran to the window and opened it. However, it flew to the top of the wardrobe and perched on the edge, looking around. Jamie flapped his arms in front of it, hoping to dislodge it, but it looked around, as if surveying its new territory. "No, this isn't your home. You can fly out to the great outdoors. Go on."

Voices outside his door marked the arrival of his mother and siblings. Before he could warn them, the door opened. "Close it, quickly," he yelled, but too late. The bird found its freedom, out onto the landing.

"Oh," his mother swivelled around. "Was that the baby bird? I thought it couldn't fly. I was just coming to see it, to decide what to do for the best."

Jamie ran past her and looked over the banister. The bird seemed to be enjoying itself, landing for a rest every now and again, on a picture rail, or the top of a portrait. "How are we going to let it out?"

Maisie came into the hall below. "What's happening?" She looked up and saw the bird. "Oo, don't let Missus Lansdowne know about it. She was only saying the other day that's it's unlucky to have a bird in the house. Can't you catch it?" Craning her neck, she followed its movements. "Shall I open the front door?"

Purvis appeared also. "I shall do that. The sooner the creature is out of the house, the better."

"You're not superstitious, are you, Purvis?" called down his mother.

Nellie ran into the hall. "Oh, no, not a bird. Remove it, someone."

While his mother took the children back to the nursery, Jamie ran downstairs, still in his nightshirt and cap. "It can't do any harm. It's only a defenceless baby bird. Why are you all so scared of it?"

"It's just unlucky, that's all. I don't know the reason why," replied Nellie, wafting her arms above her head, as if to ward off any evil spirits.

Maisie came up to him. "I think it's cute. I'm not afraid of it. Do you remember that baby bird we saved when we were at the gypsy camp, Jamie? That one died, though, didn't it?"

"Oh, yes, I'd forgotten all about that. A blackbird, wasn't it?"

"No, a starling."

"Ah, so it was. You have a good memory. You must have only been about five, if not younger."

"I remember all sorts of things from then. My ma, especially."

He put his hand on her shoulder. "Do you still miss her?"

She nodded, but then the blue tit flew down and landed right next to her, on the hat-stand. She offered her hand slowly towards it, but it flew off, out of the door and into the wide world.

"Byebye," she called, and then turned back to Jamie. "Do you think my ma's spirit could have been inside it? Was that why it came so close?"

He shrugged, unnerved by all the talk of spirits and

such, especially after the incident with Annabella's doll. "I don't know, Maisie."

She picked up the pile of serviettes she had been carrying and proceeded into the breakfast room, a smile of contentment on her face. If she wanted to believe all that claptrap, then why not, if it made her happy?

After a look outside to see if the blue tit could be hovering near the door, wanting to come back in, he made his way upstairs, and met Alice coming down.

"Oo, Jamie, you're not dressed."

"I know, isn't it awful?"

"Where's the birdie?" She looked up and around.

"It's flown away. I hope it's strong enough to survive."

"I hope it wasn't too podged, after eating all that bread. Nanny tells me I shouldn't eat too much bread. It gives one *indigisiton*."

He laughed. "Anyway, I'd better dress. It wouldn't be very polite if visitors arrived and saw me..." The front doorbell rang before he'd finished his sentence. "Oh, 'eck," he cried and ran up to his bedroom.

Tillie finished dressing Joseph. He seemed more content, having drunk all the boiled cow's milk from the glass bottle with a teat at both ends so, if she had to supplement his feeds with that, then so be it. Better for him to be satisfied, than to scream with hunger all day. Excited at the prospect of seeing her friend, Emily Thompson, the vicar's wife, who had helped her find Jamie all those years before, she fastened the ribbons on Joseph's cap and laid him in his cot. The doorbell rang. That would probably be her. "Please could you tuck him in, Nanny," she called as she ran out the door and down the stairs.

Emily stood in the hall, holding her younger son, Johnnie, while the older one, Eddie, clung to her skirts as she took off her coat.

Tillie took the baby from her. "I'm so sorry to keep you waiting, Emily. Please come into the parlour."

"I quite understand, my dear. Ah, here are your children."

Tillie looked up as Alice approached with Daniel. "Come and say hello to Missus Thompson, children."

Alice curtsied, saying, "Good day, Missus Thompson," but Daniel just stood staring at the baby. Tillie gave the child back to his mother. "You remember Edward?" she asked her son. "Why don't you take him up to the nursery and find some toys—if that's all right with his mama?" She looked questioningly at Emily.

"Yes, he would like that."

Alice lingered, clearly unsure what her position should be. Tillie took her hand. "Could you go up with them, my darling, if you would? And then you may come back down and join us."

The girl's eyes lit up. "Yes, Mama."

After they had gone, Emily sat the chubby baby beside her on the sofa and gave him a rattle to play with.

"My word, he's grown, hasn't he?" gushed Tillie, tickling him under his chin.

Emily laughed. "Yes, both boys have. I noticed my Eddie is inches taller than your Daniel. But then, his father is much larger then David, of course, so it stands to reason."

"Yes, and don't forget, Daniel was a sickly baby. Joseph, on the other hand, is thriving, although I've had to start supplementing his feeds with a bottle. I didn't want to, but he is such a greedy baby. I'll fetch him down when he's had his nap. Anyway, how have you been keeping? Have you recovered from that awful illness?"

"Well, I'm still very weak. Victoria is unwell now. She had been so looking forward to seeing you, but Edward didn't think it advisable that she come today, not that she seems to have the same malady. I think she just has a cold. Mine, I think, is much more serious. Edward says I do too much, that I should take more rest, but how can I?"

Her face looked very pale. Tillie had noticed such as soon as she had seen her, but hadn't liked to mention it. And she had lost weight. Even through the dark blue woollen dress, she could tell. She rang the bell for the maid.

Maisie came in and curtsied. "Yes, ma'am?"

Emily looked from her to Tillie. "My, my, someone else has grown, and not just in height, but in stature. Oh, you look so fine. Just think, that shy, little girl who could barely speak when we found you at the Buttons' house. What wonders have been performed! God is good." She stood up and hugged the maid.

"Yes, ma'am, God is very good. The mistress often tells me I have you to thank for rescuing me." She curtsied again. "And I can read and write now, as well. Jamie taught me."

"That's wonderful."

Tillie intervened. "Maisie, please may we have a tray of tea and cakes?"

Emily waved her hand as she sat down again. "No cake for me, thank you."

"You need to build up your strength, Emily."

Her friend smiled. "A cake will not make much difference."

Tillie nodded to Maisie, indicating that she should bring some anyway, and the maid departed.

Emily sat back and closed her eyes. Tillie worried that her friend should not have come. She would have put her off when she had asked for the visit, if she had known how ill she still seemed. She picked up the baby and he banged her head with the rattle, making her yelp. Emily's eyes shot open and then closed again. "You're a grand little chap, aren't you?" she continued, trying not to wince at the pain in her temple. Playing with Johnnie, she let her friend sleep until Maisie returned with the refreshments.

Emily sat forward. "I must apologise. I almost dropped off."

"There's absolutely no need, my dear. Like your husband said, you need rest, so what better place?"

As Maisie poured the tea, Alice returned with a sulky face. "Daniel's given that boy one of my jigsaws, Mama. I didn't say he could borrow it." She tugged on Tillie's arm. "Please come and take it away from him."

Maybe not such a peaceful house, after all.

"Alice you must learn to share. And 'that boy' has a name—Edward—as you very well know. Come and sit next to me and have some of this delicious cake."

Alice looked at the tasty delicacies arranged on a pretty plate, and her eyebrows relaxed as she mulled over the options. Tillie patted the sofa beside her and she sat down, taking a piece.

Emily put some on a plate, but sat with it in her hand. "How is Missus Button? Have you seen her lately?"

"I'm ashamed to say I have not, but Maisie goes frequently. The older girls have gone into service. I should have taken one of them, but had already taken on Ellen. I should have asked her first, I know. The latest baby is a boy, much to her husband's delight. That makes thirteen, I think. Or is it fourteen? I lose count."

"Yes, I should make more of an effort to visit them, but what with the illness and everything."

"Mama?" asked Alice, after politely putting down her cake, "I thought you said Missus Thompson would be bringing her daughter, Victoria. It's nice being the only girl for Papa to love, but sometimes I would like a girl to play with. Maybe your next baby will be a girl, eh?" She popped the remaining morsel in her mouth, and rubbed her hands together.

Before Tillie could reply, Emily raised her eyebrows. "Are you…?"

At first she didn't understand what her friend meant, but then it dawned on her. "Oh, no, I'm not expecting." *Thank goodness*, she wanted to add, but didn't, not in front of her daughter. She turned to Alice. "Victoria's poorly, my darling. If you've finished, why don't you…?" What could she offer her? She wanted to have a chat with Emily, not pander to her daughter's wiles. "Where's that book you started looking at? The one with the animals. You could study that for a few minutes."

With hands on hips, Alice pouted. "It's upstairs."

Emily stood up. "Sit here next to Johnnie and play with him, while I talk to your mama."

"Don't let him fall off," warned Tillie. "Be very careful."

"Yes, Mama, I'll be extra, extra careful."

"Good girl. We'll only be over by the window."

She and Emily sat in the window seat, looking at the clouds. "Thank God it isn't snowing anymore," muttered Emily. "I couldn't leave the house at all while it lay so long."

Thinking her friend seemed to be making small talk before coming out with her real intentions, Tillie studied her face. Her eyes looked yellowish, probably from the illness.

"I think I may have cancer."

Tillie felt the blood drain from her cheeks. Had she heard right? "Cancer?" she whispered.

Emily nodded.

"Why do you think that?"

"Because my grandmother died from it, and she was the same age as I am now."

Tillie took her hand in hers. "Oh, my dear, I don't know what to say." She could hear Alice playing with the baby over on the other side of the room. She took a deep breath, intent on remaining strong. Her friend needed her support, not a blathering milksop.

"I wanted to tell you personally, not in a letter. That's why I came today."

"Oh, Emily, you should be taking care of yourself, not worrying about me. What can I do to help?"

"Just being here for me to talk to is enough. Edward won't accept it. Being a man of God, you would think he would be used to illness and death."

"Have the doctors confirmed it?"

"Well, no, but I feel sure in my bones. I've been poorly for weeks and it can be the only reason."

"Have you even been to see a doctor?"

"What's the point?" Emily took out a handkerchief from the bust line of her dress and blew her nose.

Tillie took the chance to glance over at Alice, to make sure she was coping with the baby. "Oh, Emily, surely you should have it diagnosed before you write yourself off?" How could her friend, who came across as such a positive person, be so negative?

"That's what Edward keeps telling me. I suppose I shall do, just to pacify him."

"But he's right. You must see that." Tillie broke off, for she could see little Johnnie sitting in a precarious position, so rushed across to pick him up.

"May I hold him, Mama?" asked Alice, putting out her hands.

"Sit there—no, further back." She helped Alice make herself comfortable on the leather sofa and sat next to her while she placed him in her arms.

He reached up and grabbed Alice's nose. "Ouch," she yelled, letting go of him. Tillie grabbed him before he could fall, as Emily came to join them.

Smiling, Emily took him. "He did that to me last week. It comes keen, doesn't it? I suppose we had better be making our farewells. Edward will be here any moment to pick us up."

Tillie turned to Alice. "Please be a dear and go and fetch Eddie."

Alice ran out without any argument, and Emily put an arm around Tillie. "Thank you so much for listening to my rantings. I feel so much better already."

"You go and see the quack and make sure it is what you think. It could be just a prolonged form of influenza, or something like that." Taking the baby, she helped put his coat on and then assisted Emily. "Do you have any outward signs?" She didn't know what signs there might be, though.

"Well, not really."

Alice returned with Eddie who was crying.

"What's the matter?" Tillie rushed over to him.

"He says he doesn't want to go home. He wants to stay here." Alice spoke for him.

"Oh, is that all?" asked his mama. "He's always like that. He'll be fine once we are outside."

The front doorbell rang. "Ah," exclaimed Emily. "I expect that will be Edward now. Hurry up, Eddie, we must not keep your papa waiting. He's a very busy man." She fastened his coat buttons and rammed his hat onto his head. "Thank you again, Tillie."

"You have no need to thank me, after all the help you've provided over the past few years. Now, take my advice as soon as you return home. I'm sure you'll find your suspicions are completely wrong." After giving her friend a hug, she followed her out into the hall.

"Yes, ma'am." Emily grinned. "Just seeing your lovely face has cheered me up no end."

Tillie hugged her again and gave the baby a peck on the cheek. Eddie stopped crying and reached up to her. "Me want kiss." She bent down and gave him one. Then he turned to Alice, and she indulged him with one also, as

Jamie came running downstairs.

"Goodbye, Missus Thompson," he called as they went out the door.

"Goodbye, Jamie." She waved her hand behind her head. "Farewell, everyone."

Edward, the vicar, stood in the doorway. He doffed his cap. "Missus Dalton." As Emily climbed into the carriage and made the boys comfortable, he turned to Tillie. "Has she told you?"

"Yes." She touched his arm. "And I think…well, I hope, I've persuaded her to see a doctor. I'm sure she's worrying about nothing."

"Thank you. She won't listen to me. Good day."

After they had gone, Tillie said a silent prayer that her words would prove to be true. Her friend had looked very unwell, but cancer? She didn't know much about the illness, not having known anyone who had died from it, but she knew people sometimes did.

"I'm sorry I missed them," exclaimed Jamie. "They weren't here very long."

"No. Missus Thompson isn't very well, so it was only a fleeting visit. Anyway, from the look of the weather outside, it's a lovely day. Shall we go for a walk?"

"May I come?" asked Alice.

"Yes, of course. Let's find our warm clothes and I'll see if Joseph and Daniel are ready to come as well. The fresh air will do them good. It isn't healthy to remain cooped up indoors all the time."

"May we go to the village, Mama?" asked Jamie. "So I can have another look at that poster."

"What a splendid idea."

Anything to take her mind off her dear friend's illness. Although acquainted with all the matrons and wives in the neighbourhood, none of them meant as much to her as Emily.

Saying another prayer that the sickness would only

be temporary, she went to prepare the younger children.

Chapter 5

Jamie breathed in the cold but fresh air, wishing he could hurry on ahead. His mama seemed in a dream, pushing the pram as if she didn't realise what she was doing. Several times Daniel had tripped from jumping on shadows, but she scarcely noticed, and it had been his responsibility to pick him up and dust him off. Fortunately, the boy hadn't hurt himself. He wondered whether to say anything, to maybe cheer her up, but when he had made a remark on the wonders of Nature, how all the trees had begun to blossom, she had not replied, so he continued, forging ahead with Alice and Daniel, holding his brother's hand so he would not fall again.

Alice rubbed her gloved hands together to warm them. "Tell me, again, Jamie, what a circus is like."

"Well, I've never been to one, but from the picture it looks like animals—elephants and lions and things—doing tricks, and also clowns. You'll see when we reach the village."

"Lions?" asked Daniel. "Won't they eat everybody all up?"

"I'm not sure. They wouldn't be allowed to show them if they were dangerous, so I really don't know how they train them."

"Shall I ask Mama?"

"No, she seems…" *How can I describe her?* "I don't think she's in the mood to talk. Sometimes grown-ups just like to be quiet."

"Um, me too."

Alice laughed. "You? Quiet? You never stop talking, now you've started."

"I do. I'll show you. I won't say nothing else 'til we're there." Daniel put his finger on his lips.

"You won't manage it, I know." Alice danced around him, calling him names, asking him questions, anything to make him speak, but the child kept his mouth tightly shut.

Amazed, Jamie smiled. His little brother had more resilience than he would have had at that age.

Finally, they reached the village and he hurried towards the poster, its corners bent and ripped, but the writing still legible. They stood staring in awe at the images of a huge tent, showing clowns with painted faces and striped trousers.

"When can we go?" asked Alice. "Is it soon?"

"It's next week," cried Jamie as his mother caught up with them. "Mama, it's next week. We will be able to go, won't we? Please, please say we will."

"Well, your father didn't say we couldn't, so I'm sure we will." She peered at the picture. "Oo, it's so thrilling."

Jamie's eyebrows rose. What a transformation. One minute she had been almost in tears, maybe not quite that sad, but almost, and now she looked ecstatic.

"Why won't the lions eat us?" asked Daniel, released from his vow since they had reached the village.

"They just don't," Tillie replied, still studying the picture. "Perhaps they feed them well before the show."

"What with?"

Jamie reached down and tickled him. "With little boys who ask too many questions."

Daniel's open mouth closed quickly and his brow furrowed.

"Take no notice of your big brother, Daniel," his mother consoled him. "He's teasing you. Of course they don't do that."

"No," laughed Jamie, this time catching Alice, "they eat little girls with long fair hair and blue eyes."

She gave him a disdainful look from under her eyebrows.

"Don't you believe me?"

Her eyes half-closed, she shook her head and turned away. "Of course not. You've only just said it isn't dangerous."

"Ah, but I meant while we're watching them. I didn't say anything about beforehand."

"Jamie, stop teasing them," retorted his mother. "If you want them to come with us, you had better stop trying to scare them. We don't want either of them having a screaming fit halfway through the performance."

He turned to take another look at the poster. "Look, Alice, there's a man on horseback. Maybe you could learn some tricks from him."

She gave him another of her scornful looks. "I know enough tricks, thank you. In fact," her face became animated, "Uncle Sam says I might be able to jump over a log tomorrow."

He turned with concern to his mother. "Do you know about that, Mama? Surely she shouldn't be doing that yet?"

"Don't ask me, Jamie. I have voiced my forebodings to your father, but he brushes them aside. He won't be satisfied until your sister falls off and breaks every bone in her body."

Alice laughed. "Don't be silly, Mama. Of course I won't."

Jamie gasped at her impudence. "Alice, that's very naughty, speaking to Mama like that. Say you're sorry, now, straightaway."

Daniel's hand sneaked into Jamie's. Clearly upset at his sister being rebuked, he snuggled close to him, as Alice looked down at the ground, her bottom lip jutting out.

"Alice?" Jamie repeated.

"I'm sorry, Mama." Her thumb found her mouth. Although six years old, she still sucked it when overtired or upset.

His mother put her arm around her daughter's shoulder. "Come on, there's no harm done. Let's have a quick gander round the shops before we make our way home."

Out of the corner of her eye, Alice glanced at Jamie. He couldn't be sure whether to smile or still be cross with her, but she had apologised, so he took her hand. "What shall we buy?"

His mother stopped in front of a haberdashery shop. "Oh, just look at that beautiful parasol. Isn't it lovely? I wonder how much it costs."

"Yes, Mama." What other adjective could he call it? A parasol was a parasol to him. But then a thought struck him. Maybe he could buy it for her birthday. He had begun to walk on, but turned back. "Which one, Mama? There's several."

She pointed to a green lacy one. "That colour would match my new outfit perfectly. I'm having it made for the supper party we're hosting next month. Did I tell you about that, Jamie?"

"Um, no, I don't think so, Mama. Who'll be invited?"

"Oh, didn't I tell you? I'm sure I did. It will be just before you return to school for the summer. I thought it'd be a grand way for you to meet all the neighbours—you know, to become properly acquainted with them."

"But I know them all, already." He didn't want a party. All that false conversation and repartee didn't appeal to him at all. "Please don't put yourself to all that bother just for me."

"It isn't just for you, Jamie. Your father needs to socialise more."

"Can I come?" asked Daniel.

"No, you're much too young," replied Alice. "But I'm sure I will be able to, won't I, Mama?"

His mother shook her head. "No, my darling, I fear that neither of you will be allowed to attend. It's for grown-ups only. Now, I'm fair parched. Do those tearooms look appetising to you?"

"Yes, yes," they both squealed.

With one last look at the parasol in the shop window, to etch it in his mind so he could come back at a later time and buy it if his father would lend him the money, Jamie took Daniel's and Alice's hands and, giggling, they ran across the road, weaving in and out of the horses and carriages and bicycles.

The bell tinkled as they entered, and he held the door open until his mother caught up.

Two elderly ladies sitting at a table near the door peered at them through their hand-held spectacles. Jamie thought he discerned disapproval on their faces, but didn't care. He had as much right to be there as they did, and so did his family. After all, they belonged to one of the highest families in the area.

"Sit quietly, children," his mother ordered when Alice and Daniel began to argue over which cake they wanted.

An elderly matron at the next table smiled at him. He smiled back, his head high, as the waitress came to take their order. His breath caught in his throat when he looked at her. With her hair tied back underneath a little bonnet, he couldn't believe who stood in front of him. Her green eyes opened wider than his.

He realised his mother had been speaking to him. He closed his mouth, shifting on the hard chair, and looked down at the tablecloth, his heart thumping. How had she found a job in a posh tearoom? He had only seen her a few days before, in the woods, looking as bedraggled as she had ever done. What could have changed so quickly?

"One o' them…yellow cakes, please, Mama," he stuttered, not looking up.

Beth dropped her pencil, clearly as put out as he, and he bent down to pick it up for her at the same time as she did. Their eyes met under the table, and he thought he would pass out, his insides churning as never before.

The proprietor rushed across. "What is happening here? Hurry up, girl, you are keeping customers waiting."

Grabbing the pencil, Beth followed her back to the counter. Jamie sat up, praying she wouldn't be in trouble. It would be the ultimate in bad luck if she were to lose her job because of him.

"That's the girl we saw in the forest, isn't it?" asked Alice, her nose in the air.

He nodded, still too shaken to speak coherently.

"She looks different."

"Maybe she has only just started working here. She doesn't seem as if she knows what she's doing." His mother bit her bottom lip. "Oh, dear, she's dropped something else."

With his heart in his mouth, Jamie watched his sweetheart then pick up the tray and carry their drinks across to them. She placed it carefully on the edge of the table, took off the glasses of lemonade and placed one in front of each of them, without spilling a drop.

"Thank you very much," pronounced his mother in an extra-loud voice. "You have done very well."

He grinned at her for realising she needed encouragement, and for making sure the proprietor heard her praise.

"I want my cake," moaned Daniel.

"Be patient," hissed his mother. "She only has one pair of hands."

The cakes soon arrived on a fancy tiered plate.

With his face a picture of delight, Daniel's hand reached out, but his mother tapped it. "Wait until you are offered one, if you please. You are not in the nursery now. You need to learn how to deport yourself in public." She took a piece of plain cake and put it on his plate.

"I want a chocolate one," he complained.

"Please may I have a chocolate cake, Mama?" Alice piped up.

Jamie came to his little brother's rescue, and daintily picked a slice of the plain sponge. "That is the one I would like." He took a bite. "Um, it's scrumptious."

"That's a funny word," began Daniel, but his mother glared at him, making movements with her mouth.

Jamie whispered in his ear. "Don't speak with your mouth full."

Alice swallowed deliberately and sat with her hands in her lap. "Yes, I haven't heard that word before. What does it mean?"

"It means delicious, but even more so."

"Scrumptious." She rolled the word around her tongue, with her lips stuck out. "It's a lovely word, scrumptious."

"Scwum... I not say it," moaned Daniel, still eyeing up the chocolate cake.

His mother relented and put a small one on his plate. "Now, eat it carefully so you don't make a mess," she whispered in his ear.

The look of delight on his little brother's face as he ate the treat made Jamie smile. Not wishing to distract Beth, he tried not to watch her as she served other customers. Every now and again she would look his way, and he would give her a nod of encouragement, but his mother soon stood and declared they needed to be on their way. She paid the bill and, with a last smile to Beth, Jamie followed her outside.

"I hope Beth likes working there," he said as they walked down the street. "I hope she doesn't drop anything else."

"I wouldn't be so clumsy, would I, Mama?" Alice

looked up for approval.

"You won't have to work in such a place, so the occasion will never arise," Jamie told her. "You are privileged, and must never forget that."

"Jamie's right, my darling," added his mother.

Alice sighed as if bored with being told that. "I know, I know. I'll never forget it. I'm not allowed to."

Jamie let go of her hand. "Alice, you are such a spoilt brat sometimes."

His mother gasped. "Jamie, how can you be so mean to your sister? Please apologise."

"No, Mama, it's true."

"Then walk on your own. I will not have you maligning her like that." She grabbed both the children's hands and hurried off, leaving him standing open-mouthed, right in front of the haberdashery shop with the parasols they had been looking at earlier.

Maybe I won't buy her one, after all. I've never known her speak to me like that. Not ever.

Wandering across to the travelling circus poster, he studied the pictures of the bearded lady and the sword swallower. "I bet your mamas don't talk to you like that," he muttered to them, noticing, out of the corner of his eye, that his mother was almost pulling Alice and Daniel along. He could hear his little brother protesting, and see Alice looking back at him anxiously.

"Well, I don't need them. Maybe I'll join you lot—" He turned back to the poster "—and become—what act could I do? Not a skeleton man, or an armless lady." He took a closer look. "Oo, a hard-headed human anvil." He patted his own head. "No, my 'ead ain't hard. It's still soft, especially on the place where I hurt it, falling out of that window at school." Not seeing any act that he could mimic, he began to follow his family, thinking he could learn some magic tricks and become a magician, or even a magician's assistant.

Yes, that would be good. I'm too tall to be a dwarf, and too small to be a giant, but a magician's assistant—now, that would be right up my street. Or a clown, that would be even better.

Feeling less put out, he grinned to himself as he caught up. "I didn't mean no harm, Mama. I'm sorry."

His mother stopped and blinked. "I know, Jamie, I shouldn't have berated you like that. I'm sorry too. I have a lot on my mind."

"And me, I sorry," chimed Daniel.

Jamie bent down and picked him up. "You don't have anything to be sorry about, little brother. You've been very well-behaved."

He took a peep at his sister. She put out her arm. "Jamie, I didn't mean for you to get into trouble."

"That's cleared the air, then. Let's have a race, shall we? See who can reach that funny-shaped tree up there first." They all ran towards the tree. Alice won.

"I'm not in the habit of running," panted his mother, holding her side. "I'm fair pooped."

Alice and Daniel both laughed. "Pooped," repeated Daniel, "Me pooped." He lifted up his coat tails and touched his bottom, sticking it out.

Jamie laughed. "I hope you haven't done anything in your drawers."

Daniel merely laughed again, and they carried on in high spirits towards home.

The following week, dressed for the show, Jamie strode up and down the hall, waiting for the others. He stopped in front of the mirror and adjusted his navy cravat. "Don't I look a *cockalorum*? Is that the right word? No, what's that other one I heard? A *snoutfair*. Yes, that's the one."

"Who are you talking to, Master Jamie?" He hadn't heard Maisie come up behind him.

"Oh, just myself."

"You look very smart."

"Thank you." He looked at her wistful face. "I wish you could come with us."

She made a moue with her lips. "Me too, but I know I never shall be able to."

"But you have an afternoon off. Why don't I ask Mama if you can take it today? But, do you have any money?"

Her face took on a brighter sheen. "I've saved a shilling. How much is a ticket?"

"Um, I think it's about that, but I can't be sure."

His mother came downstairs.

"Will Maisie be able to come with us, Mama? She has a shilling."

"Um, we won't be sitting in the shilling seats, Jamie. We'll be in the most expensive ones."

"Oh." He turned back to the maid. "I'm sorry, Maisie, you can't sit by yourself."

She walked away, her head bowed. "I never thought I'd be going, anyway."

Jamie felt awful. If he hadn't raised her hopes, she would have been quite happy to just wave him off. Now she looked miserable and dejected. Why did trying to make people happy sometimes work the other way, and make them more dissatisfied? He slumped into an armchair, his head in his hands, some of his own excitement draining away.

He soon perked up, though, as he sat in the carriage.

"Are elephants very big?" asked Alice, her face also aglow with excitement, her blue eyes animated.

"They have long trunks," offered Daniel, sitting between his parents. "I seed one in a book." He made movements with his arm as if to imitate one.

Jamie expected his mother or father to correct his brother's grammar, but they didn't. They merely smiled at him.

Oh well, I shan't if they aren't going to, he thought, still surprised. "Yes, Alice, they're enormous," he answered his sister, blowing out his cheeks and trying to make himself look big by putting out his arms, although, in the confined space of the carriage, he couldn't do so very convincingly.

Daniel tried to copy him. "Normous."

"Yes, gigantic."

"Gigantic."

"Even gargantuan," their father added.

Jamie could see Alice trying to think of a word, her brow furrowed. "Massivous," she cried.

Jamie and his parents laughed.

"What's wrong with that?" The child's bottom lip jutted out.

"Nothing, darling," her mother placated her. "It's a lovely word."

"We shall have to use it every day," added Jamie, "so the whole world can learn it. Massivous, massivous." They all recited it and she cheered up.

Daniel fell asleep after a while, so his mother put him on her knee. With her head back, she dozed as well, so Jamie looked out of the window, thinking it best to keep quiet. He soon became restless, though, buoyed with the anticipation of the treat ahead.

Alice climbed onto his lap and began to draw circles on his cheek. "Oo, look, Jamie," she exclaimed, "you have hairs growing out of your chin."

Touching his face, he grimaced. "Shush, don't wake Mama," he whispered. "I shall have to start shaving soon, like Papa."

They both looked across at their father, who seemed to be deep in thought, staring through the window. Raising his eyebrows, he turned to face them. "I beg your pardon, did you address me?"

"No, Papa," answered Alice, grinning.

Jamie poked his head out to see what could be taking his father's attention. He pulled it back in. "We're nearly there. I can see houses, and…and…there's a big tent thing. Oh, my, I think I'm going to die." He clutched his chest.

"Jamie?" his mother woke up and cried. "Are you unwell?"

"Oh, no, Mama. It's just so thrilling, I can't contain myself."

Daniel began to grizzle.

"You've woken him up, now. He'll be in a bad mood until we arrive."

"Well, Mama, we have arrived. We're there. Look." No matter how much his mother grumped at him, he would not be deflated.

She turned her head and her eyes opened wide. "Oh, look, Daniel, look."

Daniel buried his face in her bosom. "I'm scared."

"What of?" Alice jumped off Jamie's lap to peer out, so he picked up his brother. "There's nothing to be frightened of, little man."

"No? Not big *lelephants*?"

"We'll be far away from them. They won't hurt us, will they, Father?"

"No, of course not." His father smiled at the boy as they pulled to a halt.

Jamie couldn't wait for the door to be opened by the coachman. He turned the handle and jumped out, still carrying his brother. His ankle twisted and he fell sideways, dropping the little boy onto the muddy carriage tracks. A scream from his mother didn't help the situation. He grabbed Daniel and stood him up, brushing off the blades of grass and the small pat of mud from his trousers.

"Is he hurt?" his mother yelled, jumping down.

"No, Mama, he's fine," came his quick reply, as he

prayed to be right. He drew in his breath as the child's eyes filled with tears and his face screwed up. "Aren't you, Daniel? You're a big, strong boy, aren't you? You're not a milksop. You're not going to cry, are you?"

His father grunted behind him as he struggled to alight from the carriage. What would he say to the situation?

When Daniel didn't cry, Jamie picked him up with a sigh of relief. "Come on." He didn't know what they should do first. Would they be allowed to go and see the animals in their cages? He could hear them growling and snuffling in the distance, and a not-very-pleasant smell drifted across. But a man, dressed in a black suit with a tall hat, ushered them towards the huge tent. "This way, please, ladies and gentlemen. Hurry along."

They joined the queue of people waiting to buy their tickets, and eventually made it to their seats. "Daniel, you had better sit next to your mother," ordered his father, "and Alice next to me."

"So I shall sit on the end, then," muttered Jamie. Nobody seemed to care where he sat. *But all the better to see,* he decided once they had sat down, Daniel still with a look of fear on his face.

Alice leaned forward from her seat furthest away from him, next to their father. "Why can't I sit next to Jamie? I want to sit next to Jamie."

"You will stay where you are," replied his father, "where I can keep an eye on you."

Jamie daren't argue with him, so sat back, taking in the enormity of the 'Big Top' as he knew the tent to be called.

Before long, music started playing and the ringmaster came in, cracking a whip, and the performances began. Jamie's sense of awe had him riveted to his seat as clowns ran into the ring, dressed in brightly-coloured costumes, and with their faces painted in funny pictures. He laughed at their antics, thinking he would love to join them. Maybe, if he became too dissatisfied, if his parents chastised him much more for doing nothing, he would run away and join them. Just think of the fun he would have, dressed like them, making people laugh. What a lark that would be.

A young man wearing hardly any clothes rode in next, standing on the back of a horse, and performed several dare-devil stunts. Jamie would have loved to share his thoughts with Alice, to tease her about her prowess, or ask her if she would dare dress like that, but couldn't with her being on the other side of his parents. He could hear her *oohing* and *aahing*, and even screaming when the rider almost fell off.

Then the elephants paraded in. His favourite— ridden by boys dressed in colourful costumes. How he would have loved to have a ride on top of one of those majestic beasts! He sneaked a peek at Daniel to see if he was enjoying himself, and saw him leaning forward as eagerly as everyone else. Thank goodness, his fear of them had vanished.

A creaking sound made him look up, and he saw two people climbing ropes up to some swings. "The trapeze artistes are next," his mother, sitting next to him, exclaimed. "Oh, look." She covered her mouth with her hand as the two men swung backwards and forwards, somersaulting and catching hold of the bars of the swings, to a collective intake of breath, everyone else clearly thinking the same as Jamie—that they would miss, plummet down and be killed.

The creaking noise increased. Jamie assumed it must be the movement of the equipment as the acrobats swung even higher and faster, criss-crossing each other, making him feel dizzy. Then, one of the trapezes came loose on one side. The man fell, but so did the supporting beam. At first, for a second, the place went silent, as everyone wondered if it could be part of the act, then they all started screaming and standing up, as more parts of the roof began falling.

"Quick, we have to get out," shouted his father.

Being on the end, Jamie easily obeyed. Grabbing his mother's hand, he pulled her, but she resisted, turning to pick up Daniel. Folk from the other rows pushed and jostled him, and before long, he could no longer see her. He thought he could hear his father calling him, but he was being washed away in a sea of screaming, milling people, helpless to defend himself against the onslaught, feeling as he had done in the sea when he had almost drowned a few years earlier. Powerless to stop, his feet barely touching the floor, he yelped as an elbow cracked against his temple.

* * * *

Tillie grabbed Daniel and clung onto David's coat tails as another beam fell, right in the place where Jamie had been sitting.

"We will have to go the other way," yelled David. "Come on."

"But, David, what about Jamie?"

"I'm sure I saw him down there." He pointed in front of him and grabbed her skirts. "Keep a tight hold on Daniel. I shall protect Alice."

She could see Alice crying, sucking her thumb, but knew David would take care of her as much as he could. Why hadn't he sat on the end? It would have made so much more sense, with his leg. They made slow progress along the row, having to shuffle all the way to the opposite side. All the while, she kept glancing around to find Jamie, but could see neither hide nor hair of him. Oh, why hadn't she gone when he'd pulled her? Or better still, kept him with her? Where could he be?

Another part of the roof collapsed behind them, causing her to yell out once more. "Can't you go any faster, David?" she shouted.

They finally made the end of the row, but were engulfed in the crowd of people, all as eager to escape. She saw a young man fall over but, however guilty she felt at not stopping to assist him, she didn't have time.

Then David lost his footing. Alice screamed. Handing Daniel to her, Tillie shrieked, "Hold him while I help your father." But the little girl just stood there, bawling. "Alice, hold Daniel," she repeated, thrusting the child at her daughter. She leant down to David, but a lady pushed past, shoving her out of the way, and knocking the children over as well. Torn, she didn't know whether to see to her husband or her children. Deciding David would be more likely to help himself, she turned to them, shaking, as she stood them up. "Are you injured?"

A red gash had appeared on her son's cheek, and Alice cried that her arm must be broken because it hurt so much.

Another beam fell between her and David, and she could no longer see him.

Chapter 6

A peculiar smell filled Jamie's nose as he came around. He could feel himself being carried. But by whom? It didn't feel like his mother, and couldn't possibly be his father. People screaming and yelling all around him hurt his ears as his saviour made slow progress through the throngs of terrified folk.

He couldn't decide if his leg hurt more than his arm, or vice-versa, and his head! He couldn't open his eyes without pain shooting through it.

A burst of cold air heralded the fact that they had reached the outside. With a curse, his rescuer dropped him in a heap on the ground. Somebody's foot engaged with his face, and he tried to turn onto his front and stand, but someone else kicked him down. The hustle of people, all shrieking and shouting, grew larger.

A clown, his made-up face looking grotesque in the circumstances, yanked him up. "Come with me," he hissed.

Jamie hobbled after him, holding tightly to his hand, wondering how the clown could walk at all with his huge feet. The roar of a lion close by startled him, the unusual sound strident in the mêlée of people's voices.

"Come on," yelled the clown. "We should be safe in my van."

Jamie hesitated. He wanted to be away from the area altogether, but ought to be going back inside to find his parents. The clown pulled him towards the caravans, almost hidden amongst the trees.

"Why have you rescued me and nobody else?" asked Jamie.

"Dunno. Maybe I liked the look of you."

"I need to go back, to find my family. Mama'll be

worried sick." He turned.

But the clown gripped his arm. "You'll never find them in the chaos. You may as well shelter here for a while."

Jamie tried to pull away, but the clown still had hold of his arm, and it hurt, really hurt. "I can't just leave them, though. They might need my help."

"They probably do but, like I said, how will you know where to look? Much better stay here until the hullabaloo's died down, and then go and look for them."

What the clown said made sense, but he thought he ought to be doing something, not hiding away.

The clown opened the door and pushed him rather roughly inside. "Let me wash those cuts on your face."

Putting his hand to his cheek, he realised his face was indeed covered in scratches. He plonked down on a chair and took stock of his whereabouts. Memories of his childhood returned, of the time he'd lived in the gypsy caravan. Life had been so simple then. He sometimes wished his mother hadn't left, hadn't gone to live with the old lady, Missus Curtis. She wouldn't have been sent to prison and he wouldn't have lost his memory and been found by Tom Briggs, the gamekeeper. But then she wouldn't have married his father.

"Ouch, that hurt," he yelped as the clown wiped his face with some foul-smelling liquid.

"Good, that means it's working."

The white make-up around the man's mouth and eyes made him look as if he had a huge smile, but his eyes didn't sparkle like Jamie would have expected them to. In fact, they looked hard and unsmiling.

"What's your name?" he asked, gritting his teeth. "Do clowns have names? I played the part of Feste in our school play. He was a clown."

"Stop drivelling. My name's Arthur."

"Arthur? I thought you'd have a funny name." He

105

tried to think what sort of name a clown would use.

"Yes, Arthur. Anything wrong with that?"

Jamie didn't like the way he screwed up his eyes, in a sort of threatening manner. "No, sir. Thank you for your concern, but I must be going now." He tried to stand as Arthur turned away, but he swivelled around and pushed him back onto the chair. "Let me look at your leg." He rolled up Jamie's trouser leg, revealing a large gash.

"Ugh, no wonder it 'urt," cried Jamie, rolling up his jacket sleeve as well. "Is me arm as bad?" It revealed a large purple bruise near his elbow, but no cut. "Me arm's more painful than me leg."

"You might have broken it. Don't keep moving. I'll make a splint."

"You a doctor, or summat?"

"No, but I treat most of the injuries the circus folk incur. We can't afford to take a doctor with us wherever we go." Arthur helped Jamie take off his jacket and seemed about to remove his shirt as well, but he would have felt too vulnerable, sitting there in his vest, so he pulled it to, shaking his head.

"Please yourself," muttered Arthur, strapping a piece of wood to Jamie's outstretched arm.

"I can't…"

"What?" Again the menacing look appeared in Arthur's eyes.

Jamie looked away. "Nothing." He tried to see out of the window. "Do you think everyone's out now?"

Arthur looked out as well. "There are still people milling about. We'll wait here until it's died down."

Jamie didn't want to wait there. He wanted to go and find his family.

* * * *

Tillie yanked at the children. "Oh, my goodness,

David, are you there?" She tried to look over the beam, but broken chairs and debris from the roof littered the space between her and the place she had last seen her husband. Alice began to wail, which started Daniel off as well. She put her arms around them, tears falling down her own cheeks.

She yelled again, "David!" and thought she heard a murmur, but it could have been anything. The wind blowing through the gaping hole in the roof, or the trapeze hanging lopsidedly from the one remaining beam.

A man ushered her away from the site. "Come on, ma'am, everyone needs to clear the area."

"But I can't go. My husband's over there."

The man looked to where she pointed. "I can't think that anyone would survive in that area, ma'am," he said in an unsympathetic tone. "Please leave straightaway."

Alice gripped her hand. "We can't leave Papa."

"I know, darling." A roar cut off her words as the remaining trapeze and its moorings fell, yards away from them. Carrying Daniel, and with Alice gripping onto her skirt, she made her way as fast as possible through the debris towards the opening, along with the crowds of other folk, all crying and yelling.

"Mama, where's Jamie?" asked Daniel as they reached the outside.

"I don't know. Oh, what a catastrophe. What are we going to do?" She looked around in desperation, for some sort of solution, but only came face to face with dozens of others doing exactly the same. A sense of unreality overcame her and she slumped down onto the muddy ground in tears, cuddling the children close to her bosom.

Clowns and other circus performers, still in their performance garb, ran around, trying to help with the wounded. It seemed incongruous to see them amongst the confusion.

After a while, she stood, determined to find

someone to help. Maybe she could find her coachman, although she didn't know what he could do, but a friendly face would be welcome. Brushing off her dress, she followed a line of people, all with probably similar thoughts.

Passing a caravan parked amongst the trees with several others, she was reminded of her former life with the gypsies. A face at the window reminded her of Jamie. He had been so carefree in those days. Now he always seemed to have the cares of the world on his shoulders. Probably that school. He hated it there, she knew that, but could do nothing about the situation. It wouldn't be for much longer, though.

Where could he be? How would she ever find him?

"Jamie," muttered Daniel, surprising her, as if her own thoughts had transferred to her little boy's mind.

"Where? Have you seen him?" She stopped and looked around. "Where's Jamie?"

He pointed behind him.

"I don't see him. Whereabouts, darling? Please tell Mama." Her eyes searched the people around her, but nobody resembling her older son stood out. She began to walk back the way they had come, a difficult feat, trying to force a way through the tide of men and women. "Show me." She turned to Alice. "Did you see him?"

Alice shook her head, clearly too traumatised to speak. Her bonnet had come off in the scuffle and her long, tangled curls covered her face.

Looking lost and frightened, Daniel merely put up his arms for her to lift him. A false alarm, clearly. If only it had been true, and he had seen him. She turned back to continue on her way, more desolate than before.

* * * *

Jamie tried to reach the door. "Please let me leave.

I'm fine now, thank you very much." But Arthur barred his way.

He scratched his head, realising he'd lost his cap. That was the least of his worries, in the circumstances. "Why don't you want me to go?"

"I think you'd be safer here." The clown lit a small stove and put a kettle on top. "A nice cup of tea will make you feel better."

"But I don't want tea. I want to go, to go and look for my father and mother."

"I keep telling you, you'll never find them." He pushed Jamie down onto the seat in the corner. "Now, stay there like a good boy."

"I'm not a boy. I'm a young man."

"You must be only about twelve. That's a boy in my eyes."

"I am fifteen, if you please, nearly sixteen."

The clown's already wide-looking eyes opened even wider. "Well, you do surprise me."

"What difference does it make? Except that I'm more likely to be able to fend for myself than you thought I would be, so please, I repeat, let me go." He tried to stand once more, but the clown kicked him in the leg. "Ouch, what was that for? I thought you were a healing person, but you're just a big bully, as bad as the boys at school." Anger rose in his throat. He'd had his bellyful of bullies trying to put him down all the time. This caricature of a man was not going to overpower him. He pushed him hard in the chest, but the man's short stature belied his strength and he gripped Jamie's arms in a vice-like hold.

"Sit down," the man yelled.

The pain in his arm from the grappling almost made him pass out, and he sagged onto the seat, holding the splinted one with his other, gritting his teeth in an effort to stay conscious. It wouldn't do to black out. Goodness knows what the man would do to him.

Maybe he could sneak over to the door while the clown had his back turned, making the tea. He waited for the right moment and made his move, stealthily creeping behind him. But Arthur must have been more aware than he realised, for he stuck out his leg, tripping Jamie. With a yelp of pain, he landed on his bad arm, and lay crying, uncaring if the man saw his tears.

Arthur merely stepped over him, put two mugs of tea on the small table and sat with his cupped in his hands. When Jamie didn't move, he sighed and walked over to him. "You may as well drink your tea, young man. You can't stay down there forever."

"Why not? If you won't let me leave, I may as well lie here as anywhere else."

"Now you're just feeling sorry for yourself."

Jamie sat up. "Of course I am. Wouldn't you, in my place?"

"No, sir, I would thank my lucky stars I had been rescued."

"But for what? I don't know what you intend doing with me, but I ain't staying here." He stood and hobbled over to the door. Wondering why Arthur didn't try to stop him, he turned the knob. Nothing happened. He leant on it with all his weight, but it wouldn't budge. Then he thought that perhaps it opened inwards, and tried pulling it, but again no movement. "It's locked," he exclaimed.

A low laugh behind him made him turn. "Well deduced, young man."

"Why have you locked me in?"

"Not just you, I'm here as well."

Jamie still couldn't understand how a man who played the part of a clown, who made people laugh for a living, could have such a menacing air about him. He shivered as the seriousness of the situation dawned on him. This so-called funny man was nothing of the sort. But what could he do? Shout for help? There were still plenty of people outside. He stopped in front of the window. Could he open it slyly without the man noticing? He felt behind him for the catch, but before he could do anything about it, Arthur jumped up and pushed him to the floor.

"You must think I was born yesterday, young sir. I know what you were trying to do, but you can rid your mind of any means of escape. You are staying, and that is that."

* * * *

"I'm cold, Mama," whined Alice. "I want to go home."

"Me cold, too," added Daniel.

Tillie had been forced to put him down, her arms aching. "I know, children. When we've found the coachman, I'll go back and see if I can find your papa."

"He's dead."

"Alice, don't give up hope. We don't know that."

"But that man said…"

Stopping, she bent down to her daughter, making several people behind her complain that they couldn't pass by without having to weave through the trees. "Don't take any notice of him. He was just trying to remove to safety everyone who could walk."

If she found the coachman, she would ask him to take the children home, and she would go back to look for David and Jamie. Standing, she craned her neck to see how far the path wound, hoping to see the clearing where the carriages had been left.

She stopped one young man. "Is it much further, sir, do you know?"

Without replying, he shook his head and hurried on,

overtaking the ones in front. Clearly, she had asked the wrong person. Try another. She asked several people, but nobody wanted to speak to her. They all had their own safety to consider. "We shall just have to carry on, children."

Alice looked up with such a pitiful expression. "But my legs ache."

"My, too, my ache." Daniel put up his arms once more. "Carry?"

Giving Alice a quick cuddle, she picked up her son and they set off once more, Alice complaining all the way.

Eventually, they reached a clearing, but how to find their carriage? Most of them looked the same. An elderly lady in a fur coat pushed past her, almost knocking her over. "Hey!" she yelled, but the lady had disappeared. Shaking her head, she took a deep breath. "Keep calm," she told herself. "Just look for the carriage."

"Is that ours?" asked Alice, pointing to the one on the end of the second row.

"Yes, I think it might be. Good girl."

They ran to it. Where was the coachman? Nowhere in sight. The lady in the fur coat appeared again, and yanked open the door.

"Excuse me, ma'am, this is my carriage," Tillie shouted at her.

The lady tried to close the door, but Tillie clung onto it, desperately trying to think how she could prove it.

She put her head inside, the lady trying all the while to block her way. "Let me see the interior."

Daniel yelled behind her. Turning, she saw him lying on the ground. "What happened?" she asked Alice as she sat him up.

"Don't know."

"Are you hurt, little one?" She felt down his legs. He seemed fine. When she turned back to the carriage, though, she found the door closed. How could she get the woman out? Certain it was theirs, she bent down and asked her daughter, "Alice, did you leave anything inside when we arrived?"

Alice shook her head, and then her face lit up. "Daniel dropped his sweetie, didn't he?"

"So he did. I meant to pick it up, but something must have distracted me." Opening the carriage door again, she felt around the floor, ignoring the lady trying to kick her. She found the sweet and held it up in triumph. "See, madam, I told you this was ours. Please remove yourself at once before I call a policeman." She didn't know where she would find a member of the constabulary in such chaos, but hoped the threat would be enough to make the person alight. However, the lady remained in the seat, her head held high, as if she hadn't heard.

"Ma'am, please leave."

Still receiving no response, Tillie lifted Daniel and sat him on the seat opposite, assisted Alice in, and then went around to the other door and opened it. Reaching in, she grabbed the lady's arm. "Out, now, if you please."

The lady broke down in tears, surprising Tillie enough to release her hold. "I can't find my husband. I don't know what to do."

Her anger at the woman receded. "Well, he isn't in here, so why are you insisting on staying?"

"He'll be angry at me for not staying close to him."

With a sigh, Tillie climbed inside and sat next to her. "Let us help you find your own carriage. Surely your husband will understand? You won't be the only one separated from your loved ones, will you?"

The lady looked up at her with sad, grey eyes. "You don't know him. He can be very vicious when I don't do as he says."

"But none of this is your fault."

"That won't make any difference."

At a loss as to what to suggest, Tillie sat holding the lady's cold hand, until Daniel began to cry. "Now what's the matter?"

"Hungry." He rubbed his belly.

She looked inside her reticule to see if she had any sweets left, and found two, to her intense relief. She wouldn't have been able to give him one and not his sister. After unwrapping them and popping one in each of their mouths, she gave her attention back to the elderly lady. "What's your name, ma'am?"

"Missus Harrison."

"Oh, we know some Harrisons. Are you related to Grace and Christine?"

"They are my daughters-in-law."

"What a coincidence. Well, Missus Harrison, if our coachman ever returns, we shall take you home. Do you live near them?"

"Yes, not very far, just over the hill, really."

"I'm surprised we haven't met before. Now I come to think of it, we probably have, haven't we? I'm Tillie Dalton, and these are two of my children."

"Yes, I know."

"You know? Then why didn't you say something earlier?"

The lady shrugged and turned her head away. The fox's head on her collar seemed to be looking at Tillie with an evil expression. She had to look away from it.

"Is your husband not with you?" the lady asked after a moment.

Tillie's shoulders slumped. "A beam fell on him. Well, I don't know for certain that it did, but it fell between us. I couldn't reach him, and a man made us evacuate the tent before I could try."

"The man said he's dead," added Alice.

"No, he did not, I told you," replied Tillie, patting her daughter's knee. "He just said…it just seemed like that was what he was saying."

"I'm sorry," whispered Missus Harrison. "I've just added to your troubles."

"Don't you worry about that. We'll sort something out, won't we, children?" Alice and Daniel merely looked at her as if she had said they could fly to the moon.

The coachman appeared as Tillie began to despair of a solution. "Ah, there you are, ma'am. Are you ready to leave?" he asked, popping his head inside the door. "Oh!" He jerked back on seeing the stranger. "Where's the master, and your other son, Master Jamie?"

As Tillie explained what had happened, and that she intended staying to look for them, Alice squealed, "You mustn't leave us, Mama. Please don't leave us."

"I can look after you," volunteered Missus Harrison. "I could take you home and make sure you're safe, and then return for your mother." She turned to the coachman. "That is, if you would be so kind as to bring me back."

"But Mister Harrison, ma'am," interrupted Tillie, "he'll be looking for you. Won't you be in even more trouble for leaving him?"

"I don't care anymore. I hope I never see him again." With an act of bravado that didn't quite ring true, Missus Harrison swept her fox-fur over her shoulder.

Not sure if she wanted to be party to the lady's split from her marital home, Tillie didn't know what to reply. But time was pressing. She had to return to find David, so she agreed. The children seemed happy enough to go with the lady, so she waved them off and turned back towards the scene of devastation.

The trail of people leaving had diminished, so she found it easier to make the return journey. The sight that met her caught her breath. Most of the Big Top had collapsed. Only one side still stood. How could her husband have survived? She couldn't make out in her mind whereabouts they had been sitting. It all looked so different, so she didn't know where to start looking. And what about Jamie? Had he managed to escape before the roof had fallen in?

A clown, still wearing his big feet, came up to her as she stood, surveying the scene. "You mustn't go near, ma'am. Please leave."

"But I need to find my husband and my son. A beam fell on him."

He pointed over to one side. "Some people have been brought out. Maybe he's with them."

Tillie looked over to see what he meant. Men and women sat on the ground, many covered with blood and, farther along, a row of what looked like bodies covered with coats and blankets. "Are those dead?" she gasped.

"Ay, ma'am, I'm afraid so."

"Oh, please don't say David's amongst them." She ran to where a different circus entertainer had just placed another shape. "Do you know who any of these people are?" she asked him, pulling at his sleeve.

"No, ma'am, I'm just making them respectable. Feel free to take a look if you're searching for somebody in particular."

Hesitating, she didn't know if she dared. What would she find? She looked up at him. "Would you…?"

"Sorry, ma'am, I don't have time. They're bringing more out every minute."

Lifting the corner of the blanket covering the body closest to her, she took a quick peek, grimacing, and shaking so hard she could barely stand. A pink bonnet presented itself. A lady. She dropped the cover as if it had scalded her. Taking a deep breath, she repeated the action to the next few. Again, either fancy hats or bald heads— no-one who could be David or Jamie.

Several other people were doing the same thing. One man asked her, "Are you looking for a man or woman, ma'am?"

"My husband."

"What was he wearing?"

She refused to use the past tense. David could not be dead. "He *is* wearing a black coat and..." What else? Could she remember? Just his usual garb—the same as the majority of men. "He has a moustache, though. That could identify him."

"So do most of us."

"Yes, I suppose so."

"He has a ring on his third finger. A garnet ring. I gave it to him for his last birthday, his fortieth, but I'm not going to pick up every hand to look for that." She flexed her back as a voice behind her called her name. She swivelled around. There he sat, hemmed in between a portly matron and a little ginger-haired man who looked like a younger replica of their friend the Major, who had been locked away in an asylum a few years previously. Too relieved to move, she drank in the sight of his bloody face, then ran across. "Oh, David, I knew you weren't dead."

He held out his arms. "Then why were you looking over there?"

"Goodness knows." Glancing back at the formidable row of bodies increasing every minute, she saw the man to whom she had been speaking earlier lift a coat, and heard him groan as he slumped to the ground. She gripped David's hand, so thankful her quest had not ended in such a manner. "Can you walk?" she asked him.

Trying to stand, he asked, "Where are the children?"

After explaining, she helped him up and he leaned on her shoulder.

"What about Jamie?"

"No." She shook her head. "I haven't seen him."

"He will turn up. You know how resilient he is. I have lost my crutch," he muttered.

"Well, if that's the only casualty, we must thank God. Where are you hurt?"

"I do not really know." He touched his cheek. "My face stings the most."

Unable to support his weight, Tillie looked around for help, but everyone seemed too busy aiding the badly injured. "I don't know how we'll manage."

They tried a few steps, but had to stop before they both keeled over. The lion-tamer saw their predicament, and came across. "Would you like to take refuge in my caravan, sir and madam? It's just over there." When they agreed, not having any other choice, he put his shoulder under David's arm, and took them there.

"This is very kind of you, sir," said Tillie, as they sat down.

"There's a kettle." The man pointed to his left. "Make some coffee. I'm afraid I don't have anything stronger. I must leave you and help others. It's a rum deal, this is." He shook his head, and left.

Tillie drew a deep breath and took David's hand in hers. "I know I said I knew you weren't dead, but I'm so relieved you're not."

He gave her an odd look from under his eyebrows. The blood covering his face had congealed. She couldn't leave him like that. "Let me wash your face, my darling, before we have a drink, parched as I am. I can't bear to see it so." She felt the kettle, but it had gone cold, so she looked around for some matches to light the burner. Once it had warmed, she poured some water into a basin and found a towel, hoping the lion-tamer wouldn't mind her soaking it with blood. Several deep scratches on David's face began to bleed when she disturbed them, so she gave up, just wiping off as much as she could.

"My back hurts a little as well," he murmured after she had poured the red water out of the door and returned to make a drink.

"Let me see. Lean forward." A huge black bruise covered his shoulders. "Cor blimey," she exclaimed, forgetting her manners. "No wonder it's painful. But thank God it wasn't your head that caught the blow." She leaned forward and kissed him. Before she could move away, he grabbed her hand and pulled her close for a more passionate embrace.

"While we are alone…" With one movement, he pulled her down beside him, and began to fondle her.

"David! Not here. That man could return any minute."

He grinned. "Pity."

"I don't know. Even the threat of death doesn't put you off."

"Actually, it turns me on. It makes me think how delicate life can be, how we should take each opportunity as it arises."

"Well, I have to inform you, sir, this opportunity is not for the taking. I would be mortified if anyone came in. We don't know if he shares this caravan. We could have an audience of three or four before we know it."

Laughing, he straightened his jacket. "Ah, well, it was worth a try." But then he took on a more serious expression. "But what are we to do? How will I manage to make my way home?"

"Um, Missus Harrison said she would return with the carriage, but that would not be for another few hours. We can't stay here."

"Why not? I am so weary, I need to sleep."

Fetching a pillow from the bed at the other end of the caravan, she made him comfortable on the seat. "Yes, my darling, you have a snooze. I'll go and see if I can find someone who might be able to take you home sooner, and search around for Jamie."

Stepping outside, she winced once more at the sight of the carnage. The situation seemed to have calmed down, and fewer people milled about. Trying not to look at the row of bodies, she wondered if she should examine them again, though. What if Jamie lay there under one of the blankets? But no. She would know if he had died. She felt sure she would feel it in her bones. Much better to look amongst the living. But where to start? Where would he go? Would he have run off, like the time he had found himself lost in the park in Harrogate? Not that she had known anything about it, from her prison cell, but he had since told her all the details. He had only been eight years old then, though. He had grown up a lot since that fateful day.

Maybe he had stopped to help other people. That would be just like him. She scrutinised the faces of all the men and boys around her, but her son's could not be seen.

Taking a deep breath, she went farther into the trees where she could see other caravans. Maybe Daniel *had* seen him. Whereabouts had they been when he had shouted his name? But why would he be in a caravan? Sheltering, perhaps? Maybe some kind circus person had taken him in, if he had been injured, just like the lion-tamer had rescued her and David? Would it be worth asking the few people who still remained, most of them looking bewildered, if they had seen him? But how would she describe him that would make him stand out from the hundreds of other boys of his age?

A scraping noise at a window behind her attracted her attention but, when she turned, she could only see the face of a clown, looking rather angry, not happy and smiling as she expected one to be. Taking a step back from the fury he exuded, she almost fell over a tree root. What a strange sight to witness. She hurried away as fast as she could.

Her initial thoughts of finding someone to take David home disappeared. Everyone needed their own transport. But what about the dead people? They wouldn't. *Well, how will they return home, then?* her inner voice asked. *Oh, stop it. Just return to David, and see how he is.*

In which caravan had she left him, though? Panicking, she swivelled around, trying to remember what it had looked like. Most of them were painted in bright colours. What colour had the lion-tamer's been? The red one over there, or the blue one closer to her? Not having taken much notice, she couldn't remember. "Oh, what am I to do?" she muttered, searching around for the lion-tamer to ask him, but couldn't see him anywhere. She would just have to return to the scene where the dead bodies had been laid out, and try to retrace her steps. She couldn't lose David as well as Jamie. Not that David would be lost, of course. He would at least find his own way home once he woke up. But he would think she had abandoned him.

She knocked the side of her head with her fist. *Think,* she screamed inwardly. *Try to remember.* Peeping inside the window of the blue one, she could see him lying there, still asleep. "Thank you, God," she cried, looking at the sky. She opened the door carefully, so as not to wake him.

The kettle sat invitingly on the unlit burner and she licked her lips. The lion-tamer had told her to make a drink, but he had said coffee. Would he have any tea? She didn't like coffee. The bitter taste made her thirstier than she had been before she drank it.

Unable to find any tea, she poured herself a glass of water and sat drinking it, watching her husband's face twitch as he seemed to be having a bad dream.

He sat up and squealed, "Where am I?" Then a look of comprehension dawned on his face and he slumped back down. "I must have been having a nightmare."

Tillie soothed his brow. "It's all right, my darling. You're safe."

121

"Have you found Jamie?"

"No." Handing him a drink of water, she shook her head. "I went out to look, but couldn't find him. I pray he's safe. I'll go back, now you're awake."

"Stay here a while longer with me." He patted the seat beside him, and she squeezed into the space.

"If we could make a crutch out of something, we could both go." Her eyes scanned the items in the small dwelling place, and she tried to imagine what could be used. Nothing seemed appropriate.

The image of the clown at the window still haunted her. "David, you'd think clowns would be nice people, wouldn't you?"

"I beg your pardon, what do you mean?"

"Well, I saw one out there—" She pointed in the general direction of where she thought she had seen him "—and he looked evil. He had the most sinister face you could visualise."

"It was probably all that make-up. It must have distorted his features."

"I suppose so, but I wonder why he isn't out there helping the injured and dying."

"Maybe he is hurt, and his face was contorted from pain. Forget about him, Tillie, and concentrate on our own plight."

"Yes, dear." She couldn't put the face out of her mind, though.

Chapter 7

Jamie crouched in the corner, too afraid to move. "Please don't kill me," he cried.

"Why would I want to kill you?" asked Arthur. "You could be valuable to me."

"In what way?"

"Well, this show is definitely over, wouldn't you say? A lump of wood fell on my partner. I don't know if he survived, but if he did, I can't see him being of any use to me any longer, so I need a new one."

"But what has that to do with me?" Intrigued as to what the clown meant, Jamie sat up.

"You look—at least I thought you did at first glance, now I'm not so sure—but you seemed the perfect choice to be my apprentice when I find another circus to join."

Tempting as the idea was, thinking of his earlier thoughts about how he would have loved to be a clown, Jamie replied, "But I can't. My parents won't let me."

"We wouldn't tell them."

"Oh, yes? And I suppose you intend to kidnap me and take me away against my will?" He had meant it to be a joke, but the look on the clown's face told him otherwise. "You do, don't you? That's why the door's locked."

Arthur merely raised his eyebrows.

"But they'll send the police to find me."

"With all this chaos, we'll be far away by the time they start looking. They have all the dead bodies and injured to attend to first."

Jamie became worried. The man's words sent shivers down his spine. "But...but you said you had changed your mind about me being perfect. Surely you can find someone else?"

"No time, now. I need to make preparations for leaving."

"But…" Jamie stood up, desperate to find a way out. "But I wouldn't be any good. I don't know how to be a clown."

Arthur began to tie pots and pans together. "I could soon teach you."

"How do you intend keeping me a prisoner? I shall just escape as soon as we arrive where we'll be going."

He didn't receive a reply so, while Arthur continued to pack up, he yanked open the window and yelled, "Help." Before he could repeat it, he felt himself being hauled away, a cloth tied around his mouth, and then being shoved onto the bed and tied down. Squirming and wriggling, he tried to free himself, but to no avail. He lay still, listening to the man walking up and down, mumbling to himself. Maybe he had gone insane, like the Major. If so, he, Jamie, would be in deep trouble. How could he escape? He had to do something. He couldn't just take it lying down.

"Be a man, not a mouse," Oswald had once told him. It was easy for him to say. He never found himself in bother.

He sat up, determined to try to think of some way out of his predicament.

Arthur looked across at him. "Decided to be a good boy, have we?"

Shaking his head and gritting his teeth, he didn't reply, just seethed inwardly. He wouldn't give him the satisfaction of speaking to him, even if he could have made himself understood through the gag. He glanced around the small caravan. Where could the clown have put the key to the door? Probably in one of his big pockets. The man looked stupid in his costume. How could he have ever thought he wanted to be like him?

A sudden urge to pee came over him. He squirmed

for a while, not wishing to give the clown the satisfaction of knowing, but the need became urgent.

"Use that bucket over there," he was told once he finally admitted it.

"But my hands are tied."

Arthur sighed and went across. "You won't try anything stupid, will you?"

"Of course not." *But I might try something sensible, like escaping,* he thought as he felt the bonds being loosed. He used the bucket and, as fast as lightening, before Arthur could realise what he intended, he dipped his hand into the clown's deep pockets from behind. For a split second he thought they were empty, but then he touched something hard and metallic. He yanked it out and ran to the door, inserted the key with one swift movement, turned it and pushed the door with all his might, the clown's breath hot on his neck. They both fell out, landing on the ground in a heap. With the gag still around his mouth, Jamie couldn't yell for help, but he didn't need to. A gentleman and lady walking past stopped.

"What is going on here?" asked the man in a haughty voice.

The clown grabbed Jamie and tried to pull him back inside, explaining that he was being punished for a wrongdoing, but Jamie ripped the gag off. "Please help," he shouted. "It's not true."

Just as he thought his plan had failed, and the clown had almost pulled him back inside, a hand gripped the arm holding him. "Not so fast."

Jamie looked up to see Sebastian, his friend who had left school a year or so earlier. "I know this boy. He lives near me. Please release him straightaway."

Jamie jerked himself free and ran to hide behind him. "Oh, fanks, fanks so much. I fought I was going to be kidnapped."

The clown slammed the door and they could hear

him lock it.

Sebastian turned Jamie around to face him. "Well, young man, this takes the biscuit. You have been in some scrapes in your short life, but I think this one must come top of the list. I shan't ask the whys and wherefores. Did you come alone?"

"No." Jamie looked down at his shoes, sheepishly. "I became separated from my parents when the roof caved in. I don't even know if they're alive."

"Same here. I've been wandering around looking for my father."

Jamie had heard that the boy's mother had disgraced the family and moved into a cottage in the village with her lover, leaving Sebastian with his father. He remembered feeling sorry for him when it had all begun, when he had been telling him about it on the train journey to school.

The gentleman and lady who had stopped came across. "Are you hurt, young man? Do you want us to call a policeman?"

Jamie looked at Sebastian. "Do you think I should?"

"Well, no harm seems to have been done. I am sure the police are too busy at the moment to bother about something like this."

"That's just what he said." Shivering, Jamie glanced at the caravan and moved away. "Let's go, before he comes out."

Sebastian put his arm around his shoulder. "He won't do anything now. Put your mind at rest." He turned to the couple. "Thank you for your intervention. I shall see Jamie is reunited with his family."

Nodding, they turned and left.

"Where shall we start, though?" asked Jamie. "Where've you already looked?"

"I've just been rambling around, really. I had a slight crack to the head." He put his hand to his forehead and Jamie could see a purple bruise forming.

"Oh, my word. You're hurt, and you still saved me. Thank you so much. You saved my life. Oh, thank you, thank you."

"All right, Jamie, don't overdo it." Sebastian blinked, clearly still dazed, as they began to walk.

"I can't believe how stupid I was, going with him. I thought I would like to be a clown. I thought they would be nice people." They passed some other caravans, and he looked up. "Mama!" he squealed, seeing her stepping down from one of them.

She turned towards him. "Oh, Jamie," she squealed as they ran full pelt towards each other. "Thank God you're safe. Where've you been?"

Sebastian intervened. "Good day, Missus Dalton."

"Oh, Sebastian, I didn't recognise you. You've grown so tall." She hugged Jamie to her bosom, pulling him towards the caravan. "Let's inform your father that you're safe."

He appeared at the door, obviously alerted by their voices. "Jamie, we have been out of our minds with worry."

"Why are you in there?"

"Never mind that. Just be thankful we are all here."

"Where's Alice and Daniel?"

His mother explained that they had gone home.

Jamie nodded. "Sebastian's lost his father. I need to help find him. He's hurt his head, too, look." He hadn't liked to mention his father's bloody face, for fear of stating the obvious and being chastised.

His mother examined the older boy's face. "My, that's bad." She pressed it. "Does it hurt?"

He winced. "Yes, ma'am."

"Mama!" shouted Jamie. "Of course it hurts, especially when you touch it like that."

She grimaced. "I'm sorry." Then she turned to his father. "I had better go with them. Will you be all right

127

here?"

"I suppose I shall have to be. I feel so useless," his father replied, sitting on the bed, holding his own head in his hand.

"Do you want us to look for a branch?" asked Jamie. "One you could use for a crutch?"

"That was what I'd been thinking," answered his mother. "Good idea. You and I can do that while Sebastian continues to search for his father."

Sebastian shuffled his feet. "I would rather wait for you, ma'am. I didn't like it on my own."

"Of course. Come on then, let's have a search around."

As they went out to rummage through the undergrowth for something suitable, Jamie looked at his friend from a different viewpoint. "You were so brave, though, standing up to that horrible man for me."

"Well, that was because you were in danger. I hadn't been thinking of myself, just about you."

His mother straightened her back, a look of horror on her face. "What horrible man, Jamie? Where on earth have you been?"

"Just a clown, Mama. I'll tell you about it later."

She shook her head, as if to clear something from her mind. "A clown? I saw one earlier. He gave me the creeps. And to think I always thought of them as cheerful, pleasant people."

"Well, they're not. Not all of them, anyway." He picked up a forked branch and showed it to her. "Will this do?"

She twisted it around. "Yes, I think it will do fine. Let's take it to him and see."

They hurried back with it. His father had fallen asleep, so she shook him gently. "David?"

He didn't awake. She shook him again, more forcefully. He still did not awake. "David!" she screamed, looking around at Jamie with fear in her eyes. "Oh, my, he must have been hurt more than I realised when that beam fell. What are we to do?"

"Don't panic, Missus Dalton," Sebastian tried to calm her, giving him another shake.

"No, Mama, I'm sure he's just…" Just what? Jamie had no idea, but he didn't want his mother having a fit of the vapours.

The lion-tamer appeared at the door. "Ma'am?" he asked, coming inside, "is anything wrong? I thought I heard screams."

"It's my husband, sir, we can't wake him."

Jamie assumed the caravan belonged to him. Being wary of circus folk after his encounter with the evil clown, he backed away as the man came to the bed.

"Did he receive any injuries apart from the cuts on his face?"

"Only one on his back, as far as I know."

"Well, maybe he took another blow." The lion-tamer felt all over his head, and then stopped. "Oh, yes, I can feel a large lump. Here, on the back." He stood up straight and looked Tillie in the eye.

"Well, what should we do?" she asked, raking her hands through her hair.

"Arthur, the clown, is the usual person to tend to our injuries. I'll go and fetch him, if I can find him."

"No!" shouted Jamie "Not him. He's evil."

"I beg your pardon, young man. How do you know anything about him?"

"He…he…"

"Is he the one?" asked Sebastian.

Jamie nodded. "Yes, he tried to kidnap me."

The lion-tamer narrowed his eyes, looking Jamie up and down. "You're slightly older than his usual boys. But, if you don't want me to call him, then, I'm afraid, I don't know what to suggest."

"Isn't there anybody else?"

"No, no-one that's free to help. They're all assisting the people at the site."

His mother tried one more time to wake her husband. "David, please wake up."

His father's eyes opened and she let out her breath in a loud whistle. "Ah, praise God." But then they closed again. "Don't go back to sleep, David," she cried. "Please. Stay with me." She slumped to the floor, crying, resting her head on his arm.

Jamie tried to pull her up, but she pushed him away. Holding out his hands, he gave Sebastian a look of bewilderment and turned back to the lion-tamer. "Is he going to die?"

The man shrugged, but touched his arm. "No, young sir, I'm sure he'll be fine in a little while. In the meantime, I must go and see to the people outside. You may stay here as long as you need."

After he had gone, Jamie sat on a chair, his head in his hands. If only he hadn't suggested coming to see the show, none of this would have happened.

Sebastian went to the door to look outside, clearly wanting to go and search for his father.

At least his predicament isn't my fault, thought Jamie. He hadn't told his friend to come to the circus. In fact, he hadn't known he would be there until he'd rescued him. Standing up, he put his arm around his mother. "Mama, shall I go with Sebastian?"

Nodding, she gave him a hug. As he was about to leave, he heard his father moan, and turned back. His eyes had opened again, and stayed open. "Papa, how are you?"

His father tried to sit up, but his mother pressed him down. "Stay there for the time being, my darling, at least until you've recovered."

"I do feel rather light-headed." He lay back, his eyes closed, but clearly awake.

Jamie looked from him to his friend, still waiting near the door. "Mama? Should I...?"

"Yes, Jamie, off you go. You know where to find us. We'll stay here for a while, until your father feels better."

He followed the older boy out. "Where shall we start?"

Sebastian pointed to where they could see several people milling around. "Over there, I think."

His own problems receded as he helped his friend, glad he could be of assistance to someone for a change. They didn't find his father amongst the walking-wounded, so then had the gruesome task of examining the dead.

"Some of these people don't look as if they have a mark on them," he muttered, more to himself than to anyone in particular.

"Many of them were trampled to death and suffocated in the rush to vacate the chaos," a man told him.

"Oh, my, that's awful." Jamie pulled back the cover of a small person and jumped back in horror. Visions of his little sister, Annabella, lying in her coffin, some four years previously, sprung into his mind. This little girl looked the spitting image of her, and for a few heart-stopping moments, he thought it was Alice. It couldn't be, of course, Alice being six years old. And, anyway, she should be home, safe and sound. He prayed she would be, and Daniel, out of the way.

Covering up the little child, he said a prayer for her. It didn't seem right that children should die in such circumstances. Not that any circumstances would be right, of course. Shaking his head, he bent down to the next body. A lady. He took a deep breath. How many more? He looked along the line. Sebastian had started at the other end, and they had almost met.

"No sign yet." Sebastian stood and flexed his muscles. "I don't know if that's good news or bad."

131

"Well, I suppose it must be good," replied Jamie, copying him. "Two more to go. We'll take one each."

The one nearest him looked certain to be a man, from the length of it. Holding his breath, he removed the cover. Oh dear, it did look like Mister Stoddart, but he couldn't be certain. He glanced across at Sebastian. He was still covering up the person he had been examining, also a man, but definitely not his father, from his white hair.

He cleared his throat. "Um, Sebastian…"

"Well, that's all of them." He looked up and noticed Jamie's screwed-up face. "What? It isn't, is it?"

"I think so."

"No, it can't be. I thought we'd seen them all and had just heaved a sigh of relief. Let me look." He hurried around to Jamie's side. Jamie had dropped the cover, so he picked it up. "No," he whispered, kneeling next to the body.

"Isn't it him? Praise the Lord. For a minute I…" Jamie began, but tailed off when his friend fell on top of the body, sobbing. "It is? Oh my, oh my." Hopping, holding one leg behind him, he didn't know what to do or say. What could he say in such circumstances? His eyes darting from his friend to the place he thought the lion-tamer's caravan stood, he wanted to ask his mother. Should he leave his friend to mourn his father alone? Would he prefer that, or would he rather have some company? Jamie daren't ask. He swapped feet, dancing on the other leg, knowing he looked stupid, but unable to decide what to do.

A man came across and pulled Sebastian up gently, asking, "Is it a relative?"

Sebastian nodded, pulled a white handkerchief out of his pocket, and blew his nose.

At last Jamie could stand on both feet.

"What do we do now?" Sebastian asked the man.

"You need to report to those people over there. They're making notes of the identifications of the deceased persons." He pointed to two ladies writing things down. "I'm very sorry, young sir, for your loss."

"Oh, yes," piped up Jamie, "me too. I'm sorry. What will you do?"

"I don't even want to think about my future, Jamie."

"No, I suppose not. You can come and stay with us if you'd like. We have plenty of room."

"Thank you, but my mother will need me."

"But I thought she didn't live with you anymore. She won't be interested, will she?"

Sebastian gave him such an angry look, he stepped back.

"Of course she will. She was still his wife. They hadn't divorced. I had heard Father say she had been thinking of coming home."

"Oh, I see. I'm sorry. I didn't mean to upset you." He began to hop again. "Shall I go and tell my parents, or would you rather me stay here with you?"

Sebastian pushed his hair back from his brow. "I don't know, Jamie. I just don't know what I want."

Should he hug his friend? No, that would be going too far. His mother could, though. "I'll run and tell my parents, and they might be able to give you some advice, eh?"

Receiving a nod, he dashed off in the direction of the caravan. The door stood open, so he ran inside. His parents weren't there, though. Had he found the wrong one? He went back out and looked it up and down, then at the others. It was certainly the right one, so where had they gone? Several people walked up and down, but he could not see his parents amongst them. "Oh, golly gosh," he muttered. "Now what do I do?"

Seeing a clown approaching, he rushed back inside and slammed the door, cowering behind it. Even if it

133

hadn't been Arthur, he still didn't want to come face to face with him. He had been put off clowns for the rest of his life, and never wanted to see another one ever again— not ever.

Peeping through the window until he had gone by, he opened the door, but turned back, remembering the branch they had found. If that had gone, it would mean his father would have been able to walk. He could see no sign of it, so took a deep breath and stepped out to return to Sebastian. What else could he do? There would be no point going to look for his parents. Hadn't his mother told him she would wait there? Why had she changed her mind?

Dragging his feet, he returned to the scene, noticing several people crying, and some wailing. Why had so many people died? He thanked his lucky stars his family had not perished. But what about Sebastian? He didn't have any brothers or sisters. He hoped he had been right about his mother, or how would he manage in that big house on his own?

Spotting his parents before he reached Sebastian, he ran to them with relief and told them the bad news.

"Oh, dear, poor lad." His mother wiped a tear on her sleeve.

"Are you well now, Father?" he asked, thinking he looked very pale and juddery.

"I shall be fine, thank you. I had been hoping we could find someone to take us home, but with this happening… We cannot just leave the boy on his own."

"I asked him if he wanted to come and stay with us, but he refused."

Sebastian came across. "I've told them the details. They said they will be in touch."

"So you are free to leave?"

He shrugged. "I suppose so. What else can I do?" He broke down in tears and Jamie felt as if he would cry as well, especially when his mother took his friend in her arms and rocked him back and forth until he calmed down.

"Come home with us. We can send word to your mother from there," she told him.

"Yes, thank you. I don't think I want to be on my own."

Jamie blew out his breath. Thank goodness, a decision of a sort had been made.

* * * *

Several days later, Jamie sat in the lounge, playing chess with his father. "Checkmate," he declared.

"Are you sure?"

"Yes, Father, of course I'm sure. That's two games in a row. You're slacking."

His father grinned. "Yes, I am, or you are becoming too good for me."

"That must be it. Would you like me to pour you a drink?"

"That would be grand."

As he twirled the golden liquid around in the glass, his father looked thoughtful. "I still cannot put that poor boy, Sebastian, out of my mind. At least his mother has returned to live at the house. I have heard rumours, though, that her lover might be joining her. I do hope not."

"Wouldn't it be better, though?"

"Better for whom? Certainly not her reputation, although that is in tatters, anyway."

His mother walked in, carrying Joseph. "Whose reputation?"

"Missus Stoddart's."

"Oh, her."

"Tillie," exclaimed his father, sitting up straight and

accepting his baby son. "It is not like you to denigrate someone of your own sex."

"No, I shouldn't judge, should I? It's just…never mind. The sun's shining, do you fancy going for a walk?"

Jamie jumped up. "Yes, what a spiffing idea. Don't you think so, Father?"

"Have you finished your packing?"

Jamie's shoulders drooped. "Nearly. Do I have to go back to school?"

"Yes, David," his mother intervened. "What's the point in him going back to that awful place just for a few weeks? I cannot see any reasoning in it at all."

Giving a deep sigh, his father handed back the baby and stood up. "Why do we have this argument every single term? The boy still has his education to finish. He is going and that is that."

Jamie looked at his mother and shook his head. Much as he would have loved to never set foot in the school again, he didn't want his parents falling out over him. He wished he hadn't said anything, and put his arm around her. "It isn't for long, Mama. I'll soon be home for good."

His father gave him an odd look.

"No, Father, I am not going to University," he insisted, his mouth set. "I am putting my foot down on that score."

"Huh. I cannot believe a son of mine…never mind. Are we taking that walk, or not? There is still time to change your mind."

"I won't."

Nanny came in with Alice and Daniel, both dressed in warm coats and hats. Jamie picked up his younger brother and swung him around, singing, "Hey ho, little bro, for a walk we all shall go."

"That sounds like a song," added Alice, trying to muster in on their merriment.

"That's good. It was supposed to."

The nanny took Joseph and put him in his pram.

Outside, the sun shone in a bright, clear, blue sky. "Maybe I'll see my buzzard, to say goodbye," chirped Jamie, swinging Daniel's hand.

Alice ran up to him. "I saw one the other day."

"Did you? Was it circling around and around?"

She thrust out her lips in thought. "Um, no, I don't think so."

"Then it was probably just a crow or a rook."

"No, I tell you it was a *buzzd*." She turned her back on him and walked over to her father. "It really was a *buzzd*, Papa."

He patted her head. "I'm sure it was, darling, if you say so."

About to refute it again, Jamie saw his mother shake her head at him, so he kept quiet. As they approached the lake, he spotted a family of ducklings. "Look," he shouted, running towards them. "Aren't they cute?"

"Don't go too close to the water," called his mother.

"I won't." A shudder ran through his body at the thought of drowning in the murky depths.

They watched the ducklings waddle after their mother. Daniel bent down to try to pick one up, but Jamie pulled him away. "No, you mustn't touch them."

"Ducky, ducky," he called to them, but they all jumped into the lake and swam away.

"I saw a new word in a book this morning," Jamie told his father as they walked on again. "Have you heard it before? What was it?" Feeling foolish, he scratched his chin, trying desperately to recall the word he had so wanted to show off with. "I looked it up in my dictionary. It's very appropriate for today. It means 'the warmth of the sun on a cold day'. Oh, what was it? I'm sure it began with 'A'."

His mother grinned. "I can't think of one starting

with 'A'."

"Apple," shouted Alice.

They all laughed. "Very good, darling," said his mother. "Apple does begin with 'A'."

His father stopped and leant on his crutch. "Do you mean 'apricity'?"

"Yes, that's it. Apricity. Isn't it a lovely word? It sounds like apricot."

"Well, I've never heard of it," retorted his mother.

"It is a very old word, rarely used nowadays. Have you heard of its derivative 'apricate', meaning to bask in the sun?" When she shook her head, his father continued, "I think it a great pity that such delightful words go out of use. I can think of several others that are no longer in circulation."

"Tell me some, so I can say them to the boys at school, and see if they know what I'm talking about." Jamie's eyes lit up with the thought of having an advantage over them.

"Let me think." They came to a tree stump and his father sat down. "There is 'jargogle'."

"Oh, that's great. What does that mean?"

"It means to confuse or bamboozle."

Jamie threw his arms in the air, a grin on his face. "Oh, don't jargogle me with such big words." He bent down and repeated the word in Daniel's ear, making the little boy giggle. "Jargogle, jargogle."

Alice tugged her father's sleeve. "Tell me one, Papa."

He took off his hat and scratched his head. "Um… What about 'jollux'?"

"Ugh, that's not a nice word."

Jamie stood up. "I think it is. I have a feeling I've heard that one before. Something to do with a fat man?"

"Yes, that's it."

His mother looked up to the sky. "Well, it's all very well, having an English lesson out here, but I think we ought to be making our way back. I can see one or two grey clouds looming."

"Ah, Mama, I don't want to go back yet," replied Jamie. "Please may I take Daniel a little further? Maybe show him my tree house? And you, Alice, if you'd like to come?"

"Well, I don't like the look of those clouds."

"It isn't such a...I mean, there isn't so much apricity in the air now, is there?" Jamie tickled his brother. "What do you think, little one?"

Daniel shrieked with laughter.

"It wasn't that funny." He turned to his mother again. "Please, Mama, it's my last day home, and the clouds don't look too dark."

She looked upwards once more. "Oh, very well, but don't stay out too long, just in case. Do you want to go with them, Alice?"

With her head to one side, his sister pondered for a minute, then shook her head. "No, thank you, Mama. I'll go back with you and Papa."

His mother turned the pram around. "Don't change your mind when we're halfway home."

Jamie waited a moment to make sure she hadn't done so, and then took his brother's hand. "Come on, then, little man, let's go." They made their way through the woods, Jamie wondering if he ought to tell Daniel about their father's brother being killed there, years before, but decided he would be too young to understand.

They reached the tree house and he helped Daniel climb up the wooden ladder. "I used to spend lots of time here when I was young," he told him. "I had blue tits and squirrels for company. That was long before you were born."

As he spoke, a bird flew into the branches above him. Of course it couldn't be the blue tit he had befriended all those years before. He knew they only lived for about a year or so, although he had read somewhere that one had survived for twenty years, so maybe it could be. It flew off again before he could identify it.

Chapter 8

With a worried expression, Tillie took Joseph out of his cot and sat him on her knee. "That's a horrible cough you have there, my little one. I hope it isn't whooping cough. That can be deadly."

Alice looked up from her dolls. "Have I had that, Mama?"

"No, thank goodness, and I pray Joseph doesn't." The baby coughed again. "I think I'll call the doctor. I'm really worried."

"Daniel was coughing in the night as well. I heard him. He woke me up three times."

Tillie walked over to look at him. "Well, he's sleeping peacefully now, so we'll leave him. Perhaps you should come out of the nursery and sleep in one of the other rooms, just until they're better."

Alice jumped up, a look of glee on her face. "You mean in one of those big beds? Oh, yes, please, Mama."

"I suppose you're old enough to have your own room, anyway. I hadn't thought of it before. Would you like that?" The nanny came in, so she laid Joseph in his crib, telling her she would be calling the doctor, and took Alice's hand and went out.

"Did you really mean it, Mama?" Alice jumped up and down in excitement. "I may have my own room. I won't have to share with the boys again?"

"If I'd known you'd be this enthusiastic, I'd have suggested it ages ago."

The little girl's laughter trilled along the landing and down the stairs.

Tillie knocked on David's study door and entered, finding the room empty. "Oh, I didn't know your papa had intended going out. He didn't say anything to me."

After taking one more glance around, she went back out, closing the door behind her.

Nellie came into the hall, looking anxious.

"Is there anything wrong?" Tillie asked.

"Well, I don't like the look of young Maisie, Mistress. I've sent her up to bed."

"What's the matter with her?"

"She has an awful cough."

"Oh, no, not her as well. Both the boys have one, too. I've been looking for the master to see if he thinks we should call the doctor, but I can't find him." She twiddled a stray curl between her fingers. "Do you know where he is?"

"I think he went out an hour or so ago."

"Did he say when he would be back?"

The housekeeper shook her head. "No, Mistress."

Tillie looked up and down the hall. "I shall call the doctor, anyway. Please would you send somebody?"

Nellie ran out. "Yes, ma'am, straightaway."

Tillie turned to Alice, who had been stroking one of the dogs. "Well, young lady, that means you'd better stay with me, today. What do you fancy doing?"

Alice stood up and pressed her lips together. "What I really, really want to do is ride my pony."

"Oh. I thought we could do something together, but very well, we'll go down to the paddock. Then we'll call on Auntie Ruby and the girls, and see how they are, warn them about the cough."

Alice clapped her hands. "I'll fetch my coat. Please may I wear the new one, the turquoise one with the black cuffs and collar?"

"Not to ride on your pony, no. You need to save that for Sunday, for going to church."

"Oh, yes." Alice ran upstairs, seemingly in agreement.

Tillie fetched her own coat and bonnet—her old

one, in case she should rub up against the pony—and waited for her daughter to return.

Skipping along, Alice hummed, clearly happy to be having her own way. How pleasant to be doing something, just the two of them. Jamie had returned to school and, anyway, she rarely had time alone with him. He had grown into a young man, and didn't need his mama fussing over him anymore. She missed him already, though, but knew it would not be for long.

After watching Alice on her pony for half an hour, she turned to Sam. "We're thinking of calling on Ruby. How is she? And the girls?"

"She's fine, for the time being, at any rate."

"Maybe she'll keep this baby."

Chewing on a blade of grass, he looked wistfully out over the hills. "I do hope so." Then he turned back and smiled. "I pray every day that she does. It would break her heart if she lost another one."

She patted his arm as Alice rode up to them. "Watch me, Mama. You weren't watching me."

"Yes, I was. You're doing very well, but we must go soon."

With a swish of her head, the child clicked her tongue and pulled on the reins. The pony cantered off across the paddock.

"Be careful," yelled Tillie.

"There's no need to worry. She's a very talented rider for her age," called Sam as he jumped over the railing and followed the fleeing pair. "But I'd better stop her before she does anything stupid." He caught up with her and walked her back. "I think that's enough for one day, lass. Down you come."

"Aw, do I have to?"

Tillie reached up to her. "Uncle Sam has other chores to complete, my darling. He doesn't have all day to take care of you."

"Do I have to brush and clean her?" Alice turned to walk away. "Can't Uncle Sam do that?"

"No, as I said, he has other jobs. I'll help you. It won't take long."

They took the pony into the stable. Taking off the saddle, Tillie yelped at a sharp twinge in her side. Fortunately, Alice didn't seem to notice, humming as she brushed down the pony—as high as she could reach, anyway.

Wondering what could have caused the pang, Tillie finished the grooming and they settled the pony in her stall with some oats.

The pain had disappeared by the time they arrived at Ruby's cottage. Her sister turned from the washing line with her mouth full of pegs, and grunted.

Tillie picked up a nappy and pegged it next to the others.

"Good day," Ruby finally offered. "To what do we owe this honour?"

"Ah, sis, do I need a reason to visit my favourite sister?"

"Well," laughed Ruby, picking up the wash basket, "seeing as how I'm your only sister."

Tillie laughed as well. "It's the boys, and it looks like Maisie as well—they have bad coughs, so I thought I'd better warn you. I've sent for the doctor just in case it's whooping cough, so I can't stay long. He could be arriving soon."

"Well, I've been told—now don't shout at me. I know you don't believe in old wives' tales—but I've heard that you should let a frog breathe into the mouth of a child who catches whooping cough."

At Alice's raised eyebrows and look of disgust, Tillie laughed. "Oh, Ruby, how on earth would that cure it? A frog's breath, of all things?"

"Or even a donkey."

"A donkey? What? Its breath?"

Ruby lifted the kettle. "Tea?"

"No, thanks, we mustn't stay."

She put the kettle over the fire, anyway. "I knew you'd scoff."

"Well, I just hope your girls don't catch it, for their sakes. Where are they, by the way?"

"Elizabeth's in bed and Eleanor is somewhere around."

"You mean you don't know where she is? Oh, Ruby, how can you let her out of your sight?"

Ruby shook her head. "Tillie, not everyone is as attentive as you. Just because you've... I'm sorry, I didn't mean..." She sat down and looked under the table. "See, she's here. I knew she wouldn't be far."

Knowing what her sister meant, Tillie drew in a deep breath as her niece came out from behind the overhanging tablecloth. Bending down to her, she scolded, "Were you hiding, you little minx?"

"I knew she was there all the time," bragged Alice, giving the little girl a hug. "Didn't I, Ellie...Eleanor?"

"Well, she's safe. That's all that matters. We must be off." She knew she should not be so protective, but her own experiences would not let her relax whenever children were not where they should be. Her sister should know that.

After she had given her sister and niece a kiss, she asked, "Are you still coming tomorrow? But no, perhaps you'd better not. I'll let you know what the doctor says."

Ruby rubbed her belly. "I definitely don't want to catch it. We all had it as children, so I shouldn't do. I'm not sure if it can affect unborn babies, but I'm not willing to take the risk. And, anyway, I don't have any spare frogs at the moment."

Tillie laughed, and she and Alice hurried home, arriving as a carriage drew up in front of the house.

"That's probably the doctor," she squealed, dragging Alice inside. They quickly took off their coats and she sent her daughter into the kitchen for a drink as she welcomed Doctor Abrahams. He had been their medic for many a year, and his advancing years showed. Grey streaks in his hair and beard gave him a distinguished look. Purvis took his hat and cane and Tillie explained the situation.

"There is an epidemic doing the rounds at the moment," he remarked, when she mentioned her fears about whooping cough.

"Will you be able to give them anything, if it is that?"

"Well, the quacks would sell you all sorts of remedies, but the ones I find the most effective are burning rags soaked in saltpetre, and placing onions in the sick person's room. I'm not sure how that works, but it seems to."

"Onions? Ah, I think my ma did that, come to think of it, when we had the illness as children. But it couldn't have worked one hundred percent, for I'm sure my youngest brother, James, who died as a baby, had it, if I remember rightly."

"Nothing works one hundred percent, I fear. No matter how hard we try, someone always seems to contract a disease worse than everybody else."

They began to walk upstairs but Tillie pulled his sleeve. "Do you mean one of my children will die?"

He turned to her. "No, no, Missus Dalton, it is not always the case. Please do not take any notice. I didn't mean to alarm you."

Seriously worried, she followed him up. Enough upset and death had occurred in the last few years, and she couldn't bear the thought of any more.

Daniel still slept, a most unusual occurrence. Normally, he would have an hour at the most. The nanny paced up and down with Joseph. "He just won't settle," she began as a fit of coughing overtook the baby.

The doctor waited until he had stopped, seemingly listening for something, and then lifted his finger in the air. "Ah, there, the familiar whoop at the end. I am afraid to say, Missus Dalton, your fears are confirmed."

"Oh, no." Tillie ran across and took him. "Can you tell whether he has a severe case or not?"

"Not at the moment. It could grow worse, or just fizzle out, as most cases do." He looked at Daniel, who had begun to stir, and felt his brow. "Does this little one seem as bad?"

"No, not yet. At least, I don't think so." Tillie glanced across at the nanny with raised eyebrows, hoping she would corroborate her story. "Does he, Maria?"

"No, ma'am."

"You had better keep your daughter away from them. Does she show any signs?" the doctor asked.

"No, not yet, and I have already arranged for her to sleep in a different room."

"Ah, good. Very sensible."

Tillie remembered what Nellie had told her a while before. "One of the maids might have it, though—Maisie, our parlour maid."

"Well, as I say, keep her away from everyone else. I...um... is there any possibility you could be...?" He looked purposely at Tillie's belly.

She followed his look, and patted it. "No, I don't think so, but my sister, Ruby, is expecting."

"Well, tell her to stay away for a few days. It shouldn't do any harm to an unborn baby, but it's better to be safe than sorry." With one last look around, he made his way across the room.

"Thank you, Doctor," she said as she showed him out of the front door.

"They should recover quickly. They are healthy children. If the onions don't work, try giving them some

Ipecacuanha with a little antimonial wine. But call me if you become seriously worried," he replied as he entered his carriage.

Tillie met Nellie in the hall and told her his diagnosis, and asked if they had any of the remedies he had recommended.

"I shall buy some in if we haven't, and I'll have a look in that book you bought the other day—the one by Missus Isabella Beeton—to see what she recommends," the housekeeper replied, stroking her arm. "I'd heard there are many cases in the village, but I'm sure it will not be severe. Don't worry."

"I can't help it, Nellie. The master calls me a worry-pot, but after all that's happened..." Tillie took a deep breath and blew it out again, lifting her shoulders, determining to remain strong for her children. There would be no point crumbling.

The following day, Joseph became more fretful, but Daniel didn't seem any worse. Tillie wanted to sleep in the nursery with her baby that night, but the nanny persuaded her that she needed her own rest. She couldn't sleep, though, and went in, in the early hours, to check on the baby. He lay still in his cot, pale and wan. For a second, she thought she couldn't see him breathing, but, just as she reached in to grab him up, he began to cough. She picked him up to rub his back and he spewed up over her dressing gown.

The nanny awoke. "Ma'am," she cried, "what are you doing in here?"

"It's just as well I am, for he would have choked on his own vomit if I had not been here." She laid the baby down and took off his nightshirt.

The nanny tried to ease her out of the way. "Allow me, ma'am. I should be doing that, not you, and I had only nodded off for a short while."

"We'll give him a hot bath. That's what the book says."

"What book, ma'am?"

"Missus Beeton's book, of course, and she recommends applying leeches to the breastbone, also."

The nanny looked at her in horror. "But, ma'am, we don't have any leeches, and I'm not going to send for some at this time of the night."

Tillie sat down on a chair. "No, of course not. I'm not thinking straight. She also says the child should be given plenty of fresh air, but we can't take him outside in the dark, either."

"Oh, no, ma'am. Fresh air would do him no good at all. He needs to be kept warm and tucked up in bed."

Joseph began to cough once more. Tillie picked him up. "Try to distract him, and he might not cough so much."

Once more the nanny gave her a disbelieving look. "Distract a baby, ma'am? How do you propose doing that?"

"Well, I don't know. The book didn't say how to." She tried waving her hand in front of his face.

"If I may be so bold, ma'am, I think your Missus Beeton is talking a load of tosh."

"Tosh? What on earth does that mean? But never mind. He seems quieter now. See, it did work, distracting him." She laid the baby back in his cot, trying to ignore the nanny's shaking head. What did she know? Surely Missus Beeton would be more qualified to give advice, if she'd had a book published?

"You had better return to your bed, ma'am." The nanny tucked up the baby, covering him with more blankets than Tillie would have used. "I shall try to stay awake, to ensure the little one is safe."

Tillie turned to the door, trying to remember what else the book had said. Something to do with vomiting.

Had it said to make the child vomit, or to try to stop it? She couldn't be sure, so left the subject hanging in the air. "Call me if you need me, then. I shall take over in the morning if you need a rest."

"Thank you, ma'am. That won't be necessary, I'm sure."

Daniel stirred, so she hurried over to him. He settled down again, without waking. "I suppose our voices disturbed him," she whispered. "I'll go now. Good night."

Sleep evaded her once more, and she tossed and turned until daybreak. Fortunately, David had slept in his own room, or she would have worried about disturbing him.

Chapter 9

The previous evening Jamie had packed his trunk for the last time. "I shan't miss this place one iota," he told Oswell as they walked around the playground during their morning break.

"Oh, I shall," his friend replied, tracing the pattern of the hopscotch lines with his foot. "I don't have many friends at home."

"You will always be my best friend. I shall miss you."

Silas Brown came around the corner, his coat flapping in the breeze, his head high, followed by several of his cronies. Just the sight of the bully gave Jamie a sick feeling in his stomach but, it being their last day, he could no longer hurt him. Best to ignore him. He turned his back on the group, trying to pretend he hadn't seen them.

"Ah, Quackers," called the hated voice. "I bet…"

Jamie pulled Oswell's sleeve and they stalked off before he could finish. He wished he could see the look on the bully's face, but didn't have enough courage to turn around and see it.

"I definitely will not miss him," he declared, once out of sight.

"No, me neither," replied Oswell. "But I've heard he has been accepted at Cambridge. I am almost tempted to refuse my place there."

"Oh, no, you mustn't do that. Your aunt would be so upset. Remember how elated she was when you were accepted. Father would have been ecstatic if I'd even tried for a place, but you know me, I'm not the academic type. I wouldn't have prospered there any better than I have here."

"What will you do?" asked Oswell, but the bell rang and they lined up to go inside in silence before he could answer.

Taking one last look up at the old brick building, having said his goodbyes to the friends he had made in the past year—ironically more than he had made in the whole of the previous years put together—he climbed into the carriage. "No regrets," the headmaster had said in his final speech to the boys who were leaving. "Do not take regrets away with you. Dwell on the happy times."

He tried to think of as many as he could. Not many at all.

Throwing his arms in the air, he flung off his cap. It almost flew out of the open-topped carriage, and he had to lean out to catch it. Grinning, he declared, "But I've survived. I hope I'm a more mature, better person for having done so."

The footman, a new one he had not seen before, turned around and asked, "Is everything all right, sir?"

"Oh, yes, everything is fine. Just fine and dandy, thank you. I shan't have to see that awful place ever again, thank the Lord." Except for prize-giving day. But he hadn't won a prize all the time he had been there, so there wouldn't be much point going back for that.

Humming, he settled in his seat, watching the green fields pass by, wishing he could speed up the carriage. He didn't even have a book to while away the miles. He smiled to himself as he recalled being tempted to sneak one into his trunk, but his innate honesty had forbidden him from doing so. It had been 'Tom Brown's Schooldays' by Tom Hughes, that he had borrowed from his housemaster. Only having read half of it, he had wanted to finish the rest. He felt sure his father would have it in his library, though, and, if he hadn't, he would buy it. Feeling an affinity to Tom Brown, he had been enthralled, and hoped it wouldn't be too long until he could catch up with his shenanigans.

His heart beat faster as he recognised the scenery. Almost home. And for good. How pleasing did that sound! He couldn't wait. Hearing a sweet, high-pitched call, he looked up, and there flew his buzzards, around and around, high above, welcoming him.

He put his hand in his pocket, remembering he had saved a sweet for the last part of the journey. They had already travelled so far, he would scarcely have time to suck it all before the house would come into view. However, he popped it into his mouth. He could always chomp the last bit, if need be. He didn't want to arrive with his mouth full. How unmannerly would that be!

And there he could see, through the trees, the chimneys. Closing his eyes, so he could savour the moment when the whole house would appear, he counted to ten, and then opened them again. How familiar it looked, the yellow stone almost blending into the background as if it had been there thousands of years. He clapped his hands, unprepared for the rush of emotion that coursed through his body. He had known he would be excited, but this sensation beat everything he had ever known before. His legs had turned to jelly by the time they drew up in front of the main door, and he daren't stand.

"Are you well, sir?" asked the footman when he remained seated.

"Oh, yes, thank you. I have never been so well in my whole life. This is the best day."

The footman gave him an odd look and stood waiting patiently, holding open the door of the carriage.

The front door opened and Alice ran out. "Jamie, you're home," she squealed, jumping up beside him.

He hugged her tightly. "I am indeed. And I never plan to leave, as long as I may live."

"How long will that be?" she asked, trying to pull away.

"A very long time, I hope."

His mother came hurrying out. "Welcome home, son," she gushed as Nellie followed her. "Aren't you getting out?"

"Yes, oh, yes."

The footman unhitched the bags and Jamie took a light one from him. "I shan't ever have to do this again. What a spiffing thought."

His mother hugged him. "No, son, you're home for good."

Alice looked up at him. "Won't you ever marry, then, Jamie?"

"Well, I hope so, and I suppose, if Father is still alive, I shall have to find somewhere else to live, but we don't want to think about that now, do we?"

"Is Papa going to die?" She stopped, blocking the doorway.

"No, of course not," cried his mother. "Jamie didn't mean that. Come on. Let's get his things inside."

Jamie looked up at the carved hall ceiling. He couldn't remember ever being so happy in his whole life.

* * * *

Jamie wandered around the old house, taking in the familiar burgundy wallpaper in the lounge, and sniffing at the faintly musty smell of books in the library.

He had been home a few weeks, and had begun to feel like a spare part. Alice had lessons in the morning with a governess, and the boys were too little to occupy his time for long, much as he enjoyed playing with them.

He saw his father go into his study and followed him. "Father, is there anything I can do to help with the running of the house?"

His father sat behind his desk, rearranging papers. "Well, I like the idea, but I am not sure what to suggest.

Are you any good with figures?"

Jamie grimaced. "Not really."

"I thought not. You could help organise the shoot, I suppose. How does that sound?"

"Ah, yes, that would be spiffing."

His father's eyebrows raised. "You still use that word, then?"

"Which word? Spiffing? Don't you think I should?" Jamie sat down on the nearest chair. "I suppose it is rather…what can I call it? Childish?"

His father laughed and lit his pipe.

Jamie hadn't realised he smoked one. Probably a diversion from his usual cigars. He rather liked the smell of the tobacco. He thought he had detected a different aroma on his clothes the last time he had been close.

"Do you not approve?"

Jamie jerked his head back. "I beg your pardon. What do you mean?"

"I thought I saw a look of censure on your face when I lit my pipe."

"No, Father, certainly not. I was actually thinking I might try it myself."

"Well, do not let your mother see you. I am only allowed to do it in here. She will not let me smoke it anywhere else in the house. She says the smell makes her ill." He offered the pipe to Jamie. He took a small puff and began choking. "Maybe not, then."

"No, Father, maybe not, I agree. But, going back to our conversation earlier, will you ask Mister Hodges if I would be able to help him. I'm sure I could be of assistance, if only in a small way."

"My, how you have grown up, son. I remember what a little scrap you were when you first came."

Jamie walked over to the window. "Yes, I was, wasn't I?" Then he ran across to hug his father. "And thank you so much for rescuing me. I heard someone say once, that you didn't want me at first."

Extricating himself, his father replied, "Well, son, maybe that might have been true in the beginning, but I soon grew to…um…love you."

"And I seem to remember loving you from the very start."

"Well, son, I have work to do. Have you any plans for today?"

"Not really. I'll probably take a stroll into the village."

"You could take Daniel. I'm sure your mother and the nanny would appreciate that. Fortunately, he has recovered from the whooping cough, as have Joseph and Maisie."

Walking down the lane a while later, Jamie thought about his reasons for going to the village. He had been once before, a week or so back, and entered the tearooms, hoping to catch a glimpse of Beth, but she had not been there. He prayed she had not been sacked for her little misdemeanours. She hadn't seemed very adept at the job. He couldn't fathom out why he felt so concerned for her. In fact, she filled his mind most of the day. Why?

"Do you think I'm in love, Danny, my boy?" he asked Daniel, who trotted along beside him.

"Yes, Jamie. Me love you, too," he replied. "Can we sing a song?"

Jamie laughed at his little brother's naivety. "Good idea. Which one? Do you know 'Come into the Garden, Maud'?"

"I can't 'rember. Will you learn it me?"

"Oh, Danny, Danny, don't let Papa hear you use the wrong word. It's 'Will you teach me', not 'learn me'."

"Who's Maud?"

"I don't know. Just the lady in the song."

They sang the chorus over and over, for Jamie

couldn't remember the verses, and soon arrived at their destination. He lingered for a short while, looking in various shop windows, not wanting to appear too eager to go to the tearooms, even though that had been his intention for the walk, but his brother looked up at him after a while, and pointed to them. "Pretty girl?"

Non-plussed, he stammered, "Um, um, which pretty girl do you mean?"

"In there."

He glanced across at the building again, replying in as nonchalant a voice as he could, "Very well, then, if you want."

A horse pulled up in front of them before they could cross the road. "Jamie," called the rider, "your father tells me you would like to help with the shoot. Is that correct?"

"Ah, Mister Hodges, yes, please."

"Then come to my house, or would you prefer me to call on you? I can be there in half an hour, if you are ready to return."

Jamie looked down at Daniel. Would the boy make it all the way back home without a drink? His own mouth felt very dry. He decided they needed the drink. "Could you make it an hour, please, sir?" he shouted back. "We had been about to take refreshments."

"Certainly, see you in one hour, then." Mister Hodges doffed his cap and rode off down the street.

Jamie grabbed Daniel's hand and they hurried to the tearooms. Disappointment flooded through him when Beth did not appear. He gave his order, hoping she would come out of the back door any moment, but she did not.

"Pretty girl?" asked Daniel, tucking into his cake.

The waitress must have heard him, for she stopped on her way to take a tray of dirty dishes to the kitchen. "Do you mean Beth?"

Jamie nodded, sipping his tea, and trying not to show

too much interest.

"She left last week. Couldn't cope."

"Ah, that's a pity," Jamie replied as she made her away through the crowded shop. "A real pity," he muttered under his breath. The cake had lost its flavour, and he toyed with it, then gave up, pushing it towards Daniel.

The boy's eyes lit up. "Me have it?"

"Yes, I've lost my appetite."

Much as he wanted it, though, two slices of cake proved too much for the little one, and they went out, leaving a large chunk on the plate. Jamie felt guilty at wasting food, but his dry mouth would not have been able to tolerate the sponge.

Down the lane on their way home, they saw some sheep coming out of a field. "I hope they're not escaping," laughed Jamie.

"Sheep," cried Daniel, running towards them, scattering them in all directions.

Dozens more followed. Farmer Askew came out, whistling to his sheepdog. Seeing Jamie, he called, "Catch that one up there, would you, please?"

Jamie looked around to see one of the woolly animals climbing the bank. He hurried to it and shooed it down to the others. The lane had become so full, he and Daniel could not make their way through, so he pulled his brother to the side and let them pass.

"Where are you taking them?" he shouted to the farmer. He obviously didn't hear him above the bleating and baaing, for he continued without replying. Another ewe made a bid for freedom, but soon changed its mind and re-joined the flock.

Once they had all passed, Jamie took Daniel's hand and hurried him along. "I don't want to be late for Mister Hodges."

"Sheep," repeated Daniel, turning as if he wanted to

follow them.

"No, Danny boy, we have to return home. Come on." He bent down to look his brother in the eye and his heart stopped. Ahead, climbing over a low hedge, he thought he saw Jake, Beth's cousin, the boy whom he had caught poaching fish some years before. But Beth had told him he had been sent to the convict place. Nobody returned from there, did they?

It dawned on him that it could be the other boy Jake had been with—his friend or cousin. He couldn't remember which. He stood up. Maybe the older boy—actually he had grown into a man—wouldn't remember him. Or, if he ignored him, or just said, 'Good day', he might not cause any trouble. Maybe he wouldn't even come their way.

However, his hopes were dashed.

"Dalton," he called.

"Who's that?" asked Daniel, hiding behind him.

Face up to him, he told himself. "Nobody," he whispered, picking up the boy, then replied aloud, "It's Bobby's cousin, isn't it? How is he? I haven't seen him for ages."

"He's moved away. Didn't you know? His father died and the family have gone up north."

"No, I didn't know that." The lady in the shop had said that Beth had left because she couldn't cope. No wonder, if her father had died.

The young man came closer. A long scar, running down his face from his eye to his chin, made Jamie wonder if he had received it in a fight. More than likely. He backed away slightly, intimidated by the lad, who seemed to grow taller and taller as he advanced.

"I must be off. Good day," he squealed in what sounded, to his ears, a squeaky voice.

"Ah, don't be in such a hurry." The lad pointed to Daniel. "Introduce me to this young man."

Jamie tried to pull the little boy away. "This is my brother and I really am in a rush."

"Not so fast, you little runt." Before he realised what he'd intended, he had grabbed Daniel from Jamie's arms and swung him high in the air.

Daniel screamed.

Jamie reached up to try to recover him, but the bully swung him higher, a look of devilment on his face.

He tried once more. "Please, put him down. You'll hurt him."

"He likes it. Just look at his happy face." He swung him even higher, saying, "I'll bet you've never had a fairground ride as exciting as this, have you, little man?"

"We don't go to fairgrounds. Now, please put him down." Jamie jumped up to try to grab him but the monster whirled the boy around. That was until he vomited his cake all over him.

"Serves you right," shouted Jamie as the lad dropped his brother in a heap on the ground but, before he could pick him up, he felt his collar being pulled.

"You won't get away with this, you snivelling wretch. You'll pay dearly." He gripped Jamie's arm in a vicelike hold behind his back.

Helpless to assist his little brother, Jamie tried to comfort him. "Don't worry, Danny boy, Jamie will soon have you home."

"Oh, no, he won't." With his free hand, the lad grabbed a handful of grass and scrubbed at the stain but, no matter how much rubbing the jacket received, Jamie could still smell the sick. "Your big, cowardly brother, Jamie, is coming with me."

"No!" He tried to pull his arm free, but the action resulted in it being gripped even tighter. "You can't do this." He looked up the lane, wishing the farmer would return, but he had disappeared around the bend.

"And who's going to stop me? Not you, that's for

certain." He yanked him over the hedge and into a field.

"What about Daniel?" cried Jamie. "You can't leave him there on his own."

"He can follow, if he wants. Or he can return home on his own. He has legs, hasn't he?"

Twisting his head around to see his little brother, he saw him squeeze through a gap and follow them, crying, "Jamie, wait."

He breathed a sigh of relief. Although the lane led straight to the house, he couldn't be sure if the child would find his own way. And, anyway, what a rumpus would be caused if he arrived home on his own. "Come on, Danny boy," he called. "Catch up."

"Yes, Danny boy," mocked the lad. "Catch up. That is, if you can."

"Why are you doing this?" Jamie asked. "What pleasure do you gain from hurting innocent people?"

"Huh! Innocent! I went to prison because of you, and Jake was deported."

"Me? What did I have to do with it?"

"You were the only one who could've snitched on us."

"But I never told nobody, honest." With one last effort, Jamie pulled his arm free and stepped back. "You must believe me, I never told no-one."

The lad looked at him through narrowed eyes.

"It's true." Jamie reached down to Daniel, who had caught up with them, and picked him up, cuddling him, and trying to pacify him. "I promise you on the life of my little brother, that I didn't tell no-one."

Jamie could tell from the screwed up eyes and furrowed brow that the lad debated with himself whether that could be true. "I don't have a brother, only three sisters, but..." He gave a huge sigh, turning his back on Jamie. "Clear off, before I change my mind."

Jamie didn't wait for him to do so. He legged it, as

fast as he could, down the field, through the gap in the hedge and onto the lane, only stopping when he didn't have breath left in his body. Obliged to put his brother down, trying to ignore his wails, he bent over double, trying to force air into his lungs, glancing back every now and again, to make sure the bully hadn't followed. He then grabbed Daniel's hand and dragged him along until the house came into view. With one last effort, he picked him up and ran the remaining distance, stopping to hide behind a bush once he felt safe, so he could regain his composure before he entered the house. Should he tell anybody about the incident? He thought not, for it would mean telling them about the original encounter that he should have reported, but hadn't.

He bent and straightened Daniel's coat and brushed off some grass and twigs from his brown trousers. Should he ask the boy not to say anything, either? Would it be fair to ask him to keep a secret? But how would he explain it away if he did say something?

"That was an adventure, wasn't it, Danny boy?" He tried to coax the child into believing it had been a game.

Daniel looked at him from beneath his eyebrows, clearly not impressed.

He took off the boy's cap and brushed his hair back from his face. Perhaps, if he didn't labour the point too much, he might just forget about it. "We're home safely now. That nasty man can't hurt us. I bet you're ready for your tea."

The boy nodded.

"Very well, then, let's go inside." Even though he knew the young man wouldn't venture so close to the house, he had one last look around, just to make sure, and opened the door, forcing a smile to his lips.

Maisie greeted them in the hall. "Master Jamie, are you well?"

He might have known his childhood friend would

pick up on his demeanour, even though he thought he had composed himself satisfactorily. "Yes, of course, Maisie, why wouldn't I be?"

She looked from him to Daniel and back. "You look a bit flustered, both of you. You've been to the village?"

"Yes, and we had to hurry home. Mister Hodges is coming to see me."

"Oh, he's been and gone. Couldn't wait."

"Aw, no. What did he say?"

She pursed her lips. "I think he said he'd return tomorrow."

Daniel had begun to jig from one foot to the other.

"I hope he wasn't too angry." When she shook her head, Jamie continued, "Thank you, Maisie, I'd better take this one up to the nursery. It looks like he needs the toilet."

On the way upstairs, he rued the fact that he'd missed his opportunity. Would his father find out? Had he ruined any chance of doing something useful? Why did his life have to be so eventful? Why couldn't he be like an ordinary boy? And what about Beth? He would never see her again. Never look into those beautiful green eyes. How could he bear the thought of that?

Chapter 10

Jamie had been forgiven for his tardiness and Mister Hodges returned the following day to organise the annual shoot. So far, nobody had found out about Jake's friend. Daniel's moans had been brushed aside with an explanation that he had been tired out. Luckily, he didn't have a big vocabulary, so couldn't expand on his efforts to describe what had happened. Jamie had told his mother he had met a relative of Bobby's, and they had been having a lark. She hadn't seemed too impressed, but hadn't questioned him further.

"The Glorious Twelfth, we call it," pronounced Mister Hodges, puffing on his pipe, filling the room with smoke.

"Because it's on the twelfth of August," replied Jamie, eager to show off his knowledge. "The start of the grouse season."

"All right, Jamie, thank you." His father took out his pipe and lit it.

Jamie held his breath and walked over to the open window. His dogs, Goldie and Lady, played on the lawn. He would much rather have gone out to join them in the sunshine than stay in that smoke-filled room, especially as Lady had become rather arthritic with age, and he didn't know how much longer she would live, but he had offered his services, so had to endure the unpleasantness.

"So, Jamie, what would you prefer?"

He hadn't realised his father had given him any options, so turned to him with a questioning look. "I beg your pardon?"

"Would you rather write the invitations?"

He pulled a face. "Oh, my writing isn't very good."

"Right, then, you shall have to deliver the letters. On

the day itself, you may help the beaters."

"But I did that last year. Can't I join the shoot? You've been giving me lessons on how to use a gun, and I'm sixteen now."

Mister Hodges tapped out his pipe into the hearth. "I think the lad's old enough, David. Shouldn't you give him a chance?"

His father shook his head. "I do not know. He finds himself in such scrapes. We would probably all be shot to death."

"Oh, Father, how can you say such a thing? I've learned from my mistakes. Just because I nearly drowned twice, and…"

"And fell out of a window that should not have been open. Your mother and I still have not had a proper explanation of how that happened, but now is not the time to go in to that. I shall have to have a very hard think on the matter."

Jamie turned away once more. He hated keeping secrets from his parents, and now that Silas Brown couldn't hurt him anymore, he could tell them what had happened. But, as had been said, now would not be the appropriate time. Maybe later, or the next day.

They continued to discuss the arrangements for the shoot, with Jamie contributing little to the conversation. Perhaps his father had been right. Something bad would most likely happen, knowing his past record. It would probably be for the best if he didn't participate, after all. But what else could he do to occupy his time? He had never had any trouble finding things to do during the holidays when he had come home from school, so why should his life be any different now?

As soon as he could make his excuses, he left the drawing room. His mother found him later, in the library, trying to find a book to take his mind off his difficulties.

"Ah, Jamie, I've been thinking."

Oh dear, what's coming now?

"You haven't seen your Auntie Annie and Sarah for so long." She picked out a book and blew off the dust from the top. "How would you like to go to Harrogate and stay with them for a while?"

"But what about the shoot? I'm supposed to be helping with that."

"Well, after it's finished, obviously." Opening the book, she sneezed. "I must get someone to come in here and dust these shelves. They're appalling."

"I could run a feather duster over them, Mother. That used to be one of my tasks at school."

The book replaced, she went across and hugged him. "Do you miss it, my darling?"

"What, school? Oh, no, not at all. I couldn't wait to leave."

"That's what I thought, but you don't seem content since you left."

He took out a handkerchief and blew his nose. "I am content, Mama, it's just... I don't know. I seem rather like a spare part. I'm not a child anymore, but I'm not an adult, either. I feel I'm in the way."

Dropping her head to one side, she looked him in the eye. "You could never be in the way, son. Don't ever think so. That's not why I suggested you go to stay in Harrogate."

"No, I didn't mean... I know you wouldn't say that." He hugged her. "But, yes, I would like to go and see Sarah. She's having a party of some sort soon, isn't she?"

"Yes, her coming-out party."

"I won't be expected to go, will I?"

"Oh, no, it takes place next week. It will all be over by the time you go."

Not enjoying formal parties, he heaved a sigh of relief. "Thank goodness for that. Are you sure she'll want me to go, though, now she's been...whatever she's been?"

"Oh, yes, I'm sure she won't act any differently towards you. In fact, I know she won't. Even though the 'coming-out' is supposed to show the world she is now available to marry, she is such an unpretentious girl, her first love will always be you."

"And she'll always be mine. I've loved her since the first time I met her. But more like an older sister, not in a romantic way."

Beth holds that position, he thought, but, of course, didn't mention such a thing to his mother. The woodland girl had gone, anyway, so what would be the point in considering her at all, ever again?

"Well, we'll see. You may come to think differently in time." She straightened his cravat, just as she'd done when he'd been a child, and crossed the room. "I'll make the arrangements. It will give you something to look forward to."

"Thank you, Mother."

After she had gone, he went to the window. "Ugh, more rain," he muttered. "Just as I'd decided to go out. Oh, well, I shall just have to find a book, after all."

He picked out 'Tom Brown's Schooldays'. He still had not finished it. But did he want to be reminded of his time at the hated school? Maybe Tom Brown had enjoyed life in his institute. Maybe he hadn't been bullied, or shouted at, or fagged. It would be worth a look. Sitting in the large armchair, he soon lost himself in the goings on at Rugby, until a voice outside called his name.

"In here, Alice," he called back.

His sister came in, resplendent in a new navy blue riding habit.

"My, you look gorgeous," he told her. "But, surely, you aren't going riding in this rain?"

She went to the window. "It stopped raining ages ago."

"Oh, did it? I must have been too engrossed in my book. But, pray, tell me why you've come to see me. I'm honoured, of course, but you don't usually seek me out."

"Mama said…"

He raised his eyebrows. Had his mother been telling the whole family he felt like a spare part? He'd hoped it would have been kept confidential, but it didn't look like it.

"Mama wondered if you would like to accompany me."

"Um, no, thank you. You know I'm not very adept at riding. I wouldn't want to spoil your fun."

"Very well, goodbye." She left without needing any further encouragement, clearly not at all disappointed at his rejection of her kind offer.

The book seemed to have lost its appeal, so he put it on the table, intending to finish it at a later time. What could he do instead, though? If the rain had really ceased, he could go for a wander around the lake. Take the dogs for a run.

He bumped into Maisie in the hall. She swapped the tray of teacups into her other hand. "I hear you're going up to Harrogate, Master Jamie. I hope you have a good time."

"It isn't for a week or so, but thank you." Why did he always feel guilty that he couldn't take his childhood friend with him whenever he went anywhere exciting? He had accepted years ago that her life had taken a completely different path to his but, as they crossed so frequently, he wanted to help her. It didn't seem fair that he had gone so far up in society, when she had only risen from being a lowly scullery maid to a parlour maid. Then a thought entered his head. Maybe he could marry her and take her out of the drudgery of her life as a servant. It was not an impossibility. His mother had done so, had married his father, when she had been an even lesser mortal, had had no job at all, only recently having been released from prison. If his father had done it, he couldn't have any objection to his son doing the same, could he?

Looking into her violet eyes, he felt a quiver of excitement course through his body. It would solve the problem, and he wouldn't have to find some bride whom he might not like, or whose irksome habits would annoy him. He had known Maisie for as long as he could remember, and she didn't have any irritating behaviour that he knew of. He wouldn't tell her yet, though. He would have to wait until he was eighteen, at least. Only two years.

"Do you enjoy your life here, Maisie? I mean…you aren't considering moving to any other place or anything?"

Her brow furrowed. "Yes, Master Jamie, I'm very happy here and, no, I have no intentions whatsoever of going anywhere else. Why do you ask?"

"Nothing."

Nellie came out of the lounge and gave Maisie a black look. The maid scuttled off into the dining room.

"You really should not keep her from her work, Master Jamie," admonished the housekeeper. "I know you feel responsible for her, but she needs to complete her chores."

"Yes, Nellie, I know, and I might have…" he had been about to say, 'a solution', but knew the housekeeper would not condone his benevolence. And, anyway, he had decided not to tell anyone, but wait to see what would happen in the future.

Outside, the rain had indeed blown over, and the sun shone in a bright blue sky. The dogs ran around, clearly delighted to be given the unexpected treat. Goldie ran up to him with a large stick in her mouth. He threw it as far as he could, reflecting on his decision to marry Maisie. Would she be in accord, though? Surely, she would. Once he had come of age, he would be one of the most eligible bachelors in the area, if not the most. Surely, she would not turn down such an offer? He would have to sound her out, somehow, without actually saying the words. How could he phrase it? He couldn't ask her if she loved him, for she would say 'yes, of course'. And, anyway, she would want to know why he'd asked.

Throwing the stick again, he tried to think of some other way. Maybe he could ask Sarah for advice when he went to stay with her. But she might be another problem. His father had hinted, once, that he'd planned on a marriage between them. But, maybe he'd misunderstood. Sarah was three years older than him. She wouldn't want to marry such a young man. But what had his mother meant earlier? Had she been hinting that as well?

* * * *

Two weeks later, having survived the shoot without any mishaps, Jamie arrived in Harrogate. Climbing up the steps to the front door, he recalled the first time he had done so, cowering behind his father, who had only been his Uncle David then.

With his heart in his mouth, he pulled the bell pull. His Auntie Annie always made him nervous, and he sensed that she still didn't approve of him. She'd had to come to terms with him, for the sake of keeping the peace with his father, but there always seemed to be an undercurrent of frisson whenever he went near her.

Sarah pushed past the footman who opened the door and rushed to him. "Jamie, how delighted I am to see you."

"And me to see you, cousin."

They stepped aside as his cases were brought in and she took his hand, leading him into the drawing room.

"Is that a new footman?" Jamie asked, sitting on the

edge of the settee, looking around for the dreaded aunt.

Sarah raised her eyes to the ceiling. "Yes, you know Mother. She never learns to keep her mouth shut. We go through more servants than anyone I know."

"And where is she, your mother?"

"Oh, out shopping. Father has been doing rather well lately with his business, so he told her—foolishly, in my opinion—that she could treat herself to a new bonnet. Why she needs another one, I cannot tell you, for she had a new hat for my coming-out party. She only has one head, so can only wear one hat at a time."

Closing his mouth when he realised it was open, he nodded, unable to think of a reply. He felt in awe of this gorgeous young lady. Her whole demeanour had changed. Could she be the same girl he had looked up to for the past eight years? How would she consider marrying him—a gawky, ungainly lad with nothing to recommend him? Obviously, his parents hadn't seen her recently or they would not be entertaining such an idea.

Relaxing against the back of the settee, he felt more at ease than he had done for a long time.

"What would you like to do while you are here?" asked Sarah after the maid had brought them some refreshments. "I have one or two parties planned, to which you would be welcome to accompany me, and I shall be holding one myself."

"Oh, I don't really feel like dancing. I don't know how to."

She jumped up and pulled him. "Well, we can soon put that right. Do you know the waltz?"

"Yes, I think I can manage that, but none of these gavort things."

"Gavotte, Jamie. The word is gavotte. Stand there and watch me, then copy what I do."

Unexpectedly, he mastered the dance within a very short time.

Sarah clapped her hands in glee. "See, it's easy. Now we'll try the polka."

Once he had grasped that, he then had to learn how to deport himself, one hand on his hip, his head high. Eventually, they fell onto the settee, laughing.

The door opened and in walked his aunt.

"My, my, it hasn't taken you long to come down to his level," she scoffed.

Sarah clearly did not suffer any pangs of remorse at being caught in such an unladylike position. "Oh, Mother, we were only having some fun."

Aunt Annie peeled off her gloves, her nose in the air. "Remember you are now a young lady, my dear, and young ladies do not behave in such a manner."

Sarah stood up and tidied her gown. "Yes, Mother, but Jamie is family. Surely I do not have to act so formally with him."

"Of course you do. It does not do to forget, even for a moment."

Jamie stood up also, and held out his hand. "Good day to you, Aunt. I trust you are well."

With a grunt, she looked down her nose at him and offered her hand, clearly begrudgingly, for he had to walk across to kiss it. It hung so limp, he thought, for a second, her wrist might be broken but, as soon as he let go, she reached up to smooth her hair.

"And Uncle Victor? I trust he is well, also?"

"Yes, yes, there is no need for all that formality."

To stop making a retort that he might regret, Jamie coughed. She had just told Sarah she had to be formal at all times. Surely she should practise what she preached?

Sarah gave him a look as if she knew his thoughts, and then turned back to her mother. "Did you have a nice walk, Mother? Buy any hats or anything?"

Her mother turned to go out the door. "No, I didn't. I could not find anything to suit me."

After she had gone, Sarah remarked, "It is no wonder she is in such a bad humour, then. She hates to be thwarted."

Jamie didn't reply. She always seemed in a bad mood to him.

"Anyway, I am forgetting my manners. I haven't even asked if you would like to brush up after your journey." She took his hand. "I'll show you to your room."

Changing out of his travel clothes, he hoped she hadn't been able to smell the sweat on him. It would have been the dancing that had made him whiffy, though, not the travelling. No wonder she had wanted him to have a wash and change his clothes.

Looking out the window at the houses lining the street, he found it so different from the views at home, or even at school. He didn't think he would like to live there. No fields to see, no birds to watch. Maybe that could be the reason his aunt always seemed bad-tempered. She would be a lot happier if she had nature on her side. But then, Sarah had the same views, and she rarely seemed out of sorts.

The following night, not very confident in his ability to dance proficiently, he escorted his aunt and Sarah to a tea dance. Fortunately, Sarah didn't expect him to stay by her side all evening. His aunt didn't give him a second glance and, once their names had been announced, she went off to gossip with her cronies.

He stood at the edge of the room, looking around at the fancy people. One young girl in a sage green dress patterned with vines and buds caught his eye—or, rather, the dress did. Because of its contrast to the gowns worn by the other ladies, he wondered if she loved nature as much as he did. Catching her chaperone glaring at him, he realised he had been staring and looked away, as the girl gave him a weak smile, peeping from under her eyebrows. Should he go and ask her for a dance? Nobody else had done so while he had been watching.

Summoning courage, he took a step forward. Maybe not. As he hesitated, she looked across at him again. He moved closer. Her green eyes reminded him of Beth. If he'd ever had the chance to take the floor with his forest girl, he wouldn't have hesitated for a second. But he never would. She had disappeared from his life forever, so this girl could take her place. Not in his affections. He had decided Maisie would replace them.

What harm could one dance do? Taking a deep breath, and before he could change his mind, he marched over to her. "Please may I have the honour of the next dance?"

The girl's chaperone stood in front of him. "And who are you, sir, to be so bold? You have not been introduced."

He stepped back. Of course. He'd forgotten about that formality. "James Dalton, ma'am. I am Sarah Smythe's cousin."

Sarah hurried over, obviously having seen his predicament. "Please may I introduce my cousin Jamie?" She bowed to the girl. "He is only recently come to Harrogate from the country."

As if that explained his bad manners, the girl bowed her head and curtsied. The grim look on the chaperone's face softened into almost a smile. "And this is Geraldine Burnyeat."

Jamie bowed, unsure of what to do next. With the introductions having been made, did that give him the freedom to dance with the girl? He held out his hand, to see what she would do. She took it and he walked towards the dance floor. She followed. Step one completed. They stood on the edge, waiting for the music to finish, so they could join in the next dance. Should he strike up a conversation? Remark on the fine weather they had been enjoying? Before he could make up his mind, the musicians fell silent, and the dancers left the floor, leaving the pair of them the only ones standing there. In a panic, he stepped back, treading on the foot of an elderly lady.

"I am so sorry," he cried, trying to move away, but impeded by the people lining up for the next dance.

Looking up, he saw his aunt watching him, shaking her head. *Oh, no, she would have to see me making a spectacle of myself,* he thought, grimacing.

The lady whose toes he had squashed patted his arm. "Do not worry, sir. It happens all the time. But, my, what a fine-looking young man you are. I have not seen you around these parts before. I would have remembered such a handsome face."

"I…um…" Jamie couldn't think of a reply. He had never been called handsome before.

Sarah came to his rescue again. "This is my cousin, Jamie Dalton, ma'am. He is recently come up from the country."

Does she have to explain that to everyone I meet?

"Well, Jamie Dalton," replied the lady. "I see you have already been introduced to my granddaughter. I should like to become better acquainted during your stay, and I am sure Geraldine would be of like mind. Enjoy your dance."

He realised he still held the girl's hand. A huge grin covered her face as he led her onto the floor. However, his concentration had been broken by the incident, and he made several wrong moves, breathing a sigh of relief when the dance finished and he could take the girl back to her chaperone.

Needing some fresh air, he went out onto the balcony. Maybe it hadn't been such a good idea to attend. His reputation would have been shattered before it had even had any chance to gain any positivism. Hopefully, it shouldn't tarnish Sarah's chances of finding a suitor.

Sarah came running out. "Do you know who that lady is?"

"Which one?"

"Geraldine's grandmother. I had forgotten until a moment ago, but she is only Lady Catherine Burnyeat, the widow of one of the richest men in Yorkshire."

"So?" Jamie wondered what that could have to do with anything.

"So?" she scoffed. "She has made a point of singling you out."

"But I don't want to be 'singled out'. It makes me uncomfortable. May we go home now?"

"Don't you want to dance with her granddaughter again? She is very pretty."

"Yes, she is, but I would rather stay out here, thank you. Let me know when it's time to leave."

"Ah, Jamie." She put her arms around him. "You'll be fine." Stepping away, she put her finger to her mouth. "Actually, I have just remembered something. Geraldine has a cousin, her father's brother's son, a grandson of Lady Catherine. He is considered to be one of Harrogate's most eligible bachelors, by all accounts. Joel, that's his name. I met him once. He's very attractive. Maybe, if you are invited to Lady Catherine's house, you could suggest you and Geraldine and I make a foursome with him."

Jamie shook his head. "I'm not going to nobody's house."

"But it would be the height of bad manners to refuse."

"I haven't had an invitation, Sarah, so don't go..." he began, but she had already disappeared inside.

As he leaned over the railing, a faint whiff of tobacco smoke drifted across, and he wished he had a cigar. His father had told him it soothed the nerves. Well, he could do with something to soothe his. A foursome, indeed! What could Sarah be thinking? Surely taking the young lady out would imply he might be interested in her as a prospective bride? He couldn't give her that impression, not now he'd decided to marry Maisie. Sarah didn't know that, of course. And if it meant she could be thrown into the path of the most eligible bachelor in the town, he shouldn't stand in her way. Anyway, hopefully he wouldn't receive any such invitation.

Sighing, he wished he hadn't come to Harrogate. If he had realised it would entail all this intrigue, he would definitely have thought twice about it.

A scent of a familiar perfume heralded the arrival of his aunt. "What are you doing out here, boy? You should be inside, dancing."

Surprised that she should be interested in his activities, he replied in as polite a voice as he could, "Yes, Aunt, I am coming. I just needed some air."

"I saw you being introduced to Lady Catherine. You shouldn't thwart her, you know. Her grandson is one of the most eligible…"

"Yes, I know, Aunt. So everyone keeps telling me." She wasn't interested in him at all. Only in the connections he had made.

She pulled his arm. "Come along, then. That nice girl, Geraldine, is waiting for you."

"But…"

"Come, come, do not be abashed. She has not had her coming-out yet, so needs all the practice she can get."

He saw her dancing with someone else, so sat down. What had he been told about partners? More than three dances with one person meant one was serious, so as long as he only danced with her two more times he would be safe. Or was it twice? What if he got it wrong, and danced three times with her? He had better only do it once more, to be on the safe side. But when? If he offered for the next one, it would mean he couldn't have another later, and she might think he had snubbed her.

Several times, as he glanced around the room, he caught Lady Catherine looking at him. Did he have a smut on his face from being outside? He reached into his pocket and, pretending to blow his nose, surreptitiously wiped his handkerchief over his cheeks and chin, and then dabbed it on his forehead, as if he were hot.

Sarah swept past in the arms of an elderly gentleman. She pulled a face which made Jamie grin, but then he looked up and saw his aunt frowning at him. *What can she be condemning me for now?* he seethed. *Aren't I allowed to smile?*

He turned away, only to be confronted by Lady Catherine. "Ah, Mister Dalton, I am leaving in a short while, but thought I would let you know I am hosting a soirée at the end of the week, and shall send you and your cousin an invitation."

Realising his bad manners at remaining seated, he jumped up, knocking over the chair beside him, sending it crashing to the floor with a bang, so everybody around them turned to see who could have made such a faux-pas. With a quick movement, he picked it up, keeping his face averted, praying the lady would not say anything to exacerbate the situation.

A slight smile at the corner of her lips proved, when he plucked up the courage to look at her, that she didn't censure him. She merely gave a slight shake of her head and patted his arm. "I shall have to take you in hand, young man. Try to curb some of that maladroit behaviour. Call around to my house tomorrow morning. You may bring your cousin, if you wish."

Sarah had hurried over. "Oh, thank you, Lady Catherine. We will be honoured, won't we, Jamie?"

Bemused at the turn of events, he merely nodded, but feeling Sarah's elbow in his side, he quickly added,

"Yes, ma'am. Thank you, ma'am."

The lady left, leaving Jamie as if he had stepped into a different world. He had not envisaged any of this sort of thing happening. A quiet holiday with his cousin had been his aim, not being thrust into society—high society, at that.

Chapter 11

Intent on taking the children out for some fresh air, Tillie walked into the nursery. Daniel sat on the floor, grappling with a jigsaw puzzle, while the nanny stood, looking into Joseph's cot.

"Is everything well?" she asked.

Feeling down the sides of the cot, the nanny turned, a worried look on her face. "I cannot find Baby's rattle, ma'am."

"Baby has a name, if you please. He is a year old now, so needs to be called by it." Tillie joined her and picked up Joseph. "Do you mean the silver one with the bells? The one that used to belong to my husband's great grandmother, and has been passed down through the generations?" At the nanny's nod, she continued, "Well, you had better find it. I know the coral teething part has almost been chewed away by the various children who have benefited from it, but it is still serviceable, and will be for many more generations. When did you last see it?"

"Yesterday, I think, ma'am."

Tillie turned to Daniel, who had abandoned the puzzle. "Have you seen it, darling? Joseph's rattle?"

He thrust out his bottom lip, his head to one side. "No, Mama, I not. Where's Jamie?"

Bending down, she sat Joseph beside him but, having learned to crawl, he soon shot off to the other side of the room. His actions could not be described as crawling, really—more like a shuffle, propelling himself forward with one leg under him. "Jamie's gone to stay with Cousin Sarah, my darling. I told you this morning."

"But I fought he be back."

"No, he won't be back for many days." Picking up the puzzle pieces, she mused, "I hope he's enjoying himself."

"Why didn't me go?"

She gave him a cuddle. "Because, my sweetheart, you're too young. Anyway, you wouldn't want to leave Mama and Joseph, would you?"

Much to her chagrin, the little boy nodded.

"Really? You would? Oh." Showing him an offended face didn't work, for he ran to the toy cupboard and took out Jamie's train.

"Play with this?"

"Yes, very well. But, no, I want to take you outside, into the fresh air." The train went back in the cupboard. "Let's take the dogs for a walk. They need some exercise."

Daniel clapped his hands. "Yes."

Turning to the nanny, she ordered, "You'd better stay here and look for that rattle. The master will be most perturbed if it's lost."

Shamefaced, the nanny lifted the cot blankets and shook them as Tillie left. With the dogs collected, they walked outside. Daniel tried to push his baby brother's pram but almost ended up in a hedge, so Tillie found a stick for him to throw to Goldie and he played with that for a while.

Wondering how Jamie fared in Harrogate, she hoped Annie wouldn't be too hard on him. David had voiced his thoughts again the previous evening, about Jamie and Sarah marrying. That was why he had been sent, to become more intimately acquainted with his cousin. Tillie thought him much too young to be thinking of an engagement but, as usual, her opinion didn't seem to count.

Lady, the older dog, seemed to be having difficulty walking. Calling Daniel to come to her side, she stopped and lifted her paw. "Can you see anything in there?" she asked her son.

He reached out towards it, but the dog snapped at him, making him back away. Tillie dropped the paw and grabbed him. "She didn't bite you, did she, darling?" she squealed, examining his hand.

With a shake of his head, he murmured, "Naughty dog."

"Yes, she is. I shall have to have words with your papa. She's never done anything like that before." After inspecting his hand again, she satisfied herself that he hadn't indeed been injured. She had heard of people dying from dog bites, and didn't want any more disasters to befall the family. "I think we'd better take her back home before she tries any more stunts like that."

They made their way back, Daniel clearly soon forgetting the incident, for he ran around, playing with Goldie as if nothing had happened.

As they neared the paddock, Daniel spotted his sister on her pony and called out to her, "Alice, cooee."

Tillie waved also. Her daughter's prowess on her pony had improved so much she could jump small obstacles with ease. Tillie went up to Sam, who had been supervising her.

He turned to smile at them. "She's doing so well, Mistress Tillie." He still found it difficult to call her or David by their Christian names, no matter how many times she insisted.

Eleanor came running up to her.

"Oh, hello, darling, I didn't see you there."

"Auntie Tillie, I'm going to have a ride on Alice's old pony."

Alice rode over to them. "I said she could, Mama."

"That's very magnanimous of you."

The child gave her such a funny look, she burst out laughing. "Haven't you learned that word, yet?"

"Magnasi...no, that's too long."

"Anyway, are you coming home or staying here a

while longer?"

Alice scratched her neck and pursed her lips. "Um…"

Tillie turned to Sam. "I'm sure you would rather have Eleanor on her own, if this is her first time."

"Can't you stay, Mama?" asked Alice, wheeling her pony around.

"Well, I need to do something with Lady. She isn't herself. I'm worried about her."

Sam bent down to the aging dog. "What seems to be the matter?"

Before she could reply, Alice had ridden across to the other side of the paddock.

"I'll watch her, if you could check Lady over, please, Sam," offered Tillie, grabbing Daniel and pushing the pram towards the fence, leaving Eleanor standing patiently next to her father as he examined the dog.

"Be careful," she called to Alice, knowing full well her warnings would fall on deaf ears.

Daniel climbed onto the first bar of the fence. "Me ride?"

"Daniel, you're four now, you should be able to speak properly. Take notice from Eleanor. You should say, 'Please may I have a ride?'"

"Please may I have a ride?" he repeated, perfectly.

"That's better. Good boy." She continued to watch her daughter, her heart in her mouth as she attempted several jumps, until she felt a tug at her skirts.

"Mama?"

"Yes, dear?"

"Please may I have a ride?"

"Oh, yes, I didn't give you a reply, did I? Silly me. Yes, I don't see why not. If Eleanor can do so, then, of course, so can you."

Joseph had awoken and began to murmur.

"Joey, too?" asked Daniel, reaching into the pram to

tickle his chin.

"No," laughed Tillie as they made their way back towards Sam, with Alice alongside them inside the fence.

"I've had enough for today," pronounced Alice, sliding down off the pony. Tillie reached out to help her, thinking she would fall, but she gained the ground effortlessly on her own. "I'll take Starlet inside."

"Good lass," Sam called to her, and then turned to Tillie. "I'm afraid it looks as if the old dog has had her day, as they say."

Tillie stroked Lady's back, and Daniel did the same. "I wondered as much, although she isn't that old, actually, only about eight. What do you suggest we do?"

Sam looked at the children before replying, "I'll make her comfortable."

"Jamie will be upset. She's been his pet since he first came."

Nodding, Sam sighed. "I'll put her in a stall and then give this little girl her wish to have a go on the old pony."

"Daniel would like to, as well, if that's all right."

"Of course, but I thought he didn't have an inkling to do so."

"It looks as if he's changed his mind."

Sam took Lady into the stable and brought out the smaller pony. Alice joined her, and Tillie picked up Joseph and stood watching as the two children took it in turns.

"Eleanor's a natural, isn't she?" remarked Tillie to Sam when he passed by. "She sits beautifully."

He smirked, agreeing, "Yes, she is, my own little daughter. Who would have thought it, eh?"

"And how's Elizabeth? Has she recovered from that ear infection?"

Chewing the inside of his cheek, he didn't reply as he rushed ahead to help Daniel who had been trying to climb onto the pony after Eleanor had slid off.

Eleanor began to walk away. "I want to go home."

"Shall I take her?" offered Alice, taking her cousin's hand.

"Not on your own."

"But, Mama, it's only down the lane."

"I know but..." Tillie turned as Sam and Daniel came around to them again. "We'll all go. Daniel has had enough as well. I can tell. Come on, sweetheart. Let's go and see Aunty Ruby." Then she added to Sam, "Thank you for his lesson. We'll take your daughter home for you."

"That would be a great help, thank you," he replied, lifting Daniel down. "I had thought Ruby would have collected her by now."

"We'll save her the bother."

With Joseph safely back in his pram, they began to walk away. Worried that something had befallen her sister, Tillie hurried as fast as the smaller children could keep up, and as fast as the pram could be pushed over the stony ground.

Ruby sat at the kitchen table, a dreamy expression on her face. Tillie stopped at the door. "Is everything all right?"

"Yes, why shouldn't it be?"

"Well, Sam expected you to collect Eleanor from the paddock." She looked around at the untidy kitchen. "Are you sure you're well? It isn't the baby, is it?"

"Possibly."

"Why didn't you say something?" Shooing the children outside, she put her shawl on the back of a chair. Then she stopped. "It isn't due yet, is it? Not 'til next month?"

Ruby stood up and flexed her back. "That's what I thought, but he seems to have other ideas."

"You think it'll be a boy, then?"

"I do hope so, for Sam's sake. He's desperate to

have a son."

"You sit back down, and I'll put the kettle on. How bad are the pains?"

"Well, I've only had a few twinges, actually."

"So it may not be?"

Ruby shrugged.

"There's no panic, then." Tillie sat down, after making some tea. "Has Elizabeth's ear infection cleared up?"

"Almost. She's sleeping. I'm a bit concerned, though. She doesn't seem to be hearing half the time."

"I'm sure it'll pass once she's recovered properly. Do you remember when Jamie went deaf after the measles? He seems fine now." She sipped her tea, hoping her sister's fears would be unfounded. "And you know children. They can have selective hearing at times."

Alice ran in, followed by Daniel and Eleanor. "Please may we have a drink, Auntie Ruby?"

Trying to hide a grimace, Ruby stood up. "Of course. I made some fresh lemonade yesterday." She went to the pantry and brought out a jug. "I hope there'll be enough to go round."

With bright, eager eyes, and licking their lips in anticipation, the three children stood watching her pour it out. Her hand wavered and some spilt on the table. Daniel scooped it up with his finger and sucked it off. "I love lemonade, 'specially Auntie Ruby's," he declared with a beam on his face.

* * * *

Jamie took off his jacket after spotting a small stain on the lapel. It had been his intention to wear it, for it fitted better than the other one. Dabbing water out of the basin onto it made it worse. "Fiddlesticks," he muttered, slinging it onto the chair.

With his head in his hands, he sat on the edge of the bed, wishing he could go home. If only he hadn't left.

A knock on the door made him jump up.

"Jamie," called Sarah. "Are you ready?"

He opened the door.

"Come on. Where's your jacket? And your cravat is skew-whiff." She put up her hands to straighten it, but he turned away.

"I can't, Sarah. I'm not the sort of person who goes visiting. What will I say?"

Following him inside, she picked up his jacket. "Jamie, Jamie, what are we going to do with you? What's this on the collar?"

"I don't know. I tried to wipe it off."

"Don't you have another one?" She opened his wardrobe and took out a green one. "Here, put this on."

"I'll have to change my shirt and everything."

"No, you won't. Grey goes with anything. And you don't need to worry about what to say. I think Lady Catherine will do all the talking."

"It's all right for you, cousin, you're used to polite society. By the way, you look pretty. That colour blue flatters you. It matches your eyes."

Twirling around, her hands accentuating the fullness of her skirts, she grinned. "Why, thank you, kind sir. It isn't like you to give compliments."

The green jacket fastened, he smiled. "No, I s'pose it ain't."

"And you'd better not talk like that, in your old manner."

"I just thought I'd see if you noticed, just in case it slips out without me realising it."

She cuffed his arm. "Well, I did, and so will everybody there, but don't let it worry you. Lady Catherine seems to have taken a shine to you, so I'm sure she'll forgive any faux-pas you might make."

"Well, if she wants to become better acquainted, as she said, she will jolly well have to put up with them, 'cos I'm bound to make many." Straightening his back, he took one last look in the mirror, patted down his hair, and put on his new top hat, muttering, "I look a proper dandy in this thing. I wish I'd had a smaller one, now."

"You look fine. You couldn't very well wear your old brown cap, now, could you?"

"I'd feel more comfortable." He ran his finger inside his collar. "Come, then, cousin dear. I feel like a calf going to be slaughtered."

Sarah giggled. "The expression is 'lamb to the slaughter'."

"Whatever it is, I feel like it. But I must be brave." His head high, he put his arm around her shoulder. "Hey, I'm taller than you, now. I've only just realised."

"Most people are," she replied as they made their way downstairs. "My mama calls me a squirt."

About to make a retort about his aunt, he changed his mind and closed his mouth, recalling the phrase 'least said, soonest mended'. Instead, he remarked, "I'd have thought she'd have insisted on coming with us."

"She did express her regret that she couldn't. In fact, she almost had a fit, but a prior engagement could not be cancelled, so here we are, off on our own." They reached the front door. "So let's make the most of it."

Outside, Jamie began to walk along the street, but Sarah called him back. "No, Jamie, we have the carriage."

"But I thought it wasn't far, and that your mother would need it."

"It isn't far, but Mama's going with her friend, so she said we could have it." The coachman opened the door and they climbed in. "And it's just as well, for it looks as if it's going to rain."

Settling inside, Jamie took off his hat and scratched his head, but received a glare from his cousin. "It itches," he complained. "What am I supposed to do if my head itches?"

"You grin and bear it."

Raising his eyes, he sighed. "I think it's the stitching around the rim."

She took the hat and ran her fingers along the lining. "Um, it is rather uneven, but there's nothing you can do about it now. As I said, you'll just have to grin and..."

"Bear it." Blowing out his breath, he settled back on the seat. "Something else to worry about, but it might take my mind off all the other stuff."

Within minutes they had drawn up at the gates of a mansion-type house. Sarah patted his hand. "Stop fretting. I had been about to say, 'Just be your normal self', but..." She bit her lip.

"I know, I know. But I can't be anybody else, so it's her hard luck if she thinks I'm going to try to be."

The rain letting up as they alighted from the carriage, Jamie tried to shield his cousin as they ran to the door of the huge house. The butler opened it and they entered, looking in awe at the beautiful chandeliers in the huge hall, and the ornate mirrors on the walls.

As Sarah took off her gloves and the butler took their coats, Geraldine Burnyeat came running down the left-hand staircase. The layout reminded Jamie of the Royal Hotel, where they had stayed in Scarborough. That didn't put him at ease, for they had curtailed that holiday due to one of his many mishaps. Before he could dwell on it too much, though, he had to go through the motions of being greeted.

The formalities over, he followed the two girls into the drawing room. "My grandmother will be down in a few minutes," Geraldine told them. "She is really looking forward to seeing you." She looked specifically at Jamie.

He licked his dry lips as he gave Sarah a look of disbelief, wondering why she should want to see him.

Sarah shrugged delicately.

"May I offer you a drink?" asked Geraldine. Her green eyes bore into him and he had to look away.

A glass of brandy would have been welcome, not that he ever drank it, but he knew she didn't mean that.

"Tea would be lovely," replied Sarah, giving him a nudge when he didn't reply.

"Oh, yes, tea, thank you."

Geraldine pulled the bell for the maid, who appeared instantly. "I prefer coffee, myself, but Grandmamma frowns on it. She says you cannot beat a good, strong cup of tea."

Unsure if he should make a reply, Jamie stood awkwardly, looking around at the large room, hoping Sarah would make all the right responses. He hated small talk, couldn't see the point in it, but knew it to be the height of bad manners to allow any silent episodes, so racked his brain to think of a new subject.

Refreshments brought in, they took their seats, Jamie as far from the girls as possible.

About to lift his cup to his mouth, the door opened and Lady Catherine entered. He dropped the cup with a clang onto the saucer as he jumped up, praying she hadn't heard it. She swept in, looking like a picture of Queen Victoria he had seen, dressed in a black outfit, with a little black hat not quite covering her white hair, her brown eyes twinkling.

"Ah, good day to you both," she offered in her soft, melodious voice, looking pointedly at Jamie's cup. She had noticed.

He put it on the table and bowed. "Good day, Lady Catherine. How pleased we are to be here. Thank you so much for inviting us."

"Yes, yes, don't overdo it."

A red stone in her brooch caught the light, attracting his gaze, and he had to drag his eyes from it, realising he was staring at her bosom. Sarah glared at him, but then kept up the conversation, allowing him to look around the large room, at the stag's head on the wall and the stuffed fish in the cabinet.

"Don't we, Jamie?" he heard her ask. Not listening, he hadn't a clue as to what she had been referring, so just nodded, hoping it to be the correct response. She seemed satisfied and continued.

As soon as a lull came in the conversation, he asked, "You must like nature, ma'am, to have all these trophies?"

Lady Catherine gave a surprised look. "I beg your pardon? Oh, you mean these ugly things. No, they are nothing to do with me. They were my husband's."

"Ah, and is he...?" He tried to remember what he'd been told about her.

"Yes, he's dead, died ten years ago. Geraldine here adored him, didn't you, darling?"

Her granddaughter nodded, a grin on her lips. "Yes, Grandmamma. He used to sit me on his knee and tell me all sorts of stories."

"You remind me of him, when we first met."

Jamie looked around, to see whom she meant, but she looked him in the eye.

"Yes, my dear, you have a certain look around your mouth. Do you resemble your father or your mother?"

"Oh, definitely my mother, although she has green eyes, rather like Miss Burnyeat's and my father has blue eyes, so..." Knowing his father to not be his biological one, he stopped.

"That is unusual, for a child to have brown eyes, when neither of his parents have."

Wishing Sarah would rescue him, he tugged at his ear, glancing towards her.

Sarah reached over and patted his arm. "Jamie was a foundling—well, sort of, for a while, anyway—but we do not like to talk about it in society."

"Oh, my dear, tell me more. We shall not broadcast the fact, shall we, Geraldine?"

Jamie stood up. "No, ma'am, please don't pursue the matter."

Lady Catherine swept her hand over her face. "Very well, if it will distress you. Pray sit down. I am not in the habit of upsetting my guests, although, I am rather disappointed that you do not feel able to confide in me. Maybe, once you become better acquainted with my granddaughter, you might feel comfortable enough to tell her."

"Oh." For a moment Jamie had thought she would not want to have anything more to do with him, knowing his background. "Yes, certainly, ma'am."

"You sound surprised, but when we do become better acquainted, you will find that I defy tradition. I am not one of those people that scorn those less well-off than themselves. In fact, I welcome them. I was not always rich. In fact, I was an orphan, brought up by an elderly aunt, in rather shady circumstances, so who am I to judge?"

Jamie could only stare at her in amazement as he sat down and crossed his legs, sensing Miss Burnyeat grinning at him, but not daring to actually look at her.

"Anyway, the sun seems to be shining now," continued Lady Catherine. "Why don't you young people take a walk in the garden?" She stood up and opened the doors leading out onto a perfectly-manicured lawn. "I can see my grandson, Joel, out there. You haven't met him, have you?"

Standing up, Jamie heard Sarah's intake of breath as she jumped off her chair and almost ran towards her. "I have been wishing to do so for a long time, ma'am," she gushed.

"Well, allow me to introduce you, then." She stepped

outside and shouted to him. He turned and waved, calling to two golden retrievers that Jamie could see over her shoulder. He was reminded of his own two dogs, and wondered how they fared without him.

They all went out, Sarah, rather hesitantly, lifting her skirt away from the wet grass. He nudged her forward, but she held back, clearly abashed, about to meet the man.

Lady Catherine made the introductions, and Joel's eyes lit up on seeing Sarah. He bowed low over her hand, as a blush crept up her face.

"I shall leave you young things to take a stroll," said Lady Catherine as she hurried inside.

Sarah opened her parasol and, head high, her cheeks still red, stepped off the lawn onto a gravel path, with Joel following.

Much to his embarrassment, Geraldine linked arms with Jamie. He held his breath, not knowing if he should allow it, but relaxed when she whispered in his ear, "We do not stand on ceremony here. They make a fine couple, do they not?"

He turned to look at her. Her green eyes sparkled, causing his legs to wobble. Trying to extricate himself from her grasp proved futile as she clung on even tighter, her gloved hand stroking his arm. But he had decided to marry Maisie. He shouldn't be feeling emotions for this girl. And what about Beth? He felt as if he were being unfaithful to her as well. Even though he knew he would never see her again, it seemed disloyal to be going wobbly over another girl so soon.

Ahead of them, Sarah giggled at something Joel said. He knew that giggle. The nervous one. She glanced around at him. He winked back to try to set her at her ease. The action took him by surprise. He had never winked before. What had made him do it? He rather liked it, though, and decided to try it again when an occasion arose. Better not wink at Miss Burnyeat, though. That would be a gaffe too much.

Sticking to safe topics of conversation, he asked, "What is your favourite pastime, Miss Burnyeat?" Not that he wanted to know. But they had to talk about something.

"I love watching birds, especially the pretty ones," she replied. "They fascinate me with their colourful plumage and their ickle beaks. What about you?"

He had been about to say he loved the feathered creatures as well, and had been excited that she did, until the last statement. Ickle beaks? He replied, "I love them, too, especially buzzards." *There, see if that surprises her.* Nobody could say the large birds of prey had 'ickle beaks'.

"Oh, you mean those horrible monsters that eat rabbits and the like?" *It worked.* "Oh, no, sir, pray do not tell me you can see any fascination in such creatures. They are positively cruel." She unlinked arms and stood staring at him, her eyes wide open in disgust.

The pair in front stopped and turned. "What is the matter?" asked Joel.

Jamie swallowed. Should he own up? Maybe in polite society one didn't confess to having such leanings.

Miss Burnyeat looked down at the ground. "Mister Dalton, here, is just trying to tease me. It is nothing."

Sarah glared at him. "Jamie? What have you been telling her?"

Looking up into the sky for inspiration to pull him out of the mess, he thought he saw one, soaring overhead in circles. The usual excitement coursed through his body, but should he point it out to the others? Would it make matters worse? He must have taken too long in his deliberation, for the others all looked up to follow his gaze.

"Ah, do not tell me that is one," screeched

Geraldine, cowering away from him, as if his liking of it would somehow put her in danger.

Sarah put her hand on the girl's arm. "It can't hurt you from there," she consoled her.

"It would not hurt you anywhere," added Joel, coming to Jamie's rescue. "They mistrust humans, so would not come anywhere near. You have nothing to fear."

"Yes, that is so true." Breathing a sigh of relief, Jamie took a step towards her, but she backed away. "And, anyway, I think it's just a crow, so there's nothing at all to be scared off." A little white lie might ease the situation.

"Come on, Geraldine." Her cousin tried to urge her forward. "Do not upset yourself. Let us continue with our walk."

Shaking her head, she turned to go back to the house. "No, I have lost my enthusiasm for the outdoors." She gave Jamie a particularly pointed glare. "I think I shall return."

He didn't feel guilty, though. Why should he? He had only been honest. But should he accompany her, or stay out with the other two? "I apologise if I offended you, Miss Burnyeat. It weren't my intention." *Oh dear, I said that wrong. Hope she don't notice.*

"Ah, look there's a blue tit, over there on that branch. They are fascinating, too, aren't they? Just look at the ickle blue head and ickle beak."

With her lips in a pout and her brow furrowed, she turned to look at the bird. "I think you are mocking me now, Mister Dalton."

"No, ma'am, not at all." Had he put his foot in further? "I can honestly say they are one of my favourites, along with blackbirds. Don't you just love to hear them sing?"

"Cousin, you have to admit you were only saying the

other day how you loved their melodic song." Joel put his arm around her shoulders. "Now, come on, give the lad a chance." He then whispered something in her ear, making her smile.

Sarah nudged Jamie.

"What?" he mouthed.

Screwing up her eyes, she indicated her head to Joel and then opened her eyes wide and shrugged her shoulders, grinning.

What could she mean? He shook his head.

With a look of despair, she turned back to Joel, surprising Jamie with her forwardness. "It is impolite to keep secrets, sir. Pray tell me what you are whispering about so furtively."

"I apologise, dear lady. It was just something we were speaking about earlier. Anyway, Geraldine, what have you decided? Are you leaving us or not?"

The girl grinned, taking Jamie's arm once more. "I forgive you, sir, for your taste in birds, but only if you agree to come for a ride in our carriage tomorrow. You too, Miss Smythe."

Sarah looked at Joel, as if asking if he would be going. When he told her he had a prior engagement, her face dropped, but she replied politely, "Thank you, we would both love to come, wouldn't we, Jamie?"

"Didn't your mother have something planned for us tomorrow?" he asked.

"No, no, I'm sure she hasn't, and even if she has, we can re-arrange it."

Jamie wondered why, if Joel wouldn't be going, she seemed so eager for the ride, but shrugged. He would never understand women.

They continued their walk in the sunshine, Sarah being particularly chatty, in Jamie's opinion. He had never known her to talk so much. He tried hard to think of meaningful conversation, but his companion made up for any shortfall in his speaking. His head buzzed by the time they went in for refreshments, and he breathed a sigh of relief as he sat and relaxed for a short while, letting his hosts do all the talking.

Lady Catherine came in as they made their farewells. "I hope we will be seeing you again soon."

Geraldine put her arm around her and kissed her cheek. "Yes, Grandmamma, we are taking the carriage tomorrow—we three young ones, anyway." She stuck out her tongue at Joel, who had snorted at her insinuation of his age. "Joel cannot be bothered to cancel his prior engagement, so will not be accompanying us."

"Grandmother," he retorted, "it is not a question of not being bothered." Glancing at Sarah, he cleared his throat. "Oh, very well, I shall see what I can do."

Jamie felt Sarah tense beside him as she dug her fingers in his back. About to admonish her, he saw the joy on her face, and stopped.

"That would be…" she began. "We would welcome your presence, will we not, Jamie?"

Why did she keep bringing him into it?

Chapter 12

Clutching David's hand, Tillie looked down at her new nephew sleeping peacefully in his cot. "Isn't he beautiful? Just perfect. He has a look of Joseph, don't you think?"

David laughed and limped across the room to thump Sam on the back. "All babies look the same to me, but, congratulations, he is…yes, he is perfect."

"Well, we think so, don't we, Sam?" beamed Ruby, sitting up in bed, looking the picture of health.

"We certainly do," replied her husband, leaning over to kiss her.

"Alice can't wait to see him," continued Tillie. "She is so excited. I thought I had better not bring my children just yet, but let you recover for a while first. I'll bring Eleanor and Elizabeth home tomorrow if you feel up to having them back. Eleanor says she'll help you. She promises to be good."

Ruby closed her eyes and laid her head back against the headboard. "Tomorrow would be lovely."

"Only if you're sure. You look tired."

"Tired, but exultant." Ruby looked up at Sam with love in her eyes. "A boy, my darling. Just what you've always wanted."

He kissed her again. "Thank you, my darling."

The baby stirred, making tiny noises. Tillie itched to pick him up. "Would you mind?" she asked, reaching into the cot.

"Go ahead. I knew you wouldn't be able to resist for long."

"Ah, he's so sweet." Tillie stroked his downy cheek. "Have you decided on a name yet?"

Rubbing her eyes, Ruby replied, "Eleanor wanted us

to call him Mark, but I'm not so sure. I prefer Richard."

"And what about you, Sam, what name do you like?"

"I like Paul, but if Ruby wants Richard, then so be it."

"As long as it isn't shortened to Dick," laughed Tillie. "I don't like that."

"Dickon is quite nice. They used to abbreviate Richard to that in the old days," added David.

Tillie looked at her husband in amazement. "I'm surprised at you, David. You insist all our children are called by their full name. You won't let any of us shorten them."

He shrugged as Ruby reached out to take her son, saying, "Dickon? Yes, I like that."

David went towards the door. "Anyway, I need to be making tracks."

"Are you sure there's nothing I can do before we leave?" asked Tillie, handing over her precious charge.

"No, I'll feed this little one, and then have a rest. Sam needs to sort out one of the horses."

"Is it the one we bought last week?" asked David, opening the door.

"Yes," answered Sam, giving his wife another kiss and patting the baby's head. "It doesn't seem to be feeding properly, and its coat doesn't shine as it should."

They continued discussing the horse as Sam helped David down the stairs and outside.

"I shall come with you to take a look at it." David turned to Tillie. "Do you want to come as well, or would you prefer to go straight home?"

"I had better go and check on the children. Poor Nanny will probably be tearing her hair out. I'll see you later." She held up her face for a kiss, but her husband had already walked away, the horse's problems more important than her.

Hurrying along the lane, she wondered if all married

couples grew apart after a while. Ruby and Sam hadn't done so, though. They still seemed as enamoured with each other as when they had married. But Sam didn't have the responsibilities that David had. Maybe running an estate like Brightmoor gave David too much to think about. She determined to lighten his load somehow. The intention had been that Jamie would do that eventually. She wondered how he was enjoying himself in Harrogate.

* * * *

Jamie couldn't believe the transformation in Sarah. All the way home, she enthused about Joel Burnyeat's bright eyes and his mannerly character.

"I do hope he doesn't change his mind about tomorrow," she moaned for the third time. "I shall be so disappointed if he does."

"Surely a gentleman keeps his word, so why would he?"

She chewed her fingernail. "Well, he only said he would try to cancel his engagement. What if he can't? My whole day will be ruined."

"I'm sure there'll be other opportunities."

She grinned at him. "Yes, Miss Burnyeat seems quite taken with you. What do you think about her?"

He puffed out his cheeks, raising his shoulders. "She's very pretty."

"And?"

"And what? What am I supposed to say?"

"Do you like her?"

He half nodded. "Well, yes, she's very nice."

"Nice? What sort of word is that? You should be saying, 'pleasant demeanour', or 'lively conversation'."

"That's not my style, and you know it." Watching his reflection in the carriage window, he muttered, "I can't use flowery words. It just doesn't come naturally to me."

"Well, if you are to marry Miss Geraldine Burnyeat, you will have to learn."

He spluttered. "Marry? Who said anything about marrying? I've only just met the gal. I don't intend marrying for a long time and, anyway…" He stopped, not wanting to give away his secret intention.

Sarah sat back and closed her eyes. "Well, I shouldn't mind marrying Mister Joel Burnyeat. He is just what I would want in a husband—lively, handsome, mannerly."

"But you've only known him five minutes. How can you possibly tell in such a short time?"

She tapped the side of her nose. "We women know these sorts of things. We are brought up to identify preferential traits in men."

He shook his head. Then a thought occurred to him. "But young Miss Burnyeat can't have been brought up in such a way, not if she wants me. I'm not husband fodder."

"Don't bring yourself down, Jamie. You are a lovely, kind, compassionate person. Any girl would be lucky to have you for a husband."

"Not you, though."

She sat forward, frowning at him. "I'm too old for you. You don't have feelings for me in that direction, do you? We are more like brother and sister."

"No, of course I don't. I'm not sure why I said that. Forget it. Anyway, we're here now. Are you going to tell your mother you're in love?"

A dreamy look came over her face. "I don't think so, not just yet. She might put her big foot in it and spoil things, like she usually does."

"What? Your mother spoil anything? As if she would!" Jamie couldn't keep the sarcasm from his voice as he grinned and they alighted from the carriage.

The following day Jamie opened his curtains to see a

drab, dreary day. "Good," he muttered. "Perhaps we won't be going for that ride, after all."

When he met Sarah downstairs, though, she waved away his concerns. "What's a little drizzle? It won't put me off."

He sat at the table and ate his liver and sausages, trying to find some enthusiasm for the trip. "Where will we go, do you think?"

Her fork halfway to her mouth, she stopped as her mother flounced in, a pink dressing gown not quite covering her ample bosom, declaring, "I should imagine you will go to the park. The one some people avoid." She gave Jamie a look from under her eyebrows, as if challenging him.

He knew she referred to the time he had become lost, the first time he had come to Harrogate. Narrowing his own eyes, he refused to rise to her bait. "There are several parks, aren't there? I don't mind which one we go to." He brushed back his hair from his forehead, and picked up his fork, defying her to goad him further.

"I was not speaking to you. I was addressing my daughter."

"The Stray would be best. It will take longer, so give us more time," answered Sarah, tucking into her breakfast once more, clearly unaware of the friction, or merely ignoring it.

Aunt Annie sat down. "I used to go to the racecourse."

"Mother, why would we want to go and watch horses race?" Sarah dabbed the side of her mouth with her napkin. "We want to become better acquainted. How will we be able to chat with people screaming down our ears?"

"Well, if you do not want my opinion, then I shall not speak."

"Mother, I had not asked for your opinion." Sarah

sighed. "Anyway, it won't be up to me. We shall go wherever Mister Burnyeat decides. I, myself, do not mind in the least."

"Oh, you young people with not a care in the world. How fortunate you are." Aunt Annie pulled her dressing gown tighter. "You soon will have, though, so make the most of your time."

"I intend doing just that, Mother." Sarah turned to Jamie. "Eat up, they will be here soon."

Jamie glanced up at the clock on the wall. "We have hours yet."

"But I have my hair to redo. I don't really like this style, and if it's windy, it will blow all over the place."

He laughed. "Well, at least I don't have that problem."

His aunt peered at him out of the corner of her eye, as if disputing the fact. "Have you shaved this morning?"

Stroking his chin, he thought to deny that he had, just to make her cross, but decided against it. "Yes, Aunt, like a dutiful nephew. I wouldn't want to let you down." He hated shaving, a task he thought futile, for the bristles only grew back again minutes later. "I had thought of growing a moustache like Father's. What do you think?"

She seemed to ignore him, chewing her sausage. Once she had swallowed, she replied, "It is no concern of mine."

"Well, I think a moustache would make you look distinguished, Jamie." Sarah turned her head to one side to gaze at his face. "Yes, definitely, but wait until you return home. I remember when Papa was growing his, it looked awful for the first few days."

"Very well. I wouldn't want to put you to shame, not in front of your beau."

"And your Miss Geraldine. Don't forget you need to give her a good impression."

His aunt stood up. "Well, dear, if you are altering

your hair, I suggest you change your dress as well. That colour does not suit you."

Sarah gulped. "But, Mama, you chose it for me."

"I tried to dissuade you at the time, but you would hear nothing of my judgment."

"Mother, that is untrue." Sarah's eyes seemed to bulge out of their sockets. "It was quite the other way around."

Her mother turned and walked out of the door without making any further reply.

From her red face and pursed lips, Jamie thought his cousin would have an apoplectic fit. She stamped her foot. "Oh, she can be so infuriating at times. Honestly, Jamie, this dress—do you think it suits me?"

Not wanting to infuriate her any further, he said the first thing that came into his head. "The blue matches your eyes."

"Thank you, Jamie. I'm glad someone appreciates it. If Papa hadn't already left for work, I would go and ask him. Oh, rats, now I am in a bad mood, and I so wanted to look my best today." Tears began to roll down her cheeks.

Jamie couldn't remember seeing her cry before. Feeling in his pocket for a handkerchief, he realised he had forgotten to put one in, so he put his arm around her. "Please don't cry, Sarah, it'll make your face blotchy."

Sniffing, she muttered, "I know. I'm sorry. It's just that I wanted today to be so perfect."

"But you should be used to your mother by now. You know how she riles everybody. You shouldn't take any notice of her."

"Yes, yes, you're right." She took a deep breath, wiping her hands across her face. "I am not going to let her spoil my day. I shall wear this dress. You don't think the stripes are too wide, do you, or the collar too high?"

What could he say? He didn't know anything about

ladies' fashions. "No, no, they're perfect. And the collar matches the cuffs."

"Oh, Jamie, thank you." She pulled the right cuff up to reveal a wire mesh bracelet. "And this matches my earrings and cameo brooch. Do you like the brooch? It was a present from Papa, along with the earrings, of course."

He studied the oval-shaped jewellery. "Very nice, but they wouldn't look very good on me."

She laughed as she reached up to kiss his cheek. "I can always rely on you to cheer me up."

"Off you go, then, and do whatever you have to with your hair, although I like the curly bits dangling down at the sides."

"So do I, but they blow about, although my bonnet should contain most of them. Anyway, we don't have long. What will you do while you wait?"

Nudging her towards the door, he shooed her out. "Never mind me. I'll find something."

What can I do? he wondered. Going over to the window, he saw the rain had blown over, and only a few puffy white clouds remained. If he'd been at home, he could have gone out to look for buzzards, but they didn't very often fly over towns, the one they had seen the previous day being an exception. He decided to go outside, anyway, much preferring fresh air to being cooped up inside, but wouldn't go far. Sarah's wrath would be too much to bear if he hadn't returned by the time the carriage came to pick them up. Smiling to himself, hands in pockets, he walked up the street, unable to imagine his cousin having a full-blown fit of fury. She was much too gentle a person, unlike her mother. She definitely took after her placid, easy-going father, Uncle Victor, whom he had scarcely seen since his arrival. The previous evening they had exchanged a few words, but that had been all.

Before he knew it, he had arrived at the dreaded park. Dare he go in? Would it bring back all those horrible memories of the time he had slept on the bench, after Sarah had been hurt when a runaway horse had almost run into them? But he had saved her then. And he had grown into a man—well, almost—so should have no fear of the place. Straightening his back, he entered through the gates. In the sunshine, it looked a pleasing location, with people strolling about, chatting, and enjoying themselves. He stepped back to allow two horsemen to pass, doffing his cap, affability oozing from his pores. All those years he had tried not to think of the place, too worried it would bring on the nightmares, but now he had seen it again, he had chased away the demons. He wanted to throw his arms up and cheer, but decided he would receive too many odd looks. Not that they should bother him—he was used to that sort of thing—but he swivelled around instead, smiling at everyone as he passed them.

When he arrived back, he found Sarah pacing the hall.

"Where have you been? I've been going frantic."

"Just for a walk." Giving his cap a shake, he grinned at her.

"What's so funny? Is my bonnet skew-whiff or something?" She hurried over to the mirror and adjusted it.

"No, dear cousin, you look lovely, absolutely ravishing, in fact."

"Are you unwell?"

He took her hands and twirled her around. "No, I feel better than I have done for many a year."

"Jamie, cease, please. Is that a carriage drawing up?" She took another look in the mirror. "Oh, my days, my legs are shaking, I am so nervous. What if he decides he doesn't like me once he knows me better? I can be a bit of a harridan at times."

Jamie patted her back. "Sarah, stop fretting. I'm sure he is already halfway in love with you, and harridan is the last word I would use to describe you."

The servant—he couldn't really be described as a butler, more a general menial—opened the door, and Sarah looked at Jamie with panic in her blue eyes.

"Just be yourself," he assured her as they stepped outside, astonishing himself at his composure and the fact that he was giving her advice for the first time in his life.

Joel Burnyeat helped Sarah into the open-top landau, and then indicated for Jamie to precede him, saying, "I hope it will not be too breezy with the top down." He turned to his cousin. "But Geraldine assured me you would prefer it."

"Oh, no, I love fresh air blowing through my...my bonnet," gushed Sarah, pushing the article further onto her head. "Don't I, Jamie?"

There she goes again, bringing me into the conversation. "We both do—love fresh air, that is." Jamie stole a peek at Geraldine, sitting demurely beside her cousin. She didn't seem her usual perky self. "Don't you, Miss Geral...I mean, Miss Burnyeat?" *Now why did I have to speak to her? I should just let Sarah do all the talking.* "How is your grandmother?"

"She is very well, thank you. She says you must call in for some refreshments before you return home."

"Thank you, that would be...um...lovely." He sat back, deciding he had spoken enough. Let someone else do the rest.

"Where would you like to go?" asked Joel, looking at Sarah as they set off.

"Um." She turned to Jamie, as if for confirmation, "The Stray would be nice? Or is that too far?"

"My thoughts exactly." Their host gave the driver their destination, sat forward, his hands on his knees, but then sat back, smiling into Sarah's eyes. As Jamie sat opposite him, he had the opportunity to study his face. Dark eyes with long black eyelashes looked incongruous on a man, as did his small nose and small teeth, but overall, the man looked personable enough. Approving of his cousin's choice, as he hoped his father would do also, he relaxed into the seat, watching the town rush by, until they reached the park at The Stray.

"Thank goodness I brought my parasol," remarked Sarah as they alighted from the carriage. "The sun feels really hot on my cheeks. I should hate them to turn red and burn. It would be most unseemly."

"Me, too," added Geraldine. "Last month a friend of mine forgot hers and she looked like a beetroot after an hour and had to stay indoors for a week."

Not having such an apparatus, Jamie hoped his face wouldn't look like a beetroot. He pulled his cap forward. He had never been burnt before, but it would be just his luck to do so in this estimable company.

"Shall we meander through the middle?" suggested Joel.

"Yes, whatever you think best," replied Sarah, looking up at him shyly. Jamie hadn't noticed the previous day how tall the older man was. Maybe his large top hat added height. He hadn't been wearing that in the garden. He would have to remember to wear one like that if he wanted to appear bigger in future, instead of the cloth cap he wore most of the time. Surprised that Sarah hadn't suggested him wearing the one he'd worn the previous time, he followed the pair in front, allowing Geraldine to make conversation, inserting a 'yes' or a 'no' every now and again.

His sleeve being pulled made him look at his companion. "I beg your pardon?" he asked, realising he was supposed to make a reply.

"Didn't you hear what I said?" she demanded

petulantly.

"I'm sorry, I was miles away. Did you say something about a duck?"

"A duck? No, silly, I asked if you had ever been to The Royal Pump Room."

"Um, no. What is it?"

"That building over there. It's renowned for its spa water. People flock to it from all over the world for its medicinal qualities."

"Oh, perhaps we should go then."

"Well, not today, maybe later in the week."

Unsure as to how long he would be staying in Harrogate, he just nodded, wondering if he should slow down to allow the pair in front to go ahead unhindered. He stopped to examine a particularly pretty flower, asking, "Isn't that lovely?"

Geraldine bent to smell it. "Ah, a red rose, and its perfume is exquisite."

With a hasty glance around, to make sure nobody could see, he picked it and handed to her.

"Oo, Mister Dalton, I thank you. Do you realise what the significance is of giving flowers? Ouch, it's pricked me." With a yelp, she dropped the flower as blood oozed from her finger.

"Oh," he exclaimed, mortified that his good intention had gone awry. "I'm so sorry." Grabbing the handkerchief he'd remembered to put in his pocket before he'd left, he wrapped it around her hand as Sarah and Joel ran back to them.

"What happened?" asked Joel, glaring at Jamie.

He gave a huge sigh, trying to ignore Sarah's annoyed face, pointing to the offending rose, lying on the path. "I just wanted to make a gesture, but it went wrong."

The pair looked at each other in surprise, and then Sarah asked, "You...you gave her a red rose?"

He grimaced. "I know I shouldn't pick the flowers, but she said it smelled lovely, so I thought..."

"But a red rose?"

"Well, it stood out from the others. Why are you making such a fuss?"

Sarah whispered in his ear, "Red roses mean passion."

He jumped back, mindful that he'd made an even bigger gaffe than usual, if he took her words to mean what he thought they meant. "I...um...I... Oh 'eck." He stared at Geraldine, who suddenly grinned.

"Do not worry, Mister Dalton. If you did not intend it as it seemed I am not going to hold you to it." She lifted off the handkerchief to check on the wound. "It seems to have stopped bleeding, so no harm done."

"Except to my frayed reputation," replied Jamie. "I shall never fit into society. I think I should go home." He turned to leave, but she pulled him back.

"No, please do not go. We shall say nothing further on the incident." Handing him his handkerchief, she patted his arm.

Stuffing the blood-stained article in his pocket, he looked at the others to see their reaction. Sarah shook her head, with a knowing smile on her lips, while Joel...well, he couldn't be sure of his thoughts on the matter, giving no indication by his facial expression.

Not wanting to spoil the outing any further, he stepped forward. If they followed him, then all well and good. If they didn't, then he would go on his own. Geraldine took hold of his arm and he could hear the other two walking behind them. "I am so sorry, Miss Burnyeat. I really didn't know."

"I quite understand. It is of no consequence, so forget it ever happened. But I shall never see a red rose ever again, without thinking I might have been propositioned."

"Oh, please, don't make fun of me. When you come to know me better, you will realise I make blunders all the time. In fact, my life seems to be one huge disaster at times."

She laughed. "Pray tell me about it."

"Oh, no, your opinion of me must be low enough already. I should hate to reduce it any further."

She turned to Sarah. "Your cousin was just telling me he is a blunderer. Is that correct?"

"Well." Sarah scratched her neck, grinning. "That's one way of putting it. But I shan't tell on him, except to say…" She opened her eyes wide "…beware, he could be dangerous."

"Thank you, dear cousin," retorted Jamie with a pout. "I love you, too."

Geraldine raised her eyebrows at his words. *Oh, no, should I have said that? Have I put my foot in it again?* "As a sister, of course," he quickly added.

"Shall we see if there is anywhere to take refreshments?" Joel asked. Jamie would have loved a stiff drink, but a hot cup of tea would be almost as welcome.

"That sounds like a good idea," replied Geraldine, giving Jamie's arm a tweak. "The building over there looks like an establishment of some sort. Let's try that."

But her cousin answered, "I know a better one, from the last time I came here."

"Do you often walk these paths with young ladies?" Sarah's voice held pique.

Jamie turned around to see Joel's eyes twinkle. "All the time, my dear. All the time."

Jamie winked at her, and she smiled back, saying, "Very well, then, show us the way. I could just do with a hot drink."

Sitting in the tearooms, Jamie felt in his pocket for his wallet. *Phew, thank goodness.* But would he have enough money to pay? Mister Burnyeat had invited them out, so would he be expected to foot the bill? He couldn't very well ask anybody, so ordered the cheapest cake he could find on the menu.

When they had all finished, he stood up and took out the wallet, but Joel pulled him down, an affronted look on his face.

"Pray, put that away, sir. This is my treat."

"But I like to pay my way."

"No, sir."

Sarah hissed, "Jamie, sit down. You're making a spectacle of yourself."

He could see Geraldine grinning and, once he'd sat down, she whispered in his ear, "Now I see what you meant earlier."

"Oh, calamities. I've done it again, haven't I? When will I ever learn?"

"Well, I think it's endearing."

He chuckled. "That's the sort of thing I would say about my little sister, but thank you for not berating me."

The ride home was full of lively conversation and, once in the house, Sarah took off her bonnet, a look of pure ecstasy on her face. "Oh, Jamie, is he not the most perfect man imaginable?"

"If you say so, cousin."

"And do you not feel the same about Miss Geraldine?"

He shrugged. "As I said before, she's very nice. I could probably grow to like her more, but I'm not staying here that long, so what would be the point?"

Checking her reflection in the hall mirror, she replied, "Yes, that is a problem. But I need you to make up the foursome. I cannot go out on my own. Couldn't you stay a while longer?"

"Huh, you just want me to act as your chaperone?"

She made a moue with her lips. "Please?"

Their conversation ceased as the front door opened and her mother waltzed in. "Ah, you are back already. I have missed seeing your young man. I would have been back earlier, but the traffic down Bath Road was atrocious. I think someone must have had an accident. It's a wonder there aren't more, the way some of those people drive their carriages, with no concern for others. Do you know? The other day I saw a young girl almost being mowed down by a reckless rider. Of course, it must have been her mother's fault for allowing her to be so close to the roadside." She took off her cloak and shook it.

Sarah took it from her. "Yes, Mother, you tell me every day. Did you have a good trip?"

"It was mediocre but, more to the point, how did yours go?"

The beam on Sarah's face told it all. "Very well, indeed, Mama. I was just asking Jamie if he would consider staying a while longer. You wouldn't have any objections to that, would you?"

Jamie kept a straight face as his aunt looked him up and down. "I shall have to ask your father," she eventually conceded.

"Oh, please do, straightaway. Please tell him I need him. You are so busy you can't always chaperone me, and I would hate you to have to cancel any of your engagements. I know how important they all are to you."

Aunt Annie removed her gloves. "I could be persuaded to cancel one or two of them. I have yet to meet the young man, and you will need my approval if things were to reach such a stage that…you know what."

They all traipsed into the lounge, where his aunt pulled the bell for the maid. "I assume you are thinking in that direction, my dear?"

With raised shoulders, Sarah rubbed her hands together. "Oh, wouldn't it be the most wonderful thing in the world, if he were to like me enough to propose!"

Her mother sat down, but then stood up and pulled her towards her bosom in the best semblance of a hug Jamie had ever seen her manage. "It would, indeed, my darling. Just think, I would be related to the famous Lady Catherine Burnyeat."

"Yes, Mother." Sarah raised her eyes to the ceiling. "Of course, I should have realised you would be the one to benefit." She plonked down on one of the settees. "My happiness doesn't come into the equation."

The maid came in with a tray of tea. When she had left, Aunt Annie took a sip of her drink. "Don't be like that, my dear. You know I always have your best interests at heart."

Twisting his head to one side, Jamie tried to contain a snort, hoping she would not hear it. From the glare she gave him, she had. She turned back to her daughter. "Would you like me to say anything to your father yet?"

"No, Mother, it might not come to anything, although Mister Burnyeat does seem to like me. But then, he could be like that with all the girls he takes out. I've not been with many young men, so may be interpreting friendship for something stronger." She turned to Jamie. "What do you think, Jamie?"

He gulped. "Me? I don't know anything at all about courtship. Miss Burnyeat seems to be much too familiar, in my opinion so, maybe, they're just a friendly family, and act in that manner towards everyone." As Sarah's shoulders slumped, he added, "But I'm probably wrong. Don't take any notice of me. You know how I open my mouth and put my foot in it, daily." Oh dear, he should have kept quiet. Now he had added to her sorrowful demeanour.

Glaring once more, his aunt stood up. "Yes, yes, take no heed of him. He is the most inept person I have ever had the displeasure to meet. I shall take a short nap, now, in preparation for my outing this afternoon." She swept out of the room without a backward glance.

Sarah squeezed his arm. "Pay no attention to her, Jamie. I apologise for her atrocious behaviour."

"That's all right. As I said earlier, we should be used to it."

"It can still cut to the quick, though, can't it?"

"Mm. I don't know how you put up with it."

She picked up a paper weight and examined it. "Hopefully, it won't be for much longer." A dreamy look covered her face as she hugged the ornament to her bosom.

Eager to change the subject, he suggested they play a game. "Chess or something like that?"

"I'm sorry, but I'm not in the mood for concentrating." She put the paperweight back in its place, lining it up exactly as it had been. "If it's all right with you, I'll go up to my bedroom and sort through my dresses?"

"Well, that's something I can't help you with." What could he do? "I think I'll go into town and browse through that book shop you told me about." The surprised expression on her face made him smile. "What?"

"You? Look around a shop? I thought you hated them."

"Well, I've finished the book I brought, and I know your father's library is quite large, but I just fancy browsing. I may not buy anything. I don't know if I could bring myself to go that far."

She laughed as she went towards the door. "I am almost tempted to go with you."

"Feel free."

"Actually, yes, I think I will, if you're sure you don't mind." She turned back.

"Why on earth would I mind? You like books more

than I do, and you can show me the exact location of the shop. I would probably get lost on my own, anyway."

As they reached the town area, a gentleman stopped to allow them to pass, fixing his eyes on Sarah in such a way as to make her blush. She grabbed Jamie's arm and they scooted along the pavement. "Don't look back," she ordered, "but is he still watching?"

"How can I tell, if I don't turn my head?"

"Oh, you men, you're so pedantic."

He glanced around, but the man had gone. "Anyway, Miss Smythe, I thought you were in love with your Mister Burnyeat. What are you doing ogling other gentlemen?"

"I'm not ogling. It doesn't hurt to keep one's options open. As you said earlier, my Mister Burnyeat might be trifling with me. I don't know his intentions at all."

"I didn't say trifling."

"Why don't you try some ogling, yourself, Jamie? It could be quite entertaining."

"Me? I wouldn't know where to begin."

"Go on. See that young lady coming towards us, the one with the pink parasol?"

"Yes, what about her?"

"Just wink or something, as she passes by. Don't let her mama, or whoever the fat lady is with her, see you, though."

"But…"

"We'll pretend to be studying the arrangement in this shop window, and when she approaches, turn around and do it."

His stomach churned at the very thought of being so bold. "No, Sarah, I can't."

The girl passed them and the moment vanished.

Sarah took his arm and they continued on their way. "Maybe another time. I'll have to teach you some techniques. Ah, here's the bookshop." The bell on the door pinged as they entered. "I shall be looking at different sections to you so we'll meet up in about half an hour, if we don't bump into each other before that."

With his eyes closed, Jamie's nostrils twitched as he sniffed the aroma of the books, old and new ones. When he opened his eyes, he saw his cousin grinning at him. "I know what you mean. It's a delicious smell, isn't it?"

A young lady turned with a book in her hand and sniffed it. "That's all I come in here for, just for the miasma."

Jamie had been about to deny the meaning of the word, but Sarah exclaimed, "Miasma? But I thought that meant a horrible stench?"

"Oh, does it?" The girl grimaced. "I knew it meant smell of some sort. I've put my foot in it again. I'm always saying the wrong thing."

Jamie had been about to add that he knew what she meant, to sympathise with her, but an older man appeared and ushered her away.

"I wish I could have become better acquainted with her," he told Sarah, as they made their way up the narrow staircase, lined from floor to ceiling with books. "She sounds like a fellow spirit, a girl after my own heart."

"The two of you would be in scrapes all the time," she laughed. "You would go from one calamity to the next. No, that's not the sort of girl you need."

"I suppose not. Ah, this looks like your department. I'll let you go and find your Jane Austen shelf and I'll carry on."

Sarah entered the small room as he continued upstairs. The rows of books in the top room reminded him of his life back at school, dusting Bullimore's, but he soon put the memory to the back of his mind. That era of his life had ended, and he would never have to recall it again, if he didn't want to. And he definitely didn't want to at that moment. Too many interesting covers to peruse.

Half an hour later, engrossed in Coleridge's 'Rime of the Ancient Mariner', he didn't hear Sarah creep up on him until she whispered, "Boo" in his ear.

"Oh, I thought you were an albatross," he exclaimed, making her raise her brow.

"I beg your pardon?"

"Have you ever read this poem?" He showed her the page. "It's about a sailor."

"Probably. I am not a great lover of poetry. I prefer stories."

"But this tells a story." Closing the book, he followed her out of the room. "I think I'll buy this book. It has lots of different poems in it."

Sarah turned around with a puzzled face. "I never took you to be a poet. You never cease to amaze me."

He laughed. "Me neither. If you'd asked me yesterday if I enjoyed reading poetry, I would've said not in the least, but I've changed my mind today after leafing through this book."

The bill paid, they turned towards the door. "Haven't you found anything?" he asked, realising she had nothing in her hand.

Shaking her head, she stepped back from the door, and put her finger to her lips.

"What's the matter?" he hissed.

"Don't look now, but I think I've just seen Mister Burnyeat walk past."

"So, why don't we go and speak to him?"

"He wasn't alone."

Jamie opened the door and peered up the street. "I can't see him," he called back. "Are you sure it was him?"

First poking her head out, she took a look, and then stepped out. "It certainly resembled him. But maybe I was mistaken."

"Wishful thinking, probably."

The girl who had been speaking to them earlier came

out, smiling at them, and Jamie was tempted to try some 'ogling' as Sarah had suggested. As soon as her guardian had passed them, he winked at her. With a giggle, she gave a little wave. He waved back—a little girly wave that made Sarah snort with derision behind him.

"What's wrong?" he demanded, once the other pair had turned the corner. "I thought you wanted me to ogle. That's what I was doing, wasn't it?"

"I suppose it was a start. Not that I know, really, what to do. I am not very expert at it myself." With a gasp, she grabbed his arm. "Don't turn your head, but I'm sure that's Mister Burnyeat over there, just gone behind that tree. Do you not think so?"

"Sarah, you are being very ambiguous today. You keep asking me to tell you about things you tell me not to look at."

"But I'm sure it's him. Come on, let's go over and casually walk past."

With a slight shake of his head, he obeyed, whistling gently through his teeth.

"Don't make that horrible noise," she ordered. "He'll be suspicious."

"But I'm trying to act in a cavalier manner, like you said."

"Well, not like that."

They reached the said tree and strolled nonchalantly past it, glancing out of the corners of their eyes to see if anyone stood behind it.

"There's nobody there," Sarah moaned, pulling up. "But I'm sure I saw him."

"Well, that's twice. Perhaps the third time will be for real, unless it was a ghost." He made a gesture with his hands in front of his face, trying to scare her.

She knocked them away. "I know it was a real person."

"So, where is he? He can't have vanished into thin

air."

A row of shops stood back from the others. The door of one of them opened, and the man in question stepped out. Sarah grabbed Jamie and hid behind the tree. "It is him. I knew I wasn't imagining it. But who is that lady with him?"

"Let's go and ask him," suggested Jamie.

"Oh, no, we couldn't do that. It would be the height of impropriety. Oh, no, he's seen us. What shall we do?"

"We shall have to act in as normal a fashion as we can."

Mister Burnyeat came across, a smile beaming across his face. "Miss Smythe, how delighted I am to see you. You didn't tell me you were thinking of shopping, or I might have suggested coming with you."

Sarah curtsied, glaring at the lady standing next to him spinning her parasol. Her face changed to one of glee, though, when he continued. "Allow me to introduce my sister, Miss Tannia Black."

"I didn't realise you had a sister, sir. You didn't mention her."

"He never does," said the girl, who Jamie realised was much younger than he had previously thought. "He forgets I exist most of the time."

"That is not true at all."

"Out of sight, out of mind, is what my mama says, Miss…?"

"Pray, forgive me, my dear." intercepted Joel. "This is Miss Smythe, and her cousin, Mister Dalton." As they bowed at each other, he continued, "Tannia was waiting at my house when I returned home. A welcome surprise. We do not often see each other, for she lives in the wilds of Derbyshire." They began walking. "My mother remarried after my father died, and moved away from Harrogate, having young Tannia late in life."

The girl pulled at his sleeve. "They do not want to

hear all about our private business, Joel."

Joel looked at Sarah as if she had been the reason he had given the explanation. "Shall we find a tearoom? It is quite some while since we had that drink earlier."

Tannia exclaimed, "Oh, Joel, is this the lady you were telling me about? The one with the 'fine eyes' whom you took for the drive this morning?"

At Sarah's intake of breath, Joel's face reddened. He took a deep breath. "Yes, I told you her name at the time."

Sarah beamed, clutching Jamie, her fingers digging into his flesh. He gritted his teeth, not wanting to show her up, but gently tried to free his arm from her grasp. "We were just suggesting the very same thing," she gushed. "Weren't we, Jamie?"

He couldn't remember it being mentioned, but humoured her by nodding, feeling a complete idiot, out of his depth at subterfuge. "Won't our lunch be ready?" he whispered in her ear as they followed the pair in front.

"Oh, never mind that. This is much more important."

Jamie imagined his aunt's face when she realised they had not returned for the meal. Not a pretty sight. But then, her daughter's happiness would be paramount in her mind, and she would be sure to understand why they had missed it, once Sarah had given her the explanation. Hopefully.

His stomach rumbled as they entered the tearoom. Hopefully, the others would not have heard it.

"May we sit near the window?" asked Tannia. "Then I will be able to see the folk walking by, the pretty dresses and the handsome faces of the men."

"Very well," replied her brother, turning to clarify her words. "As I said before, Tannia lives in the countryside, and does not very often come to town."

"I do too," began Jamie but stopped when Sarah

glared at him. *What have I said wrong now?* he wondered, but decided to keep his mouth shut, in case he disgraced her further.

Hiding behind the menu, she whispered to him, "Pray, let them do the talking."

So be it. I shan't open my mouth again, he vowed. He had no need to do so, for the girl never stopped, moving from one topic of conversation to another, scarcely taking a breath in between.

Standing on the pavement an hour later, his head buzzed with her voice. Not a pretty voice, either. Rather harsh and strident. They took their leave of the pair, after Joel had arranged to take Sarah out again at the end of the week.

"Isn't Miss Black pleasant?" Sarah asked as they made their way home.

"Isn't she a chatterbox?" replied Jamie. "Not a bit like her brother or her cousin. I suppose she is Miss Geraldine's cousin, as well, do you think?"

"Um, maybe not. If his father was Lady Catherine's son, then his mother wouldn't be related to her, so Miss Black…"

"Oh, I can never remember how cousins or second cousins or those once removed works. It doesn't really matter, does it? Hopefully, I won't be seeing her again. She's only staying until Thursday, didn't she say? And they're visiting some other relative tomorrow."

"I haven't persuaded you to stay longer then?"

He bit his lip. "Well, I think Mama would like me to return on the appointed day."

She stopped to look in a shop displaying a creamy-coloured wedding dress. "Maybe I could be wearing something like that soon. Are you sure you don't want to stay around to find out?"

"Much as I have enjoyed my stay, I would like to return home."

"But if I do marry Mister Joel Burnyeat, she will be my half sister-in-law, so will be related to you."

As he tried to suppress a groan she waved to a girl Jamie had never met before. "Ah, there is my very best friend over there. I haven't seen her for ages. She's been away to her grandmother's in the Lakes. I didn't know she had come home. Do let us go and say hello."

All these introductions. I shall never remember everyone's names, he thought, but dutifully crossed the road.

Chapter 13

David went down to the paddock to check on the horse. It still seemed poorly. Sam greeted him.

He nodded, making for the stable. "Is he any better?"

"No, sir. I'm afraid you've wasted your money on that one."

"That is a great shame. I had high hopes for breeding from him. Can we not take him back to the previous owner?"

"No, sir, he died. That was the reason for the sale."

"Oh, yes, of course." He gave a deep sigh. "I cannot believe neither of us spotted the ailment."

Sam brushed the horse, cooing in its ear. "But he seemed fine when we bought him, didn't he? This has only come on since the weekend."

The horse nickered as David stroked its flanks. Then he left, turning towards the lane that led behind the stables. Why did every venture he tried turn to dust? He had been pinning his hopes on that horse. His favourite stallion, Starlight, had died not long before. He had sired several foals that had been sold for a goodly sum, helping with his money problems, and he had banked on this one doing the same.

Clicking his tongue for his dogs to follow, he set off for a tour of the estate. Not a full one, of course—he would not be able to manage that—just a short one to check he could see nothing amiss.

His footsteps took him to the ridge, from which he could survey most of his land. Leaning heavily on his crutch, he took a deep breath of the fresh, clean air, wondering how he could involve Jamie in helping out. If the boy flatly refused to go to university, he could not make him, so he needed to find something to occupy him when he returned from Harrogate. It would have been good for him to marry Sarah, but in all truth, she would not be looking for a husband so young, and would probably not wait around until the boy became old enough, now she had had her coming out. There were not many girls of his age in the neighbourhood, though. Most of his friends had sons, not daughters.

One of the dogs growled and a movement behind made him turn. Christine sat on her horse, alone, dressed in a fetching navy blue outfit.

"Ah, good day, Missus Harrison. You startled me."

"I apologise. It was not my intention."

"No sister with you?"

She laughed; a sweet tinkling sound. He tried to remember the last time he had heard Tillie laugh. Not for a long time. Maybe he should make an effort to encourage her to do so more often.

"No," Christine continued, "Grace has returned home. She and her husband have rectified their differences. I am so pleased for them."

He had been about to declare how her life must be more peaceful without the interfering harpy, but thought better of it. Nobody could choose their relations. Look at his own sister. Instead, he stated, "I am sure you miss her."

Her head turned to the side, she looked at him with a smirk. "You know I will not."

Ah, well, she had said it, not him. He grinned in response. "And your mother-in-law? Has she been reconciled with her husband?"

"Yes. She's gone home also. She only stayed a day or so." She dug her heels into the horse and came nearer. "Anyway, what are you doing out here?"

He made a sweeping movement with his hands. "I was just surveying my lands and enjoying a quiet moment."

"Until I arrived and spoilt it."

"Oh, no, Missus Harrison, you could never do that." Fearful that he had overstepped the mark, he turned away and leaned on the fence, hoping she would not interpret his meaning in the wrong way.

A silence developed between them and, eventually, he heard her trot off into the woods to the side. Once he reckoned she would be out of sight, he turned and, drawing his lips together, made his way home. Her presence could still give him a fluttering sensation, but he had to remain faithful to Tillie. He could not allow the feelings to develop. He loved Tillie with all his heart and would never betray her.

Tillie came towards him as he approached the rear of the house. "Thank goodness you're back. I was becoming worried."

"Why?" he snapped, all thoughts of making her laugh retreating.

"David?" She took his free arm and linked it with hers. "Is everything well?"

"Yes…no. I am sorry, I did not mean to snap."

"Is it that new horse? Is it not coming up to expectations?"

"That and other things."

She helped him inside. "We've received a letter from Jamie. He asks if he can stay a few more days in Harrogate."

"He may as well. I have not come up with a plan for him here yet." David sat down and Tillie poured him a drink. "If he still insists he is not going to university, what else can he do?"

Before he could receive a reply, Alice ran in and jumped on him. "Papa, you're back."

"Anybody would think I had been out all day," he grumbled, putting his glass on the side table before she could knock it out of his hand. "I have only been gone a few hours."

"Do be careful, Alice," admonished Tillie. "Sit quietly beside your father. He doesn't want you climbing all over him."

"You don't mind, do you, Papa?" The child did as she had been bid, though, as Daniel came in, accompanied by the nanny.

"There you are, Miss Alice," declared Maria. "I have been looking for you everywhere. I told you to remain in the nursery until I said you could leave."

"But I heard Papa's voice and wanted to speak to him. I haven't seen him all day."

Maria looked at him, as if requesting him to back her up. Tillie opened her mouth as if she would, but he was not in the mood for a confrontation. He gently nudged his daughter off the sofa. "Now you have spoken to me, my dear, go with your nanny, if you please, and obey her."

Sticking out her lips, Alice stood up.

The nanny continued, "I thought I would take the children out for some fresh air, now Joseph has woken up."

Tillie nodded. "That's a good idea."

"Are you coming too, Mama?" asked Daniel.

"Not this time, darling." Tillie gave David a sideways glance. "I need to spend some time with your father."

"Can I stay with him as well?" asked Alice, jumping back onto his knee.

He pushed her away. "Another time, my darling. Enjoy your walk." Closing his eyes, he laid his head back.

When the children had left, Tillie sat beside him and took his hand. He reached out and enfolded her under his arm, and she snuggled into him with a murmur of contentment.

"We don't do this often enough," she whispered.

Guilty at his reaction to Christine earlier, it seemed as if Tillie had picked up on his feelings. "No, we do not," he murmured back, turning her face up to his, so he could reach her lips. The kiss he gave her brought his senses alive, and he shifted his position so he could gain access to her breasts.

She edged away and helped him stand. "Let's go upstairs, my darling. We don't want the servants witnessing our passion."

Eager to complete their lovemaking, he readily agreed, hoping the time it would take would not dull his ardour. They reached her bedroom and fell onto the bed, kissing and touching like they had not done in a long time, full of fervour and abandonment, unlike the dutiful lovemaking they usually experienced.

Half an hour later, they lay spent in each other's arms. He stroked her hair, kissing the top of her head. "Oh, my darling, I have not enjoyed intimacy like that for a long time."

"No, me neither. It was wonderful." She still sounded breathless.

He smiled. "I am pleased I can still satisfy you."

"Oh, my darling, you did more than satisfy my carnal longings. You brought me to life. I had been feeling useless and unwanted, but now… I could stay here in your arms forever like this."

He kissed her and passion flowed once again.

* * * *

Jamie received a letter from his mother saying he could stay as long as he wished. Drat. He'd hoped she would be missing him so much she would want him to return straightaway.

"That's wonderful," cried Sarah, when he gave her the news. "I'm glad you changed your mind, because I'm really enjoying having your company, and I can show you a few more tricks on how to flirt. Not that you need any. I'm sure Miss Geraldine has her sights on you already."

With a sigh, he put down the newspaper he had been reading. "That's part of the problem. I'm not sure I like the attention."

"She can be rather…how can I put it? Forceful?"

"Yes, very forceful. I feel as if I've been caught up in a hurricane after I've left her."

Sarah picked up the paper. "Is there anything interesting in here?"

"No, not really." He stretched, pointing his hands to the ceiling. "Only tittle-tattle and sport. Details of who's won this game of cricket and who's lost that game of football."

"Father follows the football. He declares it to be quite exciting. Didn't you play it at school? I seem to remember you writing to me about a goal you scored."

"Yes, I suppose it's quite a thrill to play, but must be boring to watch."

Sarah caught her breath, showing him a page of the paper. "Oh, my, I didn't know that."

"What?"

"There's an article about the war in Crimea. It mentions Joel's late father. It appears he won a medal for bravery."

"We had a neighbour who fought in that war. His name's Major Wallace. He went mad, you know, and had to be put away in one of those asylum places. That was very sad, after fighting for his country, to end up like that. But it was for his own good, so they say." Jamie read the article. "Mister Burnyeat must have died during the conflict. How old would you take Tannia to be?"

"About fifteen or sixteen. Yes, you're probably right. I wonder if Joel would tell me about him. You'd think he would be so proud he would shout it from the rooftops.

But then, he would not have been old enough to remember his father, so more than likely does not even think about him."

"I'm sure I would declare it to everyone I met. Not that I know my real father, of course. I've never met him."

She folded the paper and put it on the table. "Would you like to? To meet him, I mean?"

"No."

"Oh, why not?"

"Because I fear he raped my mama, from the snippets of information I've been able to glean. I wouldn't like to be associated with him at all. If I saw him in the street, I would cross over to the other side."

"Mm, I agree, if that is what happened."

Buttoning one of his jacket buttons that had come undone, he stood up. "I sometimes fear I may have inherited some of his cruel traits, though, when I have evil thoughts about people."

With a hug, she assured him he had not. "You are the sweetest, most generous of spirit, kindest person I know, Jamie Dalton, so do not ever think anything like that." She kissed his cheek. "I am honoured to be your cousin, and if you were a few years older, would not think twice about marrying you."

He hung his head. "I don't know what to say."

"You don't have to say anything. Just go and find your coat and come with me."

"Where are we off to today?"

Her eyes lit up with glee. "The Turkish Baths."

"Do we have to?"

"Not if you are really against it." The light in her face dimmed. "I had been looking forward to it, though."

"Is his lordship coming, or Miss Geraldine?"

Her face took on a coquettish expression. "Maybe."

"Would I have to wear one of those horrible

costumes we wore to the beach?"

"Well, yes, you will." At his grimace of distaste, she added, "But do not worry that Miss Geraldine will see you, for men and women do not bathe together."

"So, what is the point in you going then, if you will not be with your beloved Joel?"

"Because I heard him state he liked the effect. I have never been before, so thought it would be a lively jaunt."

"For you, maybe. I'd rather give it a miss, if you're not too disappointed. I shall accompany you there, but not enter the building. I may have a walk around the park. Fortunately for me, being a man, it's acceptable to do so on one's own."

"Very well, then, but do not tell Mother you left me. She would be horrified."

"My lips are sealed."

As they strolled along the street, she said, "I cannot believe the change in you since you came. Even your speech is more refined."

"More to the liking of the hoi-polloi, you mean. I have polished it so as not to disgrace you."

"There, that's what I meant earlier. You do everything to please other people. It is about time you thought of yourself for a change."

"Oh, my dear," he laughed. "I do that often enough, don't you worry."

She laughed as well, and they stopped to browse through a shop window. "See that fur hat over there?" she asked, pointing to a mannequin dressed in the latest fashion. "Wouldn't you just love to own one like that?"

With a sideways glance to see if she had been joking, he thought he would tease her, anyway. "Oh, yes, let's go in so I can try it on."

"Really?"

"No, dear Sarah, I would no more wear such a hat as fly to the moon, thank you."

"Ah, I am rather disappointed. You would have looked like a Russian. What's that dance they do, the Cossack? Have you ever tried doing that?"

"No, have you?"

With a quick glance around, she bent her knees and lifted her arms in the air. When she stuck out her foot, she lost her balance, dropping the bag holding her costume for the baths, and Jamie had to pull her up. Almost collapsing with giggles, they hurried away, praying nobody had seen them.

Arriving at the baths, Sarah pushed up Jamie's sleeve to look at his watch. "I can't remember what time they said they would be coming," she declared, looking around.

"Well, that was a bit silly. You can't go in on your own," he replied, also checking it.

As she hopped from one foot to the other, he thought he saw one of the boys from his old school, one of Silas Brown's buddies. He hadn't realised he lived in Harrogate. But he hadn't learnt much about any of the bullies' backgrounds. Trying to hide behind Sarah, he looked the other way. It probably only resembled him. It was more than likely someone completely different. However, a voice called, "Dalton, is that you?"

Be brave, he told himself. *He can't hurt you now.* "Well, well, if it isn't Thomas Windley." He clicked his heels and bowed, putting on a brave face. "What a lovely surprise. I didn't know you lived in Harrogate."

"And I didn't know you did." He gave a long look at Sarah.

"Oh, let me introduce my cousin, Sarah Smythe. Sarah, this is one of my friends from school. Mister Thomas Windley." He emphasised the word 'friends'.

The lad looked at the building. "Are you going inside?"

"No, I'm not, but Sarah is when our party arrives."

Jamie relaxed. The boy seemed to be amicable enough. Perhaps, without the influence of Brown, he would be a different character.

Windley tapped his cane against the pavement. "Which university will you be attending?"

Should he admit he would not be going to any? "Actually, I…"

"I hope it is not Cambridge. I heard Silas Brown's going there. I, myself, had the good fortune to be accepted at Oxford."

Before Jamie could reply, Sarah grabbed his arm. "There're coming."

Windley glanced around to see whom she meant. "Are these the friends you have been awaiting?"

"Yes, sir."

As Joel and Geraldine, and several other people Jamie did not know, approached, Thomas bowed, murmuring, "Burnyeat."

"Windley," acknowledged Joel. "I see you know my friends."

Jamie looked astonished that they should know each other.

"Dalton and I were best mates at school, weren't we, Quackers?" The lad put an arm around his shoulder.

"Well, I wouldn't quite put it in those terms."

Sarah cried, "Quackers? What sort of nickname is that?"

Jamie tried to brush it off. "You know I love birds. It was just a reference to that." So much for not having to recall his schooldays ever again, as he had been thinking earlier.

Joel interrupted. "Anyway, who's going inside? Dalton?"

Sarah showed him her bag. "Jamie does not fancy it, so would it be acceptable for me to come in with you?"

Geraldine grabbed Jamie's arm. "Oo, why aren't you

coming in? You would love it, I know you would."

Shaking his head, he saw Windley give him a knowing look. He would not back down, though, no matter how much the other boy might try to taunt him. "Maybe another time," he conceded.

"You and I could take a walk together and come back when these good people have finished," said Thomas.

"That's a good idea," said Sarah. "You could catch up on old times." She followed the others into the building, turning to give him a wave.

Did he want to go with this boy? He chewed the inside of his cheek, looking around for an excuse not to. Nothing came to mind, though, so with a sigh, he began to stroll along beside him, his hands in his pockets, head down.

"Don't look so scared, Dalton," began Thomas. "I'm not the ogre I appeared to be at school. I'm sorry for the mayhem we caused you. I hold up my hands and admit we were atrocious. I know it's no justification, but I only went along with Brown's ideas because I was too weak to resist. He had a way of encouraging us, even if we did not want to." He stopped and held out his hand. "Am I forgiven? We could become friends. Which part of Harrogate do you live in?"

Jamie watched a crow fly overhead, wondering what to reply. Ignoring the outstretched hand, he said, "I don't live here. I'm just visiting my aunt and uncle."

"Oh, that's a pity. I don't have many friends. The ones I grew up with have all moved away."

They stepped aside to allow a young lady and an older woman to pass. Jamie realised she was the one he had spoken to in the bookshop. She grinned at him from beneath her parasol, evidently recognising him. He winked. Cor, it felt good to be so bold.

After she had gone by, Thomas stopped and looked

him in the eye. "Why, Dalton, you have a way with the ladies. First Miss Burnyeat, now this madam. I would never have imagined you to be so forward. You always gave the impression of being…well, not shy. No, I wouldn't call you that, but reticent around others."

Jamie glanced back to see the girl turning as well. She winked back at him, but clearly had never done it before, for her face screwed up as in a caricature. Her chaperone pulled her around and they soon marched off out of sight.

"People change, Windley," Jamie replied at length. "I should hope I'm not the same person I was then. Even in the few short months since we left, I've matured. At least I hope I have. I'm no longer that snivelling, timid lad. I can hold my head up high." At that point, the heel of his shoe caught on a stone, and he almost fell, righting himself by catching hold of a tree trunk. The other boy's eyebrows arched and he seemed to be having trouble keeping a straight face. "Maybe not quite as high as I'd hoped," Jamie grinned.

By the time they returned to the baths, Sarah and her party had already emerged, standing talking in the shade of a large elm. Jamie hurried over to her. "Did you enjoy it as much as you'd anticipated?"

"Oh, yes, it was invigorating. You must come next time."

Geraldine sidled over to him, glancing at Thomas out of the corner of her eye. "What did you do, sirs, while we were being invigorated?"

Jamie saw Thomas glance at her. An idea began to form in his mind. Maybe, if he could pair the two off together, he could be free of her attentions. Not that he didn't like the girl. She was very presentable, but she threw a stone in the works of his plan to marry Maisie. He stepped back so Windley would be nearer her. "Mister Windley and I went for a walk, and very pleasant it was, too."

The trouble was, Joel did not seem enamoured of the man, and pulled Geraldine away from him. "We should be on our way, my dear. Grandmother will be expecting us back."

"Aw, don't be such a wet blanket, cousin. She won't be back from her visit yet. Let us take a walk through the park."

"But Mister Dalton has only just returned, and I'm sure Mister Windley has better things to do."

Sarah watched the interaction with a frown. She seemed uncertain as to what to do. "What do you wish to do, Jamie? Are you tired?"

"Me? No, not at all."

She linked his arm. "Then, yes, let us all parade through the park. It is such a lovely day. It would be a pity to waste it."

Jamie wondered if the others would follow, but they did, Thomas beside him, with Geraldine and Joel behind them, and their other friends behind them. He had not been introduced to them, so did not know their names.

Jamie whispered to Thomas, "Mister Burnyeat doesn't seem to like you. Is there any particular reason for that?"

Sarah gasped. "Jamie, you can't ask questions like that."

"Why not? If there's a genuine reason for his off-handedness, I want to know about it."

"It isn't really me he dislikes. He hardly knows me. It was my older brother. They became embroiled in a fight some years ago."

Geraldine called from behind them, "What are you three talking about? I can't hear."

Jamie grimaced, but slowed down. He couldn't very well tell her.

The others caught up and they decided to sit on the

grass for a while. Sarah managed to ease herself next to Joel, and he didn't seem to have any objection.

"The grass looks too wet for me," moaned Geraldine, standing twizzling her parasol with one hand, and stroking the organza material of her green dress with the other. Jamie debated if he should take off his jacket to let her sit on it, but was forestalled by Thomas.

"Allow me, Miss Burnyeat," he said, shaking his jacket out and laying it in front of her.

Joel's eyebrows rose at the gesture, and he half-stood, as if thinking he should have done the same for Sarah. He looked down at the velvet collar and shiny buttons and clearly decided he didn't want it to be spoiled, for he sat down again without speaking. Sarah gave Jamie a knowing look. He grinned back and made himself comfortable.

"What are your plans for the rest of the week, sir?"

Jamie realised Geraldine was addressing him, and he turned to her. "I'm not sure yet. I might go home."

Beside him, Sarah shook her head and protested, "But your mother has given you permission to stay as long as you like."

"And I had thought we might do something," added Thomas, "now we have been re-acquainted."

"And me too," added Geraldine. "There is a show on at the Royal Spa Concert Rooms I would love to see. I had been meaning to ask if you would like to go. Joel loves it there, do you not, cousin?"

A sense of being overwhelmed by everybody's attentions rose in Jamie's chest. He had thought he had overcome the reactions he used to experience. Taking several deep breaths didn't help. He stood up. "Thank you for your kindness, everybody, but I need to leave." He took some more breaths. "Good day."

Sarah jumped up and ran after him. "Jamie, are you unwell?"

More deep breaths. "I'm fine, thank you. You return to your friends. I need some time alone." He had never told her, or anybody, for that matter, about the attacks that panicked him, when everything seemed to close in on him, forcing him to run away.

She pulled his sleeve. "But, Jamie, has someone offended you?"

"No, Sarah, honestly."

Leaving her standing there, a concerned look on her face, he marched off, his feet crunching on the gravel path. When he thought he'd be out of sight, he crouched behind a tree, his head in his hands. Damn. Why did he have to spoil the day? He'd been enjoying it up until then. What would they all be thinking of him? How would he face them again?

After a few minutes, his breathing less ragged, he took off his hat and wiped his brow with a handkerchief.

Hearing voices coming towards him, he peeped around the tree. An elderly couple walked past and a little white dog ran up to him. He stroked its head. "It's all right for you, little hound. You don't have a care in the world." It rolled over for him to tickle its tummy until its master called it, and it ran off. The interaction with the animal had calmed him, though, and he shoved his hat on his head and pushed back his shoulders.

"Dare I go back to them?" he murmured but, looking up, he saw them coming towards him. Fearful of receiving a dressing down, he held his breath, but they carried on walking as if nothing had happened, Sarah linking arms with him as normal, and Geraldine smiling at him as if she understood. How could she, though? She had probably never experienced an attack like that in her life. But if they still wanted to be friends, he would not refuse.

He could not see Windley among them.

"Your friend went the other way," said Sarah, as if

she had read his mind. "He said he might call tomorrow. I gave him my address. I hope that's all right? It wasn't he who upset you, was it?"

"No, it wasn't anyone in particular. I'll explain later."

With that, she strode forward, seemingly satisfied.

Chapter 14

Tillie put down the letter from Jamie. Harrogate seemed to be entertaining, so he had decided to stay a while longer. Pleased for her son, she picked up the dress she had been sewing for her nephew but the light being too dim, she could not see well enough to do it justice. She yawned and stretched as David came in.

"Why are you sitting in the dark?" he asked.

"Because I'm too lazy to move from my chair and light a candle." Yawning again, she held out her arms. He plonked down beside her and reached over to give her a kiss. "Let's just have a quiet moment together in the dusk of the evening," she added, settling into his arms.

"You sound like a poet."

"I sometimes fancy writing poetry but, by the time I sit down to start, the moment has vanished and I give up. Maybe, when the children are grown up and off our hands, and we are alone and old, I'll give it another go."

"Mm, I look forward to that time."

She sat up with a start. "David, aren't you happy with our life now?"

"What? One moment you are looking forward to the future, then, when I agree, you berate me with being discontented." He moved away. "I cannot win with you sometimes."

Pulling him back, she moaned, "Oh, David, I didn't mean that. Please, just lie here with me—in silence, if you prefer."

Nellie found them entwined a while later, when she came in to light the oil lamps.

"Don't bother, Nellie," Tillie told her. "We're going to bed."

David had other plans, though. "I am sorry, my dear,

but I still have things to do in my study. You go on up, though. You look all in."

Rubbing her eyes, too tired to argue, she yawned once more and, taking the candle Nellie had been holding, made her way upstairs. However, once she lay in bed, her brain would not switch off, and sleep eluded her. Why had she snapped at David like that? She had a feeling she might be expecting again. Even though her monthlies were only two days late, she knew her body had changed slightly, and she had borne enough children to know the symptoms. She had been about to tell him, but not in the mood he seemed to be in. It would wait. Would he be pleased? She, herself, felt they had enough children, but if her fears were founded, there was nothing she could do about it. The child would be loved as much as the others. She would have to try to make sure it was the last one, though, somehow.

Her thoughts changed to the fate of her friend, Emily Thompson. Her last letter had not held much hope. If she could find the time to visit her, she would have to go soon by the sounds of it. What a waste of a young life. Not having any particular plans for the following day, she made up her mind she would go then if Ruby didn't need her. Her sister had not been coping very well with the new baby. The girls, especially Elizabeth, had been acting up. It was so unlike them. They were usually so well-behaved. Had she agreed to take them out, to give Ruby some respite? She couldn't remember. If she had, her visit to Emily would have to be postponed until the day after.

The following morning all thoughts of going to see her friend were put to the back of her mind when Alice came running indoors, screaming that Daniel had fallen outside. Filled with fear of finding him dead down a well, or some such similar disaster, she rushed out. However, the boy had not fallen down a well, or into the lake. She found him sitting on the back steps with the nanny, while Joseph lay in his pram, yelling, beside them.

"What happened?" she cried.

"He fell down the step," answered Alice from behind her.

"Is he badly hurt?"

She couldn't hear a reply for the cries of the baby. "Pick up Joseph, please, Alice," she ordered. "He didn't fall as well, did he?"

"No, no," replied the nanny. "He's just exercising his lungs."

Tillie took Daniel from her. His little pale face tugged at her heartstrings as she examined him. When she moved his arm, he yelped, so she unbuttoned his jacket and removed it to examine it closer. It seemed to be at a peculiar angle. "I think he may have broken it," she moaned as she removed his shirt as well.

Alice brought Joseph over to them, peering at it. "He won't have to have it cut off, like Papa had his leg cut off, will he?"

Daniel began to scream.

"No, no, my darling, of course you won't. Alice didn't mean that," she tried to console him, standing and running indoors with him. By that time, Nellie had come to see what the furore was about, and Maisie also.

"Fetch the doctor, somebody," Tillie yelled as they gathered in the lounge and she placed him gently on a sofa.

Nellie gently eased her away from the boy, who had become deathly silent, but Tillie would not leave him. "Please, God, don't let him die," she wailed, clutching him to her bosom once again.

"Mistress, of course he won't die." The housekeeper urged everyone else out of the room, ordering the footman to go for the doctor and then came back to her.

"Don't worry too much."

"But, Nellie…"

"I understand, Tillie, but this isn't Annabella. This situation is completely different."

"I know, I know, but I can't help it. The memories just come flooding back. Oh, please, God, don't let it be anything serious. Why isn't he crying?"

Nellie stroked his hair back off his forehead. "He's just shocked."

David hobbled in, clutching onto Alice. "I have just come from the stables. Alice told me what happened. How is the boy?"

"He… I don't know. Oh, David, do something."

* * * *

Jamie stood looking through his bedroom window at the rows of houses behind his aunt and uncle's street, wishing Sarah hadn't persuaded him to stay on. He had made up his mind to go home, but the previous evening, when he had explained to Sarah about his panicky attacks, she had been so sympathetic he hadn't had the heart to refuse when she had begged him to stay just a few more days.

Then she had dropped a bombshell by telling him that Tannia was to return, and Joel had suggested they all take a trip on a train to the seaside. Scarborough. How could he go to that place without remembering the episode when he had nearly drowned?

"But, Sarah, you were there. You know what happened," he had protested, when she had told him he would be in the party.

"Oh, Jamie, don't be such a milksop," she had scoffed. "That happened years ago and, anyway, we won't be bathing, only taking in the sea air."

"Of course, you're right. What could possibly

happen?" he had conceded with his fingers crossed, but now the day had arrived, uncertainty had set in once again.

But he had to overcome his fears. He couldn't go through the rest of his life forever harping back to previous mishaps, so he tied his red cravat, buttoned his brown waistcoat, and donned the matching jacket. Taking one last look in the mirror to make sure nothing was out of place, he went down to breakfast.

The train looked full when they arrived at the station, and they had to run to catch it. Joel told Sarah that Tannia had overlaid, but she protested that it was Geraldine who had delayed them. Thomas Windley stood waiting on the platform—Sarah had told him he had been invited—clearly agitated that they would not make it, rushing up and ushering them inside the train. They had hoped to find a carriage to themselves, but it proved impossible, so they squeezed into one already occupied by two elderly ladies, sitting by the window.

"We are sorry to impose ourselves on you, ladies." Joel bowed low and doffed his hat. "But there is not an inch of train to spare. Pray accept our apologies. We shall try not to inconvenience you too much."

One of the ladies gave him a brilliant smile, but it soon disappeared when the other one nudged her in the ribs.

Jamie allowed Geraldine and Tannia to take a seat first, then Thomas. He sat on the end, while Joel and Sarah sat opposite.

Tannia struck up a conversation with the elderly ladies about the pros and cons of train travel, and Jamie sat back, wishing he could have sat beside the window to look out at the scenery rushing by. Joel and Sarah sat quietly, occasionally looking into each other's eyes and smiling. He felt pleased for his cousin. If things progressed, as it seemed to be, she could soon be wearing that wedding dress she had seen in the shop window.

During a lull in the conversation, Geraldine reached forward and addressed Tannia. "Would you mind very much if we swapped places?"

Tannia frowned. "Why?"

"It would be so much easier for you to speak to your new friends."

Tannia looked around her at Windley and Jamie. "You mean so you could be nearer to the young men, you mean?"

"No, no, nothing like that."

"Well, I am quite comfortable here, thank you. It would only disrupt everybody if we moved. There isn't room in the carriage for us to move about." She turned her head to look out of the window, clearly not in a mood to accommodate the older girl's wishes.

"Now, now, girls, no bickering," cut in Joel when Geraldine opened her mouth to remonstrate. "These lovely ladies do not want to hear your childish wiles."

"We are not…" began Tannia and Geraldine together. But he did not let them finish. With a glare and a raised finger, he silently ordered them to stop. The two elderly ladies looked from one end of the carriage to the other, as if watching a game of tennis, a bemused look on their faces.

Jamie suppressed a grin. The girls did rather remind him of his sister, and she was only seven.

The following ten minutes passed in silence. Each time one of the girls seemed about to say something, Joel would raise his finger and they would stop.

Windley nudged Jamie with his elbow, whispering, "Do you think we are allowed to talk?"

Joel smiled. "Of course, gentlemen, speak as much as you would like. It is only these two I need to quieten, and that is only if they insist on arguing."

"We were not arguing, brother," insisted Tannia, pouting her lips.

"Whatever you were doing, it must stop. I am beginning to wish I had not invited the pair of you. If you are going to act in this way all day, we shall alight at the next station and catch the first train back to Harrogate and not visit Scarborough at all. Or, better still, I shall deposit the pair of you on the platform, and let you find your own way home."

"Oh, no, Joel, please don't do that," pleaded Geraldine. "We'll behave, won't we, Tannia?"

"Yes, yes, of course. My lips will be sealed for the rest of the journey."

"Good, good, that's good," said Joel, sitting back. "Now, perhaps we may enjoy our trip in peace."

Sarah raised her eyebrows at Jamie and he grinned. He could just imagine how their children would be kept in order by their strict father if today's actions were anything to go by.

The elderly lady who had smiled at Joel when they had first entered looked impressed as she turned to her companion and nodded in agreement, but then turned to stare out of the window when Tannia glared at her. That was the end of that new friendship.

They arrived at Scarborough soon afterwards. The crush of people emerging from the train onto the platform split them up. Jamie kept close to Thomas, feeling rather ungentlemanly, but not wanting to be left on his own. Once they had found each other, they walked towards the beach, along the way Jamie remembered from his first visit, before his mother had married his father. That had ended badly, he seemed to remember, but couldn't recall the exact details. Not as badly as the holiday, though.

Forget them, he told himself. *This is completely different, just a day out. Nothing can go amiss.*

Unsure as to the propriety of the order in which they should walk, he decided to partner Thomas, but his new friend had other ideas, saying, "I shall walk with Miss Burnyeat, if that is all right." Sarah had already walked off with Joel, so that left him with Tannia. Forcing a smile to his lips, he took her arm. He should be pleased, really. He had wanted to fob Geraldine off onto Windley, but had not intended ending up with the chatterbox.

At the beach, they bought ice creams, even though the day was not particularly hot, but the younger girls wanted one, then they wandered along the promenade. As they neared the harbour, Jamie watched the fishermen below tying nets. He had thought about being one when they had come on holiday, but then he had wanted to be a clown, earlier that year, and look what trouble that had given him.

Geraldine slowed down and stood beside him, while the others continued walking. "Jamie." When he seemed taken aback she continued, "You don't mind if I call you that, do you? We are almost related, if our cousins continue to look at each so goggle-eyed."

He shrugged. It didn't matter to him, not being a stickler for protocol.

"I would much rather walk with you than Mister Windley," she continued. "I think he is only interested in my money."

"Your money? How can you know that after such a short time?"

"It's just a feeling, something he said. We girls know these things. Anyway, I much prefer you. You're so gentle and kind."

Guilty at his earlier thoughts about fobbing her off, he turned to see her green eyes smiling up at him. His stomach lurched. Startled at the unexpected reaction, he started to walk on, gabbling, "We'd better catch up with the others." He had vowed to marry Maisie. He shouldn't—mustn't—allow his emotions to get in the way of that.

"Shall we go and see what those people down there are doing?" asked Tannia, after they had been reunited with the rest of the party.

"Oo, yes," agreed Geraldine, pulling Jamie's sleeve.

A man playing a drum beckoned them.

"What is it?" asked Sarah.

"It's a Punch and Judy show," replied the man, dancing around and holding out a bottle. Other people put money in it, so they all searched their pockets and reticules for some change, and settled to watch the show. Watching everyone laughing at the antics of Mister Punch, Jamie tried to find him funny, but his memories of being kidnapped by the clown kept coming to the fore. He tried pushing them away. He had to.

Face your demons, he had once been told, but the puppet's face resembled Arthur. He tried not to look at him.

Just watch the other puppets.

A hand slipped into his and Geraldine smiled up at him again. He smiled back. All of a sudden, his mind cleared. How could a stupid wooden puppet hurt him? Of course it could not. What a numbskull he could be at times. Squeezing the hand, he laughed as loudly as he could. It didn't matter if nobody else did at that moment. Sarah gave him an odd look, but by that time everyone had joined in as well, so nobody else seemed to notice.

Windley looked at him askance when he noticed him holding Geraldine's hand, but he didn't care. Well, that was until Joel glared at him too. "Wasn't that fabulous?" he declared, letting go and raising his arms in the air. "The funniest thing I have ever seen in my life. I don't think my little brother would like it, though. That Mister Punch is rather violent, isn't he?"

"Yes," said Tannia. "I didn't really like him."

Windley went across to her. "Didn't you? I thought he was hilarious."

"Well, you would, being a man."

"Do not start another argument, sister dear, I beg you," grumbled Joel. "Shall we find somewhere to eat? This sea air fair gives me an appetite."

"A friend told me you can buy something called 'fish and chips'," said Sarah as they began to walk once more. "Shall we find some?"

"It doesn't sound very appetising," replied Tannia.

"Well, this friend said they were delicious."

Joel pointed to a shop across the road. "Could that be what that is? Let's see what it's like inside." However, it didn't meet his expectations, so they found a restaurant.

Jamie found his food stuck to the roof of his mouth each time Geraldine glanced at him. He chewed valiantly, drinking water discreetly, trying to force it down. He had never had trouble eating before. Why should the girl have such an effect on him? He couldn't understand it.

The train journey home was lively with conversations about their day.

He joined in, trying not to take any notice of the glances of the girl opposite, thankful that nothing had gone amiss during the day and that he had not disgraced himself.

Eventually, his holiday came to an end, and he took his leave of his cousin.

"I hope I will have some good news to write about soon," Sarah declared, as she kissed his cheek.

"I hope so too. You make a lovely couple."

"Oh, Jamie, thank you," she laughed. "It sounds so odd to hear you making statements like that. Anyway, do you think you will keep in touch with Geraldine? She is very enamoured with you, I can tell."

Blushing, he shrugged.

"You could do a lot worse."

"I know, but I'm not really ready for marriage and that sort of thing. She's a lovely girl but..."

His aunt flounced in through the door. "Oh, are you still here? I thought you would have gone long since."

"I'm just going, Aunt. Thank you for putting up with me. You and Uncle Victor and Sarah must come to stay with us. It seems ages since the last time."

"Yes, well, we'll see." She patted her daughter's arm. "Hopefully, we will have other things to occupy our time."

Sarah grinned. "Yes, hopefully."

Chapter 15

Breathing a sigh of relief, David sat on the stone wall. The doctor had confirmed Daniel's arm was broken, but would soon mend. It had been splinted and he had been put to bed.

He had shared Tillie's fears, but she had accused him of not caring. How could she do that? He loved his son as much as a father could possibly do—more than the others, if he had to admit it, not that he ever would, especially to Tillie. She had always favoured her oldest son, naturally, of course, having experienced all the traumas in his younger days. He understood that.

Christine Harrison sometimes rode by at that time of day. He wondered if she might do so, and sat a while longer than he had intended. Not that he had any particular reason for speaking to her, but she gave him that little frisson of excitement that he lacked in his life.

Christine did not appear, however, so he returned to the stables to check on the ailing horse.

"She's perked up no end," Sam told him as they entered the stall.

"Thank the Lord for that. I hear there's a sale next week in Leeds and wondered if we might take one or two of the fillies. That dark one with the white patch on her ear could fetch a good price."

They went out across to the paddock. Sam agreed, adding, "And maybe we could take Jamie. Ruby tells me he's coming home today."

"Good idea. It would give him an insight on how these things are run. Yes, we will. I really do not know what else to do with the boy. He needs something to occupy him. If only he would go to university. I despair of him at times. But please say nothing to his mother. She does not understand the reason for my wanting him to be educated."

Sam called the filly over, and she trotted towards them. "Mm." He clearly did not either.

"She really is a beauty. I am loath to sell her."

The young horse nuzzled Sam's hand as he held out some oats. "Her sister over there is almost as fine. If we get a good price for this one, we could think about selling her next time around."

They walked back. "How is young Richard?" asked David.

"Oh, he's wonderful. I love my daughters dearly, but there's just something about a son."

David smiled, recalling his earlier thoughts, but did not reply.

Alice ran towards them and asked Sam if her pony was ready for her lesson.

"I was just about to fetch her," he replied, hurrying off.

"Daniel won't be able to ride for a very long time, will he, Papa?"

"No, my dear, I am afraid he will not. Is he sleeping?"

"Yes."

"Good, good. Ah, here she is."

"Will you stay and watch, Papa?" she asked as Sam helped her up onto the pony's back.

"Just for a little while. I have accounts I have put off sorting out, but which need seeing to urgently."

After a minute or two, he went back to the house. Things had begun to pick up financially, and he felt happier about the estate, but if they could get a decent price for the filly, he would be even happier. He might even buy Tillie a present—a trinket of some sort, or a necklace. Not that she ever went anywhere to wear such fripperies. No, she would be more content with a new toy for the baby, being the unselfish person he knew her to be.

The scrunch of gravel heralded the arrival of a carriage at the front of the house. Could that be Jamie, already? He had not expected him until much later.

* * * *

Tillie heard the crunch of gravel and looked out of the window. Jamie. She put down the pen she had been using to write a letter to Emily Thompson. Because of Daniel's accident, she would not be able to visit her. Would she ever see her again?

Hurrying out the door, she bumped into her oldest son. How different he seemed. So much more grown up, and in such a short time. When he took off his hat, she noticed his hair needed cutting.

"Have you had a good time?" she asked after the usual hugs.

"Yes, thank you, Mother, and I may have some good news to impart."

"Oo, you intrigue me. Do tell."

Before he could reply, David hobbled in. "I do believe you have grown, son. You will soon be as tall as me."

"Yes, Father. I would like to be."

Tillie wanted to hear what the news could be but had to curb her inquisitiveness while the baggage was brought in.

"Come into the lounge and tell me everything," she eventually told him when David had made his excuses and retired to his study.

After explaining why the children weren't there to greet him, they sat down, and Maisie brought in a tray of tea.

Jamie gave her a peculiar look, a sort of guilty one.

She wondered why, but did it really matter?

She couldn't control her curiosity any longer. "What were you about to tell me?"

"It's about Sarah. She's hoping to be betrothed very soon."

"Oh, who to?" *Oh, dear. David will be disappointed*, she thought, sipping her tea so as her face would not betray her.

"He's quite a catch. His name is Joel Burnyeat. We met the family when I first arrived, and have been out with them a few times." He went on to explain about the rides and the trip to Scarborough.

"Oh, I would love to go there again. Maybe we could organise a holiday for next summer," she began, but then remembered she would probably have a babe-in-arms by then, so changed the subject. "Anyway, has the wedding been arranged?"

"Oh, no, he hasn't proposed yet."

"Ah, good, I mean…" He didn't appear to be taking any notice of what she said, just sat back as if in a world of his own.

Once they had finished their drinks, she stood up. "You must be tired after your journey. I'll leave you alone. I must finish a letter." She had been about to tell him about her friend's illness, but he probably would not hear her.

I know what that expression is on his face, she thought. *He's in love. Has he met a young lady and lost his heart in Harrogate?* It can't be Sarah, if she is infatuated with this other man. But should she ask him? Not yet. Let him acclimatise himself to his home surroundings first, and then she could ease the information from him gradually. If he wanted her to know, he would tell her.

She went back to her bureau and completed her missive, hoping it would reach her friend in time.

However, the following day, a letter arrived as she

ate her breakfast. Opening it with trepidation, she read the short note from her friend's husband, the vicar, Edward Thompson, informing her that his wife had passed away the previous day. Even though Tillie had been expecting it, she burst into tears.

David took off his glasses and folded his newspaper. "Is it your friend?" When she nodded, he stood up and took her in his arms. "I am so sorry, my dear. I know what she meant to you."

"Those poor children, motherless at such a young age. I wish I could help."

"Tillie, you have enough on with your own brood."

"Yes, I know, and…" About to tell him of her suspicions, she changed her mind. There was time yet. She might be wrong.

* * * *

Jamie changed out of his travelling clothes and put on an old pair of trousers, deciding to have a walk to the lake. Seeing Maisie had put his thoughts into perspective. How could he have considered pursuing his relationship with Geraldine? His little friend needed him. His parents would not allow it for a long time, he understood that, and even then, they might never give their permission, so he would have to wait until he was twenty-one. But it didn't matter. He would bide his time.

The first bird he saw as he stepped outside was his buzzard, high in the sky and only just visible. Striding out, he walked around the lake and into the woods. A wood pigeon called in the treetops and he answered it as a fawn jumped out from behind a tree and stared at him with big, round eyes. How he had missed the countryside and nature. Town life just didn't compare in any shape or form. He belonged here, with his animals and birds.

Girls' voices alerted him, and his thoughts instantly

turned to Beth. But what did it matter if it were her? His mind had been made up. It couldn't be her, anyway. She had moved away, hadn't she?

It would be good to see her, though, if it were. His eyes opened wide. Green eyes stared back at him. He became aware of some younger children. One ran up to him and pulled his jacket. "Hey, mister, 'ave you got a farthing?"

Reaching into his pocket without thinking, he drew out a penny and handed it to the child, his eyes still on Beth.

His actions diverted her attention and she looked down at the ragged girl. "Lily, give that back. You shouldn't beg." Her sweet, soft voice made him draw in his breath.

"But Ma told me to," argued the child. "She said…"

"It's only a penny," Jamie told her. "She may keep it." He dug into his pocket to see if he had any more. "In fact, you may all have one."

"No, no, please. We aren't beggars," Beth insisted, hiding her hands behind her back.

"I'll have one, please, mister." The other child held out her hand and he deposited a coin into it. "I ain't proud."

"I understood you'd moved away," he mentioned at length.

"Yes, but I've come back to look after these two. Their mother's really poorly."

They stood staring at each other, not knowing what else to say, until the youngsters began to fidget. "Are we going home, yet, our Beth?" asked the one called Lily. "I want to show this penny to Mam. It'll cheer her up. I never had a whole penny before."

"Me neither," said the other one, examining hers. "Is it more than a farthing?"

"Yes, so look after it well," replied Beth.

"Ain't you going to have one?"

Beth looked longingly at the shiny penny piece the child held, and then at Jamie, shaking her head, but not very convincingly.

Jamie felt around in his pocket and brought out a threepenny bit. "I seem to be all out of pennies, so take this." He put it in her hand, wrapping her fingers around it, so she couldn't see it, because he knew she would protest if she did.

"Thank you," she mouthed as she turned and ran, the little girls following her, laughing and singing at the tops of their voices until they disappeared out of sight through the trees, their tones mingling with the songs of the birds up above.

What a dilemma! If he kept bumping into the woodland girl, he would never be able to fall in love with Maisie. He loved the maid dearly, as his friend, but would that be enough? The feelings Beth stirred inside him thrilled him to the core, much more even than Geraldine. But Maisie needed his protection. Could he go through life married to one female while having emotions for another? He would have to, if he really intended to go through with his pledge. He would just not come to the woods ever again. That would solve the problem. But those green eyes…

Wandering back towards the house, he wished he had someone he could talk to about his quandary. All the adults in his life would say he should not be considering marrying Maisie, so they would not be any help. His friend, Sebastian, was away at university and would not be back until Christmas.

A lady on horseback rode towards him as he strolled along the lane. He stepped back to allow her to pass, but she pulled up.

"Good day to you, sir."

Not in the mood for socialising, he barely looked at

her, but bowed his head politely, answering in a similar manner.

Thinking she would pass by, his head jerked up when she continued, "You are young Master Jamie, aren't you?"

"Yes, ma'am." He studied her features, the hazel eyes and blonde curls escaping from her riding hat. "Ah, it's Missus Harrison. I apologise. I was miles away."

"Yes, you were. Anywhere nice?"

He grimaced. "I was just trying to work out a problem."

"A problem shared is a problem halved, so they say." She raised her eyebrows, as if inviting his confidence. But he couldn't tell this lady his secrets. He hardly knew her. When he didn't reply, she added, "Well, feel free to call at my house any time you like. My door is always open." With a wave, she spurred her horse into action, calling, "Give my regards to your father, and your mother, of course."

Why did she say it like that? he wondered, but not for long, as his buzzard flew low overhead, and he could see the white markings on the underneath of the wings. It circled a few times, close by, and then dived into the field, so he could not see it over the hedge. Another vole or mouse gone to its maker, or maybe a crow, like he had seen a few years before. He decided to hurry back and ask his father if he could borrow the binoculars.

Receiving no reply to his knock on the study door, he opened it and went inside. Where did he keep them? Papers sat in an untidy pile on the desk and he remembered he had been supposed to be helping with them. Dare he pick one up? Would he understand what it was if he did? His sleeve caught the top one and, grabbing at it to stop it falling, he knocked several others onto the floor. Scrabbling around to pick them up, he saw a foot appear.

"What on earth are you doing?" his father's voice thundered in his ears.

"Nothing, Father, I was just looking for your binoculars."

"Under my desk?" His father came around and gasped. "And what are you doing with those bills?"

"They fell off. I'm sorry." Quickly picking them up, Jamie stood up and placed them back on top of the pile, trying to shuffle them so they appeared neat.

"Leave them, for goodness sake." His father sat down. "For a moment I thought you had come to help me. I might have known you had other ideas."

"Father, I do want to help. Please show me how I may."

"Well, if you really mean it, take this bill here, for fodder. I fear the price has increased tremendously in the last year or so. I would like you to compare it to last year's price and let me know how much it has increased. Do you think you could do that?"

Jamie took the bill. "Yes, of course. Where will I find last year's bills?" So much for borrowing the binoculars and studying his birds. Still, if it kept his father happy, he would oblige.

Lighting his pipe, his father pointed to a cabinet and Jamie held his breath, trying not to cough as the smoke wafted towards him.

"What have you been doing today?"

"Not a lot, I must admit, Father. I went for a walk and, oh, yes, I came upon Missus Harrison. She said to pass on her regards."

He thought he saw his father's face redden as he turned away and tapped out his pipe in the fireplace.

"She's a very pretty lady, isn't she, Father? She actually said to pass on her regards to you specifically."

"Oh, I'm sure she meant your mother as well."

"She did add her on, but only as an afterthought."

"Jamie, what are you inferring? You do not think I would look at any other woman, do you, with your beautiful mother at my side? No, son, do not ever think I would consider doing anything to hurt her, nothing at all."

"No, Father, I didn't mean anything of the sort."

"Have you found that bill yet?"

Three days later Jamie received a letter from Sarah, with a note from Geraldine folded inside. He read Sarah's first. Her words tumbled off the page as if she had been so animated she could hardly write. In fact, some of them were indecipherable and he had to imagine what they said. The gist of the matter was clear, though. Joel Burnyeat had indeed gone down on one knee and proposed to her.

"Oh, she will be so happy," he exclaimed aloud.

"Who? Sarah?" asked his father, dabbing his mouth with his serviette, and his mother stopped with her fork in mid-air, a questioning expression on her face.

"Yes, she is engaged to be married, to that gentleman I told you about, Joel Burnyeat."

His father almost choked. "But how can she be? I had hoped... What is her father thinking of to allow this?"

"David, don't have an apoplectic fit," answered his mother. "I have been telling you she is too old for Jamie. It would never have worked out. Be happy for the girl."

His father looked at Jamie for a few seconds. "Yes, I suppose you are right."

Has he decided I am not good enough for her, after all? thought Jamie. *Why else would he back down so quickly?*

He dropped his head. "I could not have made her happy, Father. She needs someone older and wiser than me."

"Too true. I do not know what I could have been

thinking." David stuck his fork in a sausage. "Tell me about him, this Mister Burnyeat. I need to know that he is suitable marriage material for my only niece."

"Oh, Father, he is that and more." In between mouthfuls he filled in his parents with as much as he knew of the young man and his family, apparently satisfying them as to his fittingness.

His mother stood up. "Pray excuse me, but we shall all have to have new dresses and suits. I need to make the arrangements straightaway." She clapped her hands. "Oh, isn't it marvellous? Does she say when the wedding might be?"

"No, Mother. They haven't even had the engagement party yet."

"No, no, of course not. Silly me. But I am so thrilled."

As she ran out of the room, his father shook his head. "I think she may be more excited than your cousin. But it is good to see her so. She deserves some happiness, especially after the bad news of the death of her friend, Missus Thompson. I fear her life is rather dull, with only the children for company."

"She has you, Father, and me. I am no longer a child."

"Yes, of course she has me." The clang of the fork dropping onto the plate made Jamie blink. "You know that. I told you the other day, she always will have me."

"Yes, Father, of course, I know. You made it very clear. I never doubted it. Pray, do not upset yourself."

"I am not upset." He wiped his serviette across his face. "Who is the other letter from? Not my sister? She would not write to you."

"No, not Auntie Annie. It's from a young lady, the cousin of Sarah's fiancé, a Miss Geraldine Burnyeat."

"Oh, and why should she be writing to you?"

"We became friendly while I was staying there. She

said she might write."

"Oh, and are you likely to be thinking of marriage? You are rather young."

"No, Father, not for a long time."

"Good, good. It does not do to marry too young. But if she is of the upper classes, you could do a lot worse. Bear that in mind when you do start thinking of it."

"Yes, Father." *Better not mention my idea, then.*

"Would you like to come to the horse fair with myself and Sam tomorrow?"

The change of conversation surprised him, but he replied eagerly, "Ah, yes please. That would be spiffing."

"Do you have to use that word? It is so old school."

"I'm sorry. I've always liked it, though. But I won't if you don't like it. If I may be excused, I shall go and read my other letter."

"Yes, yes, I have affairs...I mean accounts to complete. If you would like to help me later, I would appreciate it."

"My letter can wait. I shall come now."

"I would not like to put you out."

"No, Father, not at all. I've told you I want to help. Lead the way." The letter duly ensconced in his pocket, he followed David to his study.

Two hours later, he had successfully checked the year's accounts and found a slight mistake, much to his father's relief—for he had been going out of his mind that they would not balance—and could barely contain his sense of achievement.

His mother found him grinning at his reflection in the hall mirror. "You appear happy, son."

He told her what he had done.

"Oh, that's good. I'm sure your father appreciates it. What did your other letter say? Was it from a friend?"

"I haven't had time to read it yet." He took it out of

his pocket and smoothed it flat. Should he read it while his mother peered over his shoulder? "I think I'll take it outside."

"Oh." Her face dropped.

"It won't be anything important. I told you about Mister Burnyeat's cousin, Miss Geraldine, didn't I? It'll just be... Oh, very well, I'll read it now." He quickly scanned down the page. Just as he'd thought, chitter-chatter, nothing of any real interest. He handed her the paper. Did it awaken any feelings inside him? He had thought it would. But it didn't, not since he'd seen Beth.

Maisie came out of the parlour, her hands full of cleaning materials. His first instinct was to help her, and he made to step forward, but then remembered his place.

Her face lit up on seeing him, and she bobbed a curtsy and hurried off.

Why had he thought of Beth? His duty lay with this girl. He had to stay firm on his resolve.

His mother handed him the letter. "She seems a very nice girl. How old is she?"

His mind still on the maid, he drew back his brow. "Maisie, but you know how old she is, just a year or so younger than me."

"Maisie? What are you talking about? I meant this Geraldine girl."

"Oh, I'm sorry." *Pull yourself together.* "She's—I can't remember—about fifteen or sixteen. She hasn't had her coming out yet, anyway."

His mother linked arms with him and they went into the parlour. He had intended going out, but if his mother wanted a tête-à-tête, he would oblige. "Is she the one you've been moping about?"

"Moping? I haven't been moping, Mother. Why do you say that?"

She looked him in the eye. "Just a feeling I've had since you came home. You seem distracted, and I wondered if it had anything to do with this girl."

"Well, I had thought I might be in love while I was up there in Harrogate, but since I've returned, I've realised it was only infatuation. She means nothing to me now."

"Oh. I see." She gave him a hug. "You have grown up so much. My little boy is no longer a child. I have to stand on tiptoe to kiss you."

He smiled as she kissed his cheek. Should he sound her out while she was in an affable mood? "Mother?"

"Yes, dear?"

"Um…is Maisie likely to be promoted in the near future?"

She stepped back. "Maisie? What makes you ask that?"

"Well, you know I feel responsible for her."

She patted his arm. "That's very commendable, son, but you don't have to. She's well cared for here. I expect she'll rise in the ranks, if she continues to work as hard as she does. Anyway, about this Miss Geraldine, you're bound to see her again if we go up for the engagement party, for which I should hope we will receive an invitation, so maybe you will be able to continue your friendship, eh?"

With a nod to satisfy her, he turned and went out, leaving her with a smug face.

However, when they arrived at the party at his aunt and uncle's house in Harrogate a month later they were informed that Miss Geraldine had taken to her bed with scarlet fever.

"Oh, my dear, you must be so disappointed," said his mother.

"I'll try not to be too upset," he replied as Tannia hurried over to him.

"Mister Dalton, I've been so looking forward to seeing you again." He had forgotten how shrill her voice could be. He introduced her to his mother, his father having sat down on the other side of the room. Eager to escape after a decent interval, Jamie had left them chatting.

Not long afterwards, he felt his arm being pulled and turned to see his mother's bemused face. "Why did you leave me with that girl? My goodness, can't she talk! I never managed to slot a word in edgeways. She may be related to Sarah's fiancé but, goodness me I need a drink."

He ushered her through the mass of laughing and joking folk, and found the refreshment table.

Sarah came over and joined them. "Phew, I hadn't realised Mother had invited so many people. One can hardly move." She swallowed the contents of a glass in one gulp and picked up another. "You must be so disappointed, Jamie, that Geraldine isn't here, but she is really poorly. They are very worried about her."

"Oh, is it that bad?" He sipped his drink, half of him guilty at the relief that she had not come. But he hadn't wanted her to be so ill. The other half, antagonistically, wished she were there.

A red-faced man who seemed to have drunk too much, and could not walk straight, almost knocked over his mother and he had to steer her out of the way.

"Let's take some air," Sarah suggested. "It's such a crush in here."

"What about your fiancé?" asked his mother. "Won't he be worried where you are?"

Sarah tried to look through the throng of people, but shook her head. "I haven't seen him for a few minutes, but I'm sure he'll find me if he wants to. I don't want to be at his beck and call every minute. Or, at least, that's what Mama tells me."

"But it's your engagement party. Still, I am so happy for you, my dear, and your mother has done you proud tonight."

"Yes, I'll give her her due, she knows when to turn up trumps at the right moment." She turned to Jamie. "Tannia has been talking about you non-stop all day, so Joel says. Do you not…?"

"No, no, no," he cut in, before she could continue. "Pray do not saddle me with her. She may be a very nice girl, but I'm afraid to say I couldn't cope with her for more than a minute at a time." Looking up, he saw her heading towards them. "Oh, no, she's coming. I'd better hide."

"Oh, Jamie, you do make me laugh. Ah, Tannia, I trust you are enjoying yourself."

"Yes, it's a brilliant party. I thought I saw Mister Dalton—the younger one, that is, of course," she added. "Was he not here a moment ago?"

From his hiding place behind a large pot plant, Jamie saw her bewildered face scanning the area. He stooped even lower, pretending to tie his shoelace, just in case she spotted him.

She gave up, and went to harass someone else across the room.

Sarah poked him in the shoulder. "You may come out now, lily-liver. She's gone."

Slowly, he straightened. "I know I'm a coward."

"She's not so bad, once you become better acquainted with her. In fact, she and I have become very friendly."

"I'm pleased for you. One needs to rub along with one's relatives, doesn't one?"

"Ha ha, it's a good job I 'rub along' with you, little cousin, or I'd be mortally offended that you've snubbed my future sister-in-law. Come, let's enjoy some dancing, if we can find any space in which to do so."

"Not so much of the 'little'. I'm head and shoulders taller than you now," he retorted as they weaved their way through to the morning room where a few couples danced to the music provided by a small group.

Chapter 16

Tillie adjusted Alice's headband for the umpteenth time. "Stop pulling at it, darling, or the rosebuds will fall off."

"But it itches me. I think the maid tied my hair up too tight."

"It's too late now to adjust it, so try to ignore it, for Sarah's sake."

Daniel ran up to her, dressed in a sapphire blue velvet ring-bearer suit. "Don't you go falling over," she warned him. "I should hate you to walk down the aisle with dirty smuts on your knees."

He looked down, to make sure he didn't have any already, and grinned up at her. "All clean, Mama."

"Good boy." A look around did not pick out her oldest son. "I wonder where Jamie can be. He should be here by now."

"He said he would walk it, because there was no room in the carriage," offered Alice, scratching at her head again. In her full-length cream satin dress, with puff sleeves and a pink sash around her waist, Tillie hoped she wouldn't outshine Sarah on her big day. Not that that would be likely, of course. Everyone knew the bride would be the prettiest.

A cheer went up as a white carriage rounded the corner to the church. Craning her neck to see her niece, she gasped in wonderment. A halo seemed to hang over Sarah's head as she stepped out of the carriage, and her bridesmaids—Tannia and Geraldine, who were dressed similarly to Alice—straightened her long train. With a smile from ear to ear, she didn't appear to be at all nervous. Tillie remembered how tense and uneasy she had felt at her own wedding. But Sarah, being an even-tempered girl, would probably take the whole day in her stride.

But where was Jamie? Surely they wouldn't start without him? Maybe he had already arrived, and would be sitting in the church with David. Would there be time to send Alice inside to check?

Tannia came across and took the little girl's hand. "It's Alice, isn't it? I remember from yesterday's meeting. How are you feeling? I'm rather apprehensive, myself, but I don't know why. It's Sarah who should be, not me." She tinkled a little laugh, and Alice opened her eyes wide at Tillie, as if asking to be rescued.

"It's time for you to go now, sweetheart." She bent down and picked off a piece of fluff from her daughter's dress. "Where did that come from? Never mind. I have to leave you now. You'll be in safe hands with this lady."

Rather reluctantly, Alice went with the older girl, who still kept up a stream of conversation, even though she received no response, as Geraldine took Daniel's hand.

Feeling rather grand in her own new loose-fitting dress of peach and green stripes, with a high neck, a peach-coloured petticoat underneath, and a sash in the same colour, Tillie entered the church. Her corsets had not been laced tightly, for her belly had already expanded, but they still dug in somewhat.

The first person she saw was Jamie, beside David. Thank goodness. She had begun to doubt he would be there. He must have made good time, to have arrived before them. How handsome they both looked, dressed in differently-styled suits. Jamie had declared his father's to be not in the latest fashion when she had asked if he wanted one the same. He had preferred the light grey double-breasted style of frock coat and pin-striped trousers to his father's plain brown one. He had conceded to the same purple ascot tie, though.

A whiff of myrtle wafted towards Tillie as Sarah walked down the aisle on her father's arm. She turned to see her niece in what appeared, at first glance, to be a beautiful, simple, low-cut white dress with self-bows at the shoulders and short, sheer sleeves. A diamond necklace adorned her slender neck. When she had passed, however, the back of the dress showed a large, puffy bustle, and a long train edged with flowery lace.

Alice and the other bridesmaids followed, with Aunt Annie, demurely dressed much to Tillie's surprise, in a purple organza outfit, and Daniel, holding his cushion. After giving him a smile of encouragement, she turned to David. She loved him so dearly and knew he still loved her. He smiled at her. His blue eyes could still fill her with a longing, deep inside, and she determined to banish any negative thoughts that day. Holding his hand, she listened to the couple taking their vows, repeating them in her head as if she were renewing her own.

Once the service was over, they assembled outside for the photos. Tillie found the nanny, who had stayed at the back of the church with Joseph, and took the child. She didn't want him to be missing when the family perused the pictures after the couple had returned from their tour. They had decided to go to Venice, for Sarah had declared she had always wanted to ride on a gondola. Tillie had heard it to be a smelly place, with no roads on which to walk. People had to go everywhere on boats, but if Sarah had her heart set on it, then who was she to argue?

* * * *

David sat watching his wife across the flower-strewn table. Her cheeks bloomed with the aura of her pregnancy. He had been surprised when she had told him, but delighted also. After the two boys, maybe another daughter would be agreeable, but he did not mind in the least what gender it would be, as long as it was healthy. Tillie had not had any complications so, hopefully, it would be strong and robust.

She turned and smiled. What a lovely smile she had. It could still brighten his day. How could he ever have looked at Christine Harrison? He could barely believe his actions. It could not be blamed on what was known as the seven-year itch, for they had been married for over nine years. Whatever it had been, it had finished, well and truly. If he ever came across the lady he would not look her in the eye, but merely bow and pass on. She would have to understand he would never betray his wife, especially in her condition.

Jamie appeared to be enjoying himself, dancing with any manner of females, one of them in particular—one of the bridesmaids, in fact both of them, in turn—paying him special attention. His hopes for him marrying Sarah had been idiotic.

His niece looked so beautiful—radiant, rather. He thoroughly approved of her choice of husband, especially so when he thought of the young man's income. She would be set up for life, not that she had ever wanted for anything before. Her father's millinery business had flourished, so he would have been able to provide her with a sizeable dowry.

Tapping his foot to the music, he wished he could dance, but knew it would be impractical to even try. Someone would be bound to knock his crutch from underneath him, and he would go flying. It would be a cause for hilarity, though, for most people laughed at others' misfortunes, but he did not intend being such a cause.

The groom came across and, after a quick word, invited Tillie to dance. She hesitated, as if asking his permission, but he waved her on. "Go and enjoy yourself, my darling. I shall be fine here, surveying all the lovely ladies in their finery."

"That's what I was afraid of." She grinned, but stood and joined the dancers.

* * * *

Jamie's feet ached from dancing. He had stood up with nearly every young lady in the room, and his dancing skills had improved in leaps and bounds. He had tried to avoid Tannia, but it had been impossible, for she seemed to appear every time he turned around. There she was again, heading in his direction.

"I have already danced twice with you," he proclaimed when she looked up pleadingly at him. "You know three times would count as an engagement."

She pouted. "I'm sure you have danced with Geraldine three times."

"I have not, have I? No, don't tease me."

"Well, it seems as if every time I look up, you are with her, even if you aren't waltzing or gavotting. I am quite jealous. I am sure you prefer her to me."

"Miss Brown, I…" What could he say to the contrary? She had spoken the truth, but he couldn't hurt the girl by admitting it. "Miss Brown, my affections are not limited to one female. I love you all equally." Would that satisfy her? His words had not sounded like him, and he grinned inwardly at them.

"Then you are a dissolute profligate, sir, and I want nothing more to do with you." She flounced off and he watched her try her wiles on another young man whose acquaintance he hadn't made.

Could he be what she had called him? He hoped not. He had spoken in jest, but at least it'd had the desired effect.

The music stopped and Geraldine came over, her

green eyes sparkling. Would it do any harm to have some amusement? After all, he would not need to see her again, once he had returned home.

"Shall we sit over there?" he asked. "Or would you like to take a walk outside?"

Her eyes opened wide. "A walk would be lovely. It is such a lovely day, it seems a shame to stay inside, doesn't it? But I may need a shawl. I'll ask my grandmother if I may borrow hers."

They found Lady Catherine ruling the roost with some of her friends. "Ah, Mister Dalton, Jamie," she exclaimed, "just the person we were talking about."

"Oh, dear, that sounds ominous."

"No, no, not at all. Let me introduce you to my friends." He bowed to all the elderly ladies, some of whom seemed to have an extra twinkle in their eyes. What could she have been telling them?

Geraldine interrupted. "We were just going to take some air, Grandmother. It is rather stuffy in here, don't you think? I wondered if you would lend me your shawl for a few minutes. We will not be long."

Lady Catherine took off her shawl and placed it around the girl's shoulders. "Certainly, my dear. We wouldn't want you catching a chill." She gave Jamie a look as if warning him, but then winked.

Holding in a gasp of astonishment, he wondered if he'd imagined it. Surely an elderly lady would not be so bold as to wink at a young man? In a daze, he followed Geraldine out through the French doors.

Had the woman been implying that she had been hoping he might be serious about her granddaughter? That he was about to propose? Oh, goodness, what should he do? Had that been Geraldine's thoughts as well? Goodness, goodness, goodness. How could he extricate himself without hurting her feelings?

They reached a secluded bower and, wrapping the

shawl around her more tightly, she asked if he wanted to sit there.

"Um, no, I think we should return. It looks like rain, and your grandmother said you mustn't catch a chill."

"But there is scarcely a cloud in the sky," she protested. "Admittedly, there is a chill breeze."

He took her arm and led her back into the hall, muttering, "Ah, my mother is beckoning me. Pray, excuse me," and he left her, looking bemused. His mother had been having a conversation with a bald-headed man, and had probably not even seen him enter, but he'd had to make up some excuse.

"Ah, Jamie," she said as he approached. "I was just telling this gentleman about your love of birds. He is an ornithologist."

Bowing to the man, he sat down quickly. "Oh, really? I'm fascinated by the feathered creatures. Pray tell me, which is your favourite?"

His mother left them to their musings, and he hoped the man didn't want to circulate with the other guests. He seemed content to talk about his given subject, though, so they remained chatting.

After the man had told him about his collection of owls, he replied, "I would love to come and see your aviary, sir, but I think we will be returning home tomorrow." Having kept out of her way for the past hour or so, he checked that Geraldine was not in the vicinity. He would have to face her, eventually, but would stay out of her way as long as possible.

Finally, the announcement was made that the bridal couple would soon be leaving. Thank goodness. He would be able to find his family and they could return to their inn, hopefully, not having to mingle any longer.

However, once the party began to break up, he saw Lady Catherine bearing down on him. "I am disappointed in you, sir, but you are very young. There is time yet. I trust you will be gracing us with your presence again soon, once your cousin has returned from her travels?"

"I'm not sure, Lady Catherine. We haven't arranged anything."

"Well, make sure you do. Good day to you, sir. Give my regards to your parents."

He bowed as she swept off, her dress rustling.

Geraldine made as if to approach, but clearly changed her mind and, with a slight incline of her head, she followed her grandmother. He had avoided a confrontation and, hopefully, not had his reputation torn to shreds. They wouldn't have told anybody, so nobody else would have known. Anyway, he might have been mistaken. Perhaps they hadn't had an engagement in mind at all.

Breathing a sigh of relief at his easy escape, he went in search of his parents and siblings, eager to return home and help his father run the estate.

Romance could wait.

About The Author

Married to Don, Angela has 5 children: Darran, Jane, Catherine, Louise, and Richard, and 8 grandchildren: Amy, Brandon, Ryan, Danny, Jessica, Charlotte, Ethan, and Violet Alice.

Educated at The Convent of Our Lady of Providence, Alton, Hampshire, Angela was part owner of a health shop for 3 years and worked for the Department of Work and Pensions for 16 years until her retirement, when she joined the Eastwood Writers' Group and began writing in earnest.

Her hobbies include gardening, singing in her church choir, flower arranging, bingo, scrabble, and eating out.

Her first novel 'Looking for Jamie' was released as an eBook in November 2010 and in print in February 2011. It has been hailed as 'one of those books you can't put down'.

Without the help and encouragement from the writer's group, she says her book would never have been finished.

Lightning Source UK Ltd.
Milton Keynes UK
UKOW02f0609260516

275023UK00001B/9/P